Hiya!

It feels kind of sad to have come to the end of the Chocolate Box Girls series . . . If you're having trouble letting go, you might like this cool collection of stories from the viewpoints of some of the minor characters. Five of the stories were first published as ebook shorts, but lots of you have requested that the stories be brought together in book form – so that's just what we've done! I couldn't resist writing one last exclusive story, from Ash's point of view . . . I think you'll like it!

Reading these stories will give you a few extra insights into the plot and characters of the series . . . some behind-the-scenes glimpses of Tanglewood, if you like! Time to snuggle up with a hot chocolate and dip into the stories . . . enjoy!

Keep reading, keep smiling . . . and follow your dreams!

Cathy Cassidy xxx

Cathy Cassidy

Life is Sweet

six fabulous chocolate box stories

PUFFIN

PUFFIN BOOKS

UK | USA | Canada | Ireland | Australia
India | New Zealand | South Africa

Puffin Books is part of the Penguin Random House group of companies
whose addresses can be found at global.penguinrandomhouse.com.

www.penguin.co.uk
www.puffin.co.uk
www.ladybird.co.uk

Bittersweet first published by Puffin Books as a World Book Day book 2013
Chocolates and Flowers first published as a digital edition by Puffin Books 2014
Hopes and Dreams first published as a digital edition by Puffin Books 2014
Moon and Stars first published as a digital edition by Puffin Books 2014
Snowflakes and Wishes first published as a digital edition by Puffin Books 2014
Hearts and Sunsets first published as a digital edition by Puffin Books 2015
This collection first published by Puffin Books 2015
Reissued in this edition 2016

001

Text copyright © Cathy Cassidy, 2013, 2014, 2015
Illustrations copyright © Sara Chadwick-Holmes, 2015

The moral right of the author and illustrator has been asserted

Set in 11.79/17.15 pt Baskerville MT Std
Printed in Great Britain by Clays Ltd, St Ives plc

A CIP catalogue record for this book is available from the British Library

ISBN: 978–0–141–37433–8

All correspondence to:
Puffin Books
Penguin Random House Children's
80 Strand, London WC2R 0RL

Thank you . . .

As always, thanks to my fab family, Liam, Cal and Cait; and to all of my lovely extended family for the support and love! Also to my friends, who happen to be the best friends ever . . . you know who you are!

Thanks to my agent, Darley, and his amazing team; to Ruth, who keeps me organized (well, almost!); Annie, who sorts my events; and Martyn who handles the numbers stuff. A huge thank you to my editors, Amanda and Carmen, and to Roz, Julia, Sam and the whole fab Puffin crew. A special shout-out goes to lovely Sara, whose cover artwork and inside illustrations have helped to make this book so gorgeous.

A shout-out also to lovely Teresita, whose mum won the chance for her name to be used in the book in a recent charity auction for Authors For Nepal. See if you can spot her name!

Last but not least, a huge thank you to YOU, my awesome readers. You are the ones who have made the Chocolate Box Girls such a success . . . You fell in love with the Tanberry-Costello sisters just as much as I did. I hope you'll enjoy this last peek into life at Tanglewood . . . and don't worry, there will be lots more books in the pipeline, promise!

Cathy Cassidy, xx

Contents

Bittersweet was the first 'extra' mini book I wrote that linked to The Chocolate Box Girls series . . . my readers were a little bit in love with the character Shay Fletcher, and wanted a story from his viewpoint. It was fun to look into what made Shay tick . . . and to see how Honey might feel about him a year on from their split. Even the path of true love doesn't always run smoothly! I hope that **Bittersweet** will give you a whole different slant on life in Kitnor . . . take a little bit of time to chill out and enjoy it!

Cathy Cassidy ♥ xxx

Bitter Sweet

A seagull's call cuts through the misty morning
Sunlight hasn't touched the blankets yet . . .
I hear your voice whisper in my waking dream,
And tell myself you're here, and I forget –
How yesterday your smiling eyes they left me;
How yesterday your heart it turned away;
Last night I dreamt of cherry-blossom trees, but now
Comes the bittersweet reality of day . . .

Cherry-blossom sweet, bitter taste of pain
Say you won't forget me, love me still.
Cherry-blossom sweet, bitter taste of pain
Give me one more chance . . . be mine again.

I sit down by the waterfront, it's evening.
The tide comes washing in over my feet.
It's so like you in every move it makes . . .
It rushed forward to me then, but now retreats.
If there's one thing I know about the ocean
The same thing I can hope for your heart.
The sea will always find its way back to the shore . . .
Can we both find our way back to the start?

Cherry-blossom sweet, bitter taste of pain
Say you won't forget me, love me still.
Cherry-blossom sweet, bitter taste of pain
Give me one more chance . . . be mine again.

1

Sometimes, your life can change in a moment and you might not even know it.

You could be sitting on a beach at sunset with a bunch of friends, playing guitar and singing while people laugh and chat and toast marshmallows, a party going on all around you. You might not notice the tall bearded guy listening intently, or know that he has the power to turn everything upside down for you. Doors could open, opportunities could unfold. Fame and fortune could hook you in, and nothing would ever be the same again.

My friend Finch jabbed me in the ribs, grinning.

'See that guy with the beard, over there?' he asked. 'He's a friend of Mum's, from back home in London. She told him about your playing, and he said he'd come down one weekend and listen. He's called Curtis Rawlins. You should say hello.'

'Yeah?' I echoed, peering into the twilight. 'You think?'

Things had been crazy lately – a TV company was making a film in the village, and Finch's mum Nikki was the producer. She and Finch had been staying with my girlfriend's family for the summer, but the film was all wrapped up now. Nikki and Finch were ready to head back to London – the beach party was a kind of goodbye get-together.

Nikki had heard me play a few times over the holidays, though I'd never thought anything of it. The guy with Nikki looked like your typical film-crew type, youngish and London-cool with a goatee beard and a red trilby hat. I lifted a hand to wave at the two of them, and they grinned back.

'Curtis is a talent scout for a record company,' Finch said into my ear. 'Wrecked Rekords . . . you've heard of them, right?'

I blinked. Everyone has heard of Wrecked Rekords – some of my favourite bands are signed to them.

'Hang on, Finch,' I frowned. 'Did you just say . . .'

'Curtis is a talent scout, yeah,' he repeated.

'Wow. But no, the other bit . . .'

'Right. The bit about Mum telling him about your playing?' Finch checked. 'Yeah. She sent him a copy of that CD you made for me, and a link to your online stuff, and he liked it and decided to come down and meet you. He's been listening to you for the last hour. So . . . are you going to say hi?'

He nudged me forward.

'Hey, Nikki, Curtis,' I said politely.

The beardy guy grinned and shook my hand, and up close I could see he had about a dozen piercings in one ear. 'Shay, isn't it?' he said. 'Nice playing. And they're all your own songs?'

I said that they were, and Curtis asked if I'd ever recorded anything or if I might like to. Wrecked Rekords were always on the lookout for new talent. According to Curtis, I was just the kind of thing they were looking for.

'Seriously?' I remember saying. 'Me?'

Curtis was serious.

It could have been that easy, I swear. I could have had a recording contract right there and then, with a cool London

9

label. Curtis said he thought I had something special – raw talent, awesome songs, an offbeat kind of charm. Plus, I was young and keen and had the right look.

Me. Really. He said I could have a career, a future. They'd put down a few tracks, arrange some showcase gigs, get media coverage.

'You could be big,' Curtis told me. 'That indie-ballad vibe, the bittersweet songs, the surf-boy looks . . . it's unique. They're going to love you!'

My life could have changed in that moment, but . . .

Well, it didn't. Just my luck.

Thing is, I am fifteen. I am still at school, and Curtis said that was no problem at all, but that obviously my parents would have to be on board with the whole thing.

'Don't worry,' he told me. 'I'll talk to them, explain it all. Trust me!'

That's when I knew I was doomed. My parents were never going to listen to a bloke with a goatee beard and piercings and a red trilby hat, talking about bittersweet songs with a surf-boy twist. It just wouldn't happen.

'I'm heading back to London tomorrow, but I'll call in before I go,' Curtis said. 'When would be a good time?'

❀❀❀❀❀❀❀❀❀❀❀❀❀❀❀❀❀❀

'We work Sundays,' I told him. 'My dad runs the sailing centre in the village, and Sunday is one of our busiest days . . .'

'I'll definitely need to speak to him,' Curtis said.

I sighed. 'Well . . . our bookings don't start until eleven on weekends, so if you called in around ten Dad should still be home . . .'

'Cool,' Curtis grinned.

But it wasn't cool at all, and I wasn't the only one who thought so.

'D'you think you'd better tell your dad first?' my girl-friend Cherry said. 'Just mention it, set the scene a bit. So it doesn't come as too much of a shock?'

'Maybe,' I said.

'I think you should,' she persisted. 'You know what he's like. A bit cynical? You have to give him time to get used to the idea, prepare him a bit, or else he'll never even let Curtis over the doorstep!'

I looked up at the moon, a crescent of silver in the dark September sky. I was looking for inspiration, ideas, but the moon just blinked back at me, impassive.

'I'll tell him first thing tomorrow,' I promised Cherry.

Let's just say it didn't go too well.

I spilled the beans over breakfast – Dad's favourite scrambled-egg feast. I even made him a banana smoothie with cinnamon sprinkles, but it was no use. He said no – actually, he yelled it, and there was a lot of swearing mixed in there too, so I knew he wasn't about to change his mind. I texted Cherry to tell her, and she rang back right away, telling me not to give up.

'Give him time to mull it over,' she insisted. 'You might be surprised.'

'Doubt it,' I huffed. 'He won't listen . . . He hates the whole idea. Hopeless.'

'Nikki and Curtis can explain things better, though,' Cherry pointed out. 'The whole thing will have more weight, more gravity, coming from them. You've done the groundwork . . . relax, Shay. They'll soon talk your dad round.'

Ha. Pigs might fly.

Now, half an hour later, I'm sitting on my bedroom window sill wishing I had never heard of Curtis Rawlins. I don't think Dad has calmed down and started to accept the idea of me getting a record deal, not from the dark, brooding look on his face or the way he is stomping around the kitchen. Mum and Ben have made themselves scarce and headed down to the sailing centre to set up.

'Not looking good, little brother,' Ben said as he left. 'Sorry.'

I'm sorry too. I press my face against the bedroom window, watching the path, hoping to spot Curtis coming and head him off before Dad gets hold of him. Things could get messy. In the end, I am not fast enough – Dad whips the door open just as Curtis and Nikki are striding up the path, their faces bright with opportunity and hope.

'Whatever you want from us, it's not happening,' Dad is roaring even before I can get down into the hallway. 'I know your sort. Whatever kind of deal you are offering, forget it – my son wants nothing to do with you!'

'Please, Mr Fletcher,' Finch's mum says. 'Hear us out. I can assure you that Curtis is making a very genuine offer here –'

'Not interested,' Dad snaps, and my heart sinks. He is not going to budge, not even for a film producer and a London record company talent scout. Especially not for them.

❀ ❀

'I'm not sure if you realize,' Curtis says, 'but Shay here could really make his mark in the music business. Wrecked Rekords would nurture him, develop him, perfect the product and polish up his performance skills . . .'

'I don't think so,' Dad says.

'But, Mr Fletcher – Shay's got it all. Looks, skill, a unique style . . .'

Dad's eyes skim over Curtis with his goatee beard and piercings and red trilby hat. He grits his teeth, struggling not to share his opinion of the talent scout's own unique style.

'Nothing doing,' Dad repeats firmly. 'The music business is all drink and drugs and debauchery. It's corrupt, that's what it is. No son of mine is going in for all that malarky!'

'It doesn't have to be like that,' Nikki argues. 'You could manage him, make sure he was looked after. Shay has a talent. You wouldn't want him to waste that, Mr Fletcher, would you?'

'Talent?' Dad snorts. 'When has talent ever been enough? You've been watching too much X-Factor. Listen, because I don't think you heard me the first time. Over. My. Dead. Body. Clear enough for you?'

I cringe. How can he be so rude, so aggressive? I bite my lip and roll my eyes, and hope that Nikki and Curtis know how mortified I am feeling.

'All that showbiz nonsense,' Dad rants on. 'Ridiculous! Shay is fifteen years old. He's still at school, and I need him here at the sailing centre too. This is a family business, in case you haven't noticed. And it's real work, proper physical work, not your airy-fairy music rubbish!'

'Dad!' I cut in. 'Please? This is a once-in-a-lifetime chance! If you'd just give Nikki and Curtis a fair hearing –'

'I've listened,' he huffs. 'And I didn't like what I heard. It's a con, Shay, can't you see that? So, thanks, but . . . no thanks.'

He smiles icily and tries to shut the door, but Curtis turns back at the last minute, sticks his foot against the door frame and hands Dad his card and a sheaf of forms and leaflets.

'Think about it,' he says. 'No pressure. You know where to reach me if you change your mind.'

He steps back just in time to avoid a bunch of broken toes as Dad slams the door. The forms and leaflets go straight in the bin, of course. Much later, when the worst day of my life is finally over and Dad has gone to bed, I fish the papers out and stuff them into my rucksack, even though they are slightly crumpled and have a nasty brown stain from where a tea bag has landed on them.

I am not about to give up that easily.

2

It's not that my dad doesn't believe in talent – I think he believes in it too much. He knows that fame and fortune can be very fickle things. It's just that as far as Dad is concerned, all of the talent in our family belongs to my big brother.

Ben is a bit of a legend around here. He's brilliant at sport, football especially . . . he was playing for Bristol City FC Youth Squad by the time he was fourteen, and Southampton FC scouted him when he was sixteen, but he had an injury and things didn't work out. It wasn't majorly serious, but it was enough to wipe out Ben's chances of a premier-league football career.

Dad didn't cope too well when it all went pear-shaped. He couldn't believe you could play so well and work so hard and have it all end in nothing, and I suppose that has made him suspicious of chances and opportunities and promises of fame and fortune.

Anyhow, Ben went off to uni to study sports science and said it was the best thing he ever did. He went out every night and partied hard, doing all the stuff he hadn't done when he was younger because of training so hard, and this summer he graduated with a 2:1 degree and started working full time at the sailing centre. He works hard, but he parties hard too.

'You're only young once, Shay,' he likes to tell me. 'Take my advice – loosen up, little brother. Live a little!'

I don't take Ben's advice, though.

I haven't done that since I was five years old. Ben had made a go-cart and he told me I could be the first person to test it out. I felt like the most important boy in the world as I followed him up the hill behind our cottage.

'You have total control,' he told me. 'Just yank on the steering rope to turn left or right, or to slow down. You're so lucky I chose you to be the test driver, Shay! It's going to be epic!'

It was epic all right. I wedged myself into the driver's

18

seat and Ben pushed me off down the hill at about a million miles an hour. Three seconds into the ride, the steering rope came off in my hands and, of course, there were no brakes. By the time I got to the bottom of the hill I was yelling like crazy. A wheel came off as I sped across the yard and crashed into the cottage wall, and I fell out of the go-cart and squashed Mum's flowers and broke my arm in two different places.

Ben was the first to reach me.

'Don't tell,' he hissed into my ear as I lay in a mangled heap beneath the lupins. 'I'll get into terrible trouble, and you wouldn't want that, would you?'

So I didn't tell, not even when Dad shouted at me for taking Ben's go-cart without permission, not even when Mum grumbled about the squashed flower beds, not even when the doctors at A & E prodded about at my broken arm and put a plaster cast on it. I cried a bit because I was only five, remember, and it hurt a LOT. But Ben told me not to make a fuss, so after a while I just bit my lip and tried to be brave.

'How did you manage to get yourself into such a mess, Shay?' Dad huffed. 'Why can't you be more like your brother?'

✿✿✿✿✿✿✿✿✿✿✿✿✿✿✿✿✿✿✿✿✿

That's the question they've all been asking, my whole life pretty much. I wish I knew the answer, but the truth is I am not like Ben. We are chalk and cheese, day and night, sunshine and shadow.

I sigh, prising the lid off a fresh tin of paint, dipping my brush neatly and stroking the foul-smelling stuff across the upturned hull of yet another dinghy.

It's Monday evening, almost two whole days after the legendary moment that didn't change my life. Things have continued to go downhill. Finch and Nikki headed back to London along with Curtis, and with them leaving it felt like summer was well and truly over, all the fun squeezed out of it. I will miss Finch, miss the freedom of long hot days that blur into lazy nights of music and laughter.

It's like Dad has slammed the door on all of that too.

To top it all, today school started up again. I managed to survive it, but only just – my mind switched off as the teachers began to talk about how important Year Eleven is, how hard we'll need to study to pass our GCSEs and get that golden ticket to a shining future – it is hard to get worked up about exams right now. What's the point? I will probably flunk my GCSEs and drop out of school to face

❀❀❀❀❀❀❀❀❀❀❀❀❀❀❀❀❀❀❀❀❀❀❀

a life of slavery at the sailing centre, scraping barnacles off boats and teaching little kids how to kayak.

I kept my head down and hoped that nobody was talking about what happened with Curtis, but word had definitely leaked out because at break a few kids asked if it was true I was going to be recording with Wrecked Rekords. I pretended not to know what they were talking about, but that just fuelled the rumour.

Wait till they get the whole story – the boy who was offered a record deal from Wrecked and turned it down? Yup, that's me.

I'll look like the biggest loser in the universe.

It is a relief to be back here, away from the gossip, away from the sad glances Cherry keeps shooting me when she thinks I'm not looking. Nobody likes to be pitied, right?

I dip my brush again and focus on painting.

So, yeah . . . my brother, the legend.

When I was seven, Ben scored three goals in the final match of the Under Thirteens' Somerset football league and got his picture in the paper holding a shiny silver cup up in the air. Dad put up a shelf in the bedroom we shared to display the trophy, and when that shelf got crowded he put up another. When that one was full, Dad cleared my shelves so that Ben could use them too. It's not like I was going to win any trophies – that sporty, competitive gene must have skipped me completely.

'Shay Fletcher?' a whole bunch of teachers have said over the years, usually out on the sports field. 'Ben's little brother? Goodness, you don't take after him, do you?'

Ben is popular with the girls, of course. They look at his blond hair and his athletic build and his skin tanned golden from working outside at the sailing centre, and they swoon. There are always little gangs of them cheering him on from the sidelines at any given football match. All he has to do is smile and reel them in. He has a girlfriend from uni, but she lives miles away in Sheffield, and that's probably a good thing. At least she's not around to watch my brother flirting with every female within a fifty-mile radius.

I do not have an athletic build or a budding career in football, but I have the wheat-blond hair and the sea-green eyes and the tan. It took me a while to suss that not every girl who asked me if I was Ben Fletcher's little brother was angling for his mobile number. Some of them were actually interested in ME.

'Way to go, little brother,' Ben laughed, when I started dating Honey Tanberry back in Year Nine. I had my brother's approval at last.

I probably wouldn't have dated Honey for half as long as I did if it hadn't been for that. She was hard work – behind the party-girl facade, she was all anger and hurt and hopelessness. Neither of us got along with our families, and for a while that kept us together. I thought I could make her happy, but it turns out I was wrong about that, and after a while her drama-queen stuff started to get to me a bit.

I couldn't see why Honey lashed out against her mum, why she hated her new stepdad. They both seemed pretty cool to me, but when I said that she called me a traitor. After a while I started to feel like I was just some kind of cool accessory she liked to have in tow, a boy with a guitar who was good for her image.

The two of us were just marking time, hanging out together until something better came along . . . at least, that's what I thought.

It ended badly, of course.

I met Cherry, and that was it – ka-boom, it blew everything

❀❀❀❀❀❀❀❀❀❀❀❀❀❀❀❀❀❀❀❀❀❀❀

I'd felt for Honey right out of the water. Honey would never have forgiven me anyhow for ditching her for someone new, but I guess I didn't make it easy for her. As far as she was concerned, I'd chosen the worst possible girl to fall for. I might as well have stabbed her through the heart, she raged at me – that was how cruel, how callous I'd been. It was bad, I admit – about as bad as it was possible to get.

Cherry was her new stepsister.

The whole thing was a nightmare, a mess, a massacre.

Honey screamed and yelled and threw stuff at me, and even now, more than a year on, she looks at me with such coldness I can feel icicles form in my hair, frost chilling my skin. Like I said, it's a nightmare.

I finish painting the last dinghy, press the lid down on the paint and walk across to the storeroom to clean the brush. Over the last few years, I have turned the storeroom into a kind of den – there's an ancient, paint-spattered sofa and a kettle to boil water for a pot noodle or a hot chocolate. It's a good place to curl up with my guitar, a place to think and dream and write songs in the evening without Dad breathing down my neck.

There are plenty of pot noodles on the shelf and half a

bar of Dairy Milk left over from the weekend. I reckon I've missed supper already, and it's not like I'll be missing much if I stay out another hour or two. Just the odd cutting remark from Dad, a few frosty silences, the occasional pitying glance from Mum or Ben.

It's almost sunset, and the September sky is streaked with pink and gold, but the storeroom is dark and shadowy as I step inside. I don't notice her at first, and when I do I just about jump out of my skin.

Honey is perched on the worktop in the corner, half hidden in the shadows, her long legs swinging, her jaw-length blonde hair rumpled. Her eyeliner is smudged and the lashes that fringe her wide blue eyes are damp, as if she's been crying.

'Shay?' she says, her voice small, uncertain. 'I need your help. I'm in trouble – big trouble.'

3

Honey is no stranger to trouble, of course. It's her talent, her skill. If there was an exam in it she would get an A* without even trying . . . she's a natural.

I got used to mopping up the fallout, back when we were together; Honey messing up, me sorting things out – it was just what we did. Still, I cannot for the life of me figure out what Honey is doing here now.

'OK,' I prompt, one eyebrow raised. 'What is it this time? Fire, flood, plague of frogs? Or have you just broken a fingernail?'

Harsh, I know, but you have to remember that Honey and I are not exactly friends these days. Her lips begin to quiver and her eyes blur with tears, and right away I wish

I could take the words back. What if something really serious has happened?

Honey is crying harder now, her shoulders shaking, mascara running down her cheeks in ugly black streaks. I hate it when girls cry. I never know what to do.

'Hey, hey,' I say, patting her arm awkwardly. 'It can't be that bad!'

Honey burrows her head against my neck and I panic because this clearly means that things are that bad, or possibly worse. Me and my big mouth. What if Honey's mum has been diagnosed with a life-threatening illness or her no-good dad has finally gone bankrupt and topped himself by jumping off the Sydney Harbour Bridge? And here's me making jokes about broken fingernails. Nice one, Shay.

Meanwhile, Honey is clutching on to my T-shirt and making a wet patch on my shoulder. I can smell her favourite vanilla and almond shampoo, the scent of peppermint from the gum she likes to chew. I put an arm round her, then withdraw it again because it all feels a bit too close for comfort. This is not good.

27

'Shhh, Honey,' I say gently. 'Don't cry. Why don't you tell me about it?'

We sit down side by side on the beat-up sofa, the way we used to back when we were dating, and Honey dries her eyes with a corner of my T-shirt, leaving smudges of eyeliner and glittery shadow.

'They hate me,' she announces finally, her voice a whisper. 'They really do. Just because I was a little bit late home last night . . .'

Back when I used to date Honey, her curfew was 11 p.m., earlier on a school night, but Cherry tells me that those days are gone. These days, Honey is either 'grounded' or 'ungrounded', and right now I am pretty sure it's 'grounded'. Just a few weeks ago she accidentally set fire to a stable while sharing a forbidden ciggy with one of the boys from the film crew, and her sister Summer fainted while trying to fight the flames and ended up in hospital. How did Honey handle it? By taking a handful of cash from a kitchen drawer and running away. They found her at Heathrow airport trying to buy a ticket to fly out to her dad in Australia, and the last I heard she was grounded until Christmas.

Unless I am mistaken, it is not Christmas yet.

✿✿✿✿✿✿✿✿✿✿✿✿✿✿✿✿✿✿✿✿✿✿✿✿

'I stayed over with a friend, obviously,' Honey is saying. 'No big deal, right? I've done it before. And it was the last night of the school holidays – you'd think they'd give me a little bit of leeway!'

But Honey is the kind of girl who takes a little bit of leeway and turns it into a wagonload of chaos, as far as I can remember.

'So I bent the rules a little,' she goes on. 'So what? I stayed with a friend and I would have gone straight to school from there, but I accidentally slept in. It was unlucky, sure, but it's not a crime, is it? Only Mum had to go and call the school, then the police . . . you name it. Talk about overreacting!'

I frown.

'Let's get this straight,' I say. 'You stayed out all night and didn't come home in the morning, and then you skipped school too. Plus, three weeks ago you ran away from home . . . Honey, don't you think your mum had reason to panic?'

'No!' she argues. 'I didn't skip school, I just slept in! And I was perfectly fine all the time, just staying with a friend, I told you! They practically had a search party out looking for me, I swear . . . crazy. So now I am in trouble at school and if that's not bad enough, the police have been on my case, telling me I am treading a very fine line . . . what does that even mean?'

'Dunno,' I shrug.

'I'll tell you exactly what it means,' Honey says, and her eyes brim with tears again. 'It means they'll get social services involved if I land up in trouble again. Can you believe that? SOCIAL SERVICES! Like I'm some kind of problem teen or something! It's just TOTALLY unfair – I wasn't even trying to run away! It's all Mum and Paddy's fault – they want rid of me! They'd be GLAD if I was taken into care!'

Honey is sobbing again now, and I am praying for rescue because I so do not want to be here right now. I spot a clean paint rag on the arm of the sofa and hand it to Honey to wipe her eyes, but she ignores it and burrows in against my shoulder again. Loads of boys I know would love to get up close and personal with Honey Tanberry, but I am not one of them.

Not any more.

My mobile rings, and Cherry's name and picture flash up on the screen. This is not the kind of rescue I was hoping for – I jump back from Honey as if I've been stung.

'I don't bite, you know,' she says, looking hurt.

❀❀❀❀❀❀❀❀❀❀❀❀❀❀❀❀❀❀❀❀❀❀

'No. I know. It's just – well – it's Cherry.'

'Don't answer,' Honey begs. 'Not right now. Just give me five minutes, please? I know you don't think much of me, Shay, but surely I'm worth that much? For old time's sake?'

I hesitate, frowning.

'Call her back later,' Honey prompts. 'Please?'

I let my mobile ring out. I feel bad, but I am not sure how I would explain to Cherry that I am holed up in the storeroom den with my ex-girlfriend, mopping up her tears with my T-shirt. It would sound a whole lot worse than it actually is.

'Thanks, Shay,' she says in a tiny voice. 'I can talk to you – I always could. Nobody else understands. And . . . well, you don't judge me.'

I'm not sure about that.

'Look,' I tell her, exasperated. 'I can see why you're upset, Honey, but you need to calm down, get a bit of perspective. This isn't Charlotte and Paddy's fault – they must have been worried sick when you went missing!'

'I wasn't missing!' Honey sulks.

'So they knew where you were?'

'Well, no . . . but . . .'

31

'Honey, you were grounded,' I remind her. 'You vanished without telling anyone where you were going, and you were out all night and most of the next day. You didn't turn up at school. What were they meant to think?'

Honey hugs her knees, suddenly looking about ten years old instead of fifteen.

'How come you're always so smart?' she whispers. 'OK. So I messed up . . . but the point is, I'm in trouble. I have some sort of weird police record now for running away, and the threat of social services hanging over my head. That's really not fair. And Mum and Paddy hate me, Shay, they really do! I may as well be taken into care because they're threatening me with some kind of boarding-school boot camp anyhow. I mean, just shoot me now. Really. My life sucks.'

I shrug. 'You think you're the only one who's had a bad day?'

Honey gives me a sideways look. 'Yeah,' she says. 'Cherry mentioned about that whole Wrecked Rekords thing. Not to me, of course . . . your little girlfriend doesn't chat to me much, funnily enough. But . . . yeah, I heard. Bummer. Your dad's still being his usual charming self then?'

'You could say that.'

❁ ❁

'Basically, we've both been dumped on,' Honey declares. 'You just got offered the chance of a lifetime, the chance to make your dream happen – and your dad shot the whole thing down in flames. Nice.'

The anger I have been trying to keep buried all day comes bubbling up to the surface, seeping through my veins like bitter poison. It hurts, like an ache inside, a sickness. No matter how hard I work, I know I will never be able to please my dad or make him proud; Ben seems to do all of that without even trying.

Somehow, I am always second best. The things I want, the things I am good at, never count for anything.

'My family want rid of me,' Honey is saying. 'Whether it's social services or boarding school, they don't especially care which. I might as well just run away . . . it's like they expect me to anyway.'

'They were just worried,' I echo, but Honey's eyes darken and gleam.

'We could, you know,' she whispers. 'Run away, I mean. You and me. We could jump a train up to London and lie about our age and find a flat. You could record your songs with Wrecked after all, and play gigs . . . maybe you'd be famous. And I could be a designer or something, I could make really cool dresses and have a stall in Camden, and perhaps I'd get spotted too . . .'

The tiniest spark of excitement, of possibility, runs through me before the cold water of reality extinguishes it. Running away is not about finding flats and getting famous, it's about sleeping rough and going hungry night after night, and being dragged into a scary, predatory underworld. It would not be fun or cool or daring, it would be crazy, dangerous, totally disastrous.

Besides . . . Honey and me? I don't think so. Where has that even come from?

'Forget it, Honey,' I say. 'It wouldn't work out like that.'

'It might!' she argues. 'We could show them – our families, everyone – prove we can make it without their help. They'd be sorry then! And what have we got to lose?'

'Plenty,' I tell her. 'Better to stay and grab some GCSE passes and maybe some A levels . . . that could be our passport out of here. I want to go to uni and study music. London or Leeds or Liverpool, somewhere miles from here. And you could go to art college, Honey. That used to be what you wanted, not so long ago.'

❀❀❀❀❀❀❀❀❀❀❀❀❀❀❀❀❀❀❀❀❀❀❀

'My grades aren't so good lately,' she admits sulkily. 'And uni is still years away . . . we're only fifteen. I don't know if I can survive that long!'

'If I can, you can,' I point out. 'Besides, if you run away the police will track you down. And what then? Social services will wade in, just like you said. That's just what you don't want.'

'I guess . . .'

Her shoulders slump and she looks suddenly vulnerable. I've always known that underneath the stroppy, rebel-girl surface Honey Tanberry is just a kid, hurt and lost and angry because her dad went away and left her just when she needed him most.

'What is it about us that's so awful, Shay?' she asks in a small, sad voice. 'What makes us so difficult to love?'

'I don't know,' I sigh.

This time, when she leans against me and drops her head against my shoulder, I don't pull away.

4

When I get on the school bus next morning, Cherry waves me over and I flop into the seat beside her. My eyes slide to the back of the bus where Honey usually holds court, but there is no sign of her. Last night I talked her out of running away to London and into sticking things out at school. I talked her into going home and at midnight I walked her along the lane to her gate. What if she didn't go home after all? What if she waited in the trees until I'd gone, then headed off into the darkness along the lane, hitching a lift to London?

Were the late night heart-to-hearts and pep talks all for nothing?

'What happened to you last night?' Cherry is asking. 'I kept calling, but no reply.'

❀❀❀❀❀❀❀❀❀❀❀❀❀❀❀❀❀❀❀❀❀

'Sorry . . . my mobile died, and I didn't notice till this morning . . . I've left it at home on charge.'

'Oh? It seemed to be ringing . . . it didn't go to voicemail or anything . . .'

'My mobile does that sometimes,' I bluff. 'It acts kind of weird when the battery's flat.'

The lie drips too easily off my tongue, but it's safer than the truth. I am not sure how Cherry would feel if she knew I'd sat up till midnight in the storeroom den with Honey, telling her every single thing about Curtis and Dad and how let down I felt. I don't think she'd understand – I'm not even sure I do.

'No worries,' Cherry says. 'I guessed it would be something like that – I know you wouldn't just ignore me. I just wanted to make sure you were OK – thought you might be feeling low.'

'I'm fine,' I tell her. 'Or I will be, anyhow. I just don't want to be around Dad right now – I stayed late at the sailing centre last night, painting boats. It was OK . . . boring, I guess, but after a while your head just switches off and the job takes over. Then I holed up in the den and played guitar. I totally lost track of the time . . . didn't get to bed till late.'

'Aw, I bet,' Cherry sighs. 'Poor Shay. You must be so

❀❀❀❀❀❀❀❀❀❀❀❀❀❀❀❀❀❀❀❀❀❀

hacked off with your dad – all your dreams shattered before they even got off the ground.'

'What can I say?' I shrug. 'Dad's a nightmare. It's nothing new, and it's not the end of the world. You know me, I'll bounce back.'

'Of course you will. But if you ever want to talk about it . . .'

I sigh. I've done all my talking for now, but it wasn't to my girlfriend – it was to my ex. She was in the right place at the right time, and somehow the hurt and the anger I was feeling about Dad came spilling out. Now, in the cold light of morning, I wish I'd kept my mouth shut; it feels like a betrayal, somehow.

Cherry is looking at me, her dark eyes anxious. She's cute, she's kind and she cares about me far more than Honey ever did, I know. I would be crazy to screw all that up by trying to rebuild a friendship with Honey . . . not that that's what I'm doing.

Last night was a one-off.

'I don't really want to talk about it,' I say, pushing aside the guilt. 'I can't, not just now. But I know you're always there for me, Cherry . . . that means a lot.'

❁❁❁❁❁❁❁❁❁❁❁❁❁❁❁❁❁❁❁❁❁❁

The bus chugs on, navigating the winding country lanes, and without warning a wave of anger and frustration washes over me; I'm trapped in this sleepy corner of Somerset for three more years at least. My days will unfold in exactly the same way as they always have done: breakfast, bus ride, school, sailing centre, maybe some time out with Cherry or a quiet hour with my guitar. It's not bad, and many people have it a whole lot worse, I know, but suddenly it's not enough.

I want to change the rules, push the boundaries, shake things up. I want to stop waiting for my life to begin and make things happen.

Is this how Honey feels?

'Hey,' Cherry says, nudging my arm. 'You're miles away, Shay!'

'Sorry,' I say, but a part of me wishes I was. Miles away from grumpy parents and perfect big brothers; from crazy ex-girlfriends and guilt-inducing current ones; from school and work and looming exams. With an effort, I drag my focus back to Cherry.

'I was trying to tell you about Honey's latest exploits,' she goes on. 'Boy, she's really blown it this time! Out all Sunday night and truanting school – we thought she'd run

❀❀❀❀❀❀❀❀❀❀❀❀❀❀❀❀❀❀❀❀❀❀

away again! Yesterday was a total nightmare – Dad and Charlotte were arguing; Skye and Summer were crying; and Coco locked herself in her room and wouldn't talk to anyone. And what does Honey do? Rage at Dad and Charlotte for calling the police and then slam out of the house and disappear again . . .'

Unease seeps through me. 'So . . . she's vanished again?' I check. 'I couldn't help noticing she's not on the bus . . .'

'Couldn't you?'

Cherry looks confused and a little hurt, and too late I realize that it's not too tactful to tell your girlfriend you've been scanning the school bus for your ex. Oops.

'Honey hasn't vanished again, Shay, so you don't have to panic,' she says. 'Charlotte drove her into school for a pre-school meeting with the Head and some of her class teachers. That's why she's not on the bus. OK?'

'I just happened to notice,' I shrug. 'It's not like I was looking out for her or anything. I mean . . . why would I do that?'

Stop digging, Shay, I think. You're in enough trouble as it is.

'Whatever,' Cherry huffs. 'She didn't vanish, but she may

✿✿✿✿✿✿✿✿✿✿✿✿✿✿✿✿✿✿✿✿✿✿✿

as well have – she didn't get home till gone midnight, so everyone was worried sick all over again. Goodness knows where she was because Dad and Charlotte rang all her friends . . .'

I can't meet Cherry's eye, but of course she has no idea that Honey was with me. It's not something she needs to know. Ever.

The school bus shudders to a halt outside Exmoor High, and the crush of kids carries us forward and out into the bright, cool morning. Cherry's other stepsisters, the twins Skye and Summer, walk past us. Skye reaches out to swipe my beanie hat, laughing, then chucks it back at me. I struggle to dredge up a smile.

'Why would Honey even DO that?' Cherry is asking, and I seriously, seriously wish she would just drop the subject. 'Stay out so late when she was already in so much trouble? I don't get that girl, not at all. It's like she WANTED them to call the police again.'

'Maybe she just wanted you all to back off,' I sigh. 'Take some time to cool down. I don't suppose she even considers what it might be like for all of you – she's hurting too much to think about anyone else.'

Cherry frowns. 'Shay, you seem to know an awful lot about what my stepsister is feeling all of a sudden!'

The air between us crackles with tension – in a year of being together, this is the closest Cherry and I have ever been to a row. She's angry, I know, and hurt too . . . Honey has made both our lives difficult over the last year. For me to start defending my ex must seem like a betrayal, but a little bit of me can't help feeling sorry for Honey. And right now I am also irritated, annoyed; with Honey, with Cherry, with myself. I wish I could rewind, start the day again.

The last thing I want is to fall out with my girlfriend.

'I don't really know how Honey feels, I'm just guessing,' I shrug, sliding an arm round Cherry's waist as we follow the crowd into school. 'It's just the way she is – most of the time she just thinks of herself, how she's feeling. Nobody else is even on her radar. That's all I'm saying . . .'

'I suppose,' Cherry says. 'Sorry, Shay, I didn't mean to be clingy. You were with Honey for months – you're bound to care about her, just a bit . . . that's only natural.'

'Hey,' I tell Cherry. 'You have nothing at all to worry about, I swear.'

✿ ✿ ✿ ✿ ✿ ✿ ✿ ✿ ✿ ✿ ✿ ✿ ✿ ✿ ✿ ✿ ✿ ✿ ✿ ✿

'Sure,' she grins. 'I'm being silly, right? But it's just because I care.'

'I know,' I say. 'I'm sorry too . . . I'm not in the best of moods lately, as you might have noticed. Blaming my dad for that. Plus, I am shattered – I didn't get to bed till the early hours. I lay awake most of the night, but I must have dropped off in the end because I slept in and almost missed the bus. It's just not my day.'

'I bet you skipped breakfast as well,' Cherry frowns. 'You should grab something from the canteen, or you'll be tired all day. I need some stuff from my locker, but can you get me a Twix bar too? Reckon I need chocolate today!'

She hands me some silver and peels away towards the lockers while I lope along the corridor to the canteen and queue for a smoothie, a muesli bar and Cherry's Twix. The day has to get better, right? I have had enough bad luck for one lifetime, surely.

Or not.

I'm sitting on one of the tables slugging back the smoothie when Honey Tanberry walks in, her jaw-length hair perfectly tousled, her school skirt inches shorter than every other girl's, her white shirt a shrunk-in-the-wash special.

She looks a little too St Trinian's to have just come from an emergency meeting with the Head, but of course Honey makes her own rules. She's so catwalk cool and carelessly confident I guarantee nobody will have dared to challenge her.

'Sheesh,' she says, flopping down beside me. 'I hate this dump, I swear. Thanks to Mum, the teachers are going to be watching me like hawks this term. I might as well be in prison.'

She picks up the Twix I bought for Cherry, tears open the wrapper and bites a piece off.

'Hey!' I protest. 'That was for Cherry!'

'Get her another,' Honey shrugs. 'Cheers for putting up with me last night, Shay. I don't think anyone else would have had the patience to listen, and I can tell you right now that nobody else could have talked me into going home. I don't know if that's a good thing or a bad thing . . .'

'A good thing,' I say. 'Definitely.'

'Maybe. Anyhow, I just wanted to thank you for last night.'

Without warning, she flings her arms round me in a dramatic hug that has heads turning all around the canteen.

❁❁❁❁❁❁❁❁❁❁❁❁❁❁❁❁❁❁❁❁❁

I am trying to untangle myself when over her shoulder I see Cherry standing in the canteen doorway, her face frozen, her eyes wide.

I have no idea at all how long she's been there.

5

'Hang on, Cherry . . . this is NOT what it seems!' I yelp.

Honey steps back from me, amused and apologetic. 'Oops!' she says. 'Didn't know you were there, stepsis!'

'Obviously,' Cherry says, her voice a whisper.

'I was just saying thank you,' Honey explains. 'Shay was a total lifesaver last night. He sat up talking to me till all hours, then walked me home.'

My heart sinks so low it's probably in my Converse trainers. I am in trouble – big trouble, serious trouble.

'Cherry, I can explain,' I protest, although I'm not sure I can.

'Don't bother,' Cherry says. 'I think I can see what's going on.'

A small crowd of kids has gathered to gawp at the showdown. They remember the days when I used to date Honey and are putting two and two together, coming up with all the wrong answers. Just like Cherry.

'Are you cross because he didn't return your calls?' Honey asks brightly. 'Because that was totally my fault. He wanted to, but you called right in the middle of a big heart-to-heart so I asked him not to answer . . . honestly, blame me!'

I wish the ground would open up and swallow me.

Cherry doesn't even glance at her stepsister. She looks straight at me and I can see disappointment, disgust, dismay in her eyes. I hate myself for putting those things there.

'So your phone was out of battery?' she asks quietly. 'Nice one, Shay. Next time just tell me straight that you don't want to talk to me. Except that there won't be a next time, OK?'

The kids crowded round hold their breath, and I stifle the urge to tell them all to get lost. It wouldn't help.

'Cherry, listen –'

'There's nothing you can say that I want to listen to,' Cherry says. 'Why would I believe anything you have to say? You're a liar and a cheat!'

There is no comeback to that. I am not a cheat, but a

47

liar? Guilty as charged. I have lied to my girlfriend and been caught out; it doesn't matter that I lied for all the right reasons, to stop her from worrying, stop her from getting the wrong idea. She got the wrong idea anyhow.

'Harsh, Cherry,' Honey says, clearly amused. 'But then again . . . well, now you know how it feels.'

'Honey!' I argue. 'Cherry – it's not the same at all, if you'd just listen –'

'I've heard enough,' Cherry says, and her voice cracks a little as she speaks. 'Stay out of my way, Shay Fletcher. We're through. I never want to see you again!'

She turns on her heel and walks away, and the watching crowd whoop and cheer their support and solidarity as she goes.

'Loser,' one girl snarls at me.

'Idiot,' another spits.

The bell rings out for the first lesson, way too late to save me, and at last the crowd splinters away, heading to different corners of the building, different classes. I am left alone in the empty canteen with Honey.

'So . . . that was interesting,' she says. 'Who knew your little girlfriend could stand up for herself like that?'

48

'Ex-girlfriend,' I sigh. 'Thanks to you.'

'How was I to know you'd lied about your mobile?' she asks. 'And I take it you didn't tell her you were with me last night. You should have known she'd find out some time . . .'

I glare at Honey. 'Yeah, I should have known. Like I should have known you'd stir things up, make it look a million times worse than it actually was. Thanks a bunch.'

As I grab my rucksack and head to lessons, Honey shrugs and picks up the half-eaten Twix, taking another bite and wiping the chocolate from her mouth with a grin.

My life sucks, it's official. My mates Luke and Chris tell me I must be mad to go messing around with Honey again, and when I tell them I really wasn't, they smirk, disbelieving, and tell me Cherry's way too good for a Romeo like me. Skye and Summer, Honey's younger sisters, ambush me in the corridor at lunchtime, demanding to know why Cherry's so upset.

'What have you done to her?' Skye demands, furious. 'Every time I ask, she just starts crying again! There's a rumour going round that you kissed Honey in the school canteen, and if that's true I think I might have to strangle you.'

✿✿✿✿✿✿✿✿✿✿✿✿✿✿✿✿✿✿✿✿✿✿✿

'It's not true,' I huff.

'You're not welcome in our house any more,' Summer chips in. 'You cheated on Honey last summer and ditched her for Cherry – now you've dumped Cherry! What's wrong with you, Shay? Do you enjoy hurting people?'

'I haven't – what? Of course I don't!'

But the twins turn tail and are gone.

I scrape through the day, flunking a maths test, spilling ink all over my pencil sketch in art, breaking a guitar string in music. Yesterday's gossip about my possible contract with Wrecked Rekords has been replaced with a twisted story of how I'm way too full of myself these days and how I think Cherry's not good enough for me now.

It makes me sick.

I want to talk to Cherry, but her friends form a wall round her, warning me off. I try texting, until Cherry's friend Kira tells me to stop, that Cherry's deleted all my messages and blocked my number.

'Give up,' Kira tells me. 'Haven't you caused enough trouble?'

'It's all a mistake,' I argue. 'If I could just talk to Cherry, explain . . .'

✿✿✿✿✿✿✿✿✿✿✿✿✿✿✿✿✿✿✿

'Take the hint,' Kira says. 'It's over.'

I make it to the end of the school day, then have to endure the bus journey home. Surprise, surprise, Cherry is not saving me a seat; she is guarded by her friends who glare at me as I mooch past, looking for somewhere to sit. Luke and Chris both live in town, so they're not around for moral support. Summer and Skye and their friends give me the cold shoulder; Alfie, who's been hanging out with us all though the holidays and has just started dating Summer, shrugs awkwardly, mouthing an apology, turning away as I pass.

'There's a spare seat here, Shay,' Honey calls from the back, and everyone watches to see what I'll do.

I am pretty sure they'd lynch me if I took that seat, so in the end I squash in beside Anthony, a quiet loner-kid from the village, who is known as a maths and computer whizz. His hair is greasy and still cropped into a little-boy bowl-cut, his shirt is greyish and un-ironed and his school trousers flap an inch above his ankles. Anthony doesn't notice things like that, but he notices my misfortune all right.

'Hear you've blown it with Cherry,' he says brightly. 'Too bad.'

'It's a glitch,' I say. 'A misunderstanding. Trust me, it'll all be sorted by this time tomorrow.'

'How?' Anthony asks reasonably. 'As far as I can see she wants nothing to do with you.'

'I'll email,' I say confidently. 'Or send her a message on chat, or on her SpiderWeb page.'

'Don't think so,' Anthony says. 'This afternoon she was asking me how to block people on email and chat and defriend them on SpiderWeb.'

'She wouldn't do that!' I argue. 'I haven't done anything wrong!'

Anthony smiles. 'I know a lot about computers. If I wanted to, I could probably show you how to get past Cherry's security settings . . . it'd cost you, mind. But that still doesn't mean she'd read your messages. Too bad, huh?'

'Thanks for the sympathy vote,' I huff. 'If you've heard the rumours, they're all rubbish – I was just talking to Honey, that's all. It was totally innocent, like when you did that maths tutoring with her last term . . .'

He just shrugs. 'I know her better than you think,' he says. 'We're really close. Obviously, I didn't believe the rumours. I don't think anything's going on with you and

Honey – but Cherry does and that's what matters. I happen to know that Honey wouldn't take you back anyway. She says you're vain and shallow –'

'I'm vain and shallow?' I echo. 'That's rich! This is all Honey's fault!'

'Is it?' Anthony asks. 'Are you sure?'

I scowl, staring out of the window for the rest of the journey. If I stay angry, the self-pity can't creep in, prickling my eyes with shameful tears. That can't happen, it really can't; boys don't cry.

6

I learnt not to cry early on, soon after the incident with Ben's go-cart. In my family, crying doesn't earn you sympathy or hugs, just harsh words from Dad and smirks from Ben and pitying glances from Mum. It's safer to put on a brave face, smile and hold your head high and pretend that nothing matters. You can build a wall round yourself that way, keep the hurt inside.

The trouble is, Cherry learnt the same lesson. She lost her mum when she was a little kid, and got picked on at school too; she perfected the don't-care mask, the smile that hid a whole heartful of pain. When we got together, it was pretty much the first time either of us had learnt to be open and honest with anyone else – we taught each other to trust.

I've destroyed all of that now.

Days crawl by. I fix my brave face on each morning and cycle to school – let's just say it beats the school bus. After the first day or two, I begin to enjoy the cool breeze on my face, the misty mornings, the fast pedalling along twisty moorland lanes . . . but school itself is grim.

Cherry acts like I don't exist. I knew she was hurt, I knew she was angry, but I thought she'd calm down and let me put my side of the story. I didn't think she'd shut me out, push me away, block my texts, my emails, my messages.

Why would she do that? I've messed up, I know, but surely I deserve the chance to explain?

'Maybe she was getting fed up with you anyhow,' my friend Luke says helpfully.

'Maybe she was planning to finish with you,' Chris chips in. 'Maybe all you've done was give her a good excuse.'

'Thanks, mate,' I say. 'That makes me feel a whole lot better. Not.'

'It was just an idea,' Luke shrugs.

I don't like their idea, but I start to wonder if it might be true.

Back home, I eat tea while listening to Ben's latest exploits,

55

teach the evening kayak club at the sailing school, mop out the shower block and tidy up the reception area, hide out in the den and play guitar for hours. No matter what I do, everything seems grey and pointless without Cherry.

I sleep, and somehow I forget. I dream of moonlight and stars and sitting on the steps of the gypsy caravan with Cherry, last summer when we first met. In my dreams, the air is warm and the trees are strung with fairy lights and the two of us are talking, laughing, holding hands. We have big dreams, big hopes; and all of them are still possible.

And then I wake up, and grim reality crashes back in.

Tuesday turns into Wednesday, Wednesday into Thursday, and still Cherry won't even look at me.

What do you do when you feel so low you don't even want to lift your head up off the pillow? When your dreams of stardom bite the dust and bring you crashing down with them? When your dad treats you like dirt and your friends think you're crazy and the only girl you ever really cared about ditches you because you tried to stop your ex running away to London?

You write a song.

❀❀❀❀❀❀❀❀❀❀❀❀❀❀❀❀❀❀❀❀❀❀❀

You stay up late night after night down by the ocean, playing sad melodies until the words you cannot say to her in the daytime fall out of your mouth and drift into the darkness, making patterns with the music, pulling the sadness from your soul and turning it into something new, something better, something beautiful.

The song is called 'Bittersweet', and it's probably the best thing I've ever done – it's a pity Cherry won't ever get to hear it.

'Bittersweet' says all the things I want to say but can't – if Cherry heard it she would understand, surely? She'd know that I'm sorry.

If I had the guts, I would pick up my guitar, walk over to Tanglewood House and play my new song in the moonlight beneath her window. The trouble is Cherry has the attic room; she might not even hear me, and knowing my luck Summer and Skye would spot me first and chuck a bucket of water over me. Or possibly boiling oil?

I sink on to a rock at the water's edge instead, pick up my guitar and start to play, losing myself in the song:

✿✿✿✿✿✿✿✿✿✿✿✿✿✿✿✿✿✿✿✿✿

A seagull's call cuts through the misty morning
Sunlight hasn't touched the blankets yet . . .
I hear your voice whisper in my waking dream,
And tell myself you're here, and I forget —
How yesterday your smiling eyes they left me;
How yesterday your heart it turned away;
Last night I dreamt of cherry-blossom trees, but now
Comes the bittersweet reality of day . . .

As the last chorus fades away, I hear gentle clapping from behind me and jerk round to see a shadowy figure against the cliffs.. Hope floods me and I drop the guitar, scramble to my feet.

'Cherry?'

But Honey Tanberry steps out of the shadows, and my heart sinks.

'Sorry to disappoint you, Shay,' she says. 'Of course, there was a time when you'd have been pleased to see me . . .'

'Huh,' I snap. 'What are you doing here?'

'It's a free country, isn't it? Last time I checked, this wasn't your private stretch of beach.'

I scowl. 'Haven't you caused enough trouble?'

'Me?' she echoes, wide-eyed. 'Shay, it was you who lied to Cherry!'

'But you stirred things up,' I remind her. 'And you enjoyed it.'

'Maybe I did,' she admits. 'The way I see it, Cherry had it coming – she did the same to me, didn't she?'

'It wasn't the same at all,' I say firmly. 'What happened last summer was my fault, not Cherry's, but you've never let either of us forget it. In fact, I wouldn't be surprised if this whole thing wasn't one big set-up, designed to split us up!'

'Yeah, right,' Honey huffs, her eyes flashing anger. 'Don't flatter yourself, Shay. What happened last summer is over with – I've moved on. I had way bigger things on my mind this Monday than you and your moody little girlfriend!'

I sigh, sitting down again as the truth of this sinks in.

'I guess,' I admit. 'Sorry, Honey.'

'I have to admit I've kind of enjoyed the fallout, though,' she grins. 'I didn't think you had it in you to mess up so spectacularly, Shay, but I was wrong. And Cherry is just as stupid and stubborn as you are, moping and mooning

❁ ❁

around like it's the end of the world but too proud to do anything to fix it. Too bad.'

'She's moping?' I say, suddenly hopeful. 'She misses me?'

'Like I told you, she's not very bright,' Honey shrugs. 'She misses you, but she's really hurt . . . Skye and Summer and Coco are telling her to be brave, stay strong. And none of them will talk to me! What a joke!'

'But we didn't do anything,' I argue. 'Nothing wrong, anyway!'

'Tell her that,' Honey sighs. 'I already know.'

'She won't take my calls or read my messages or texts,' I say. 'I'm doomed.'

'Maybe you're better off without her?'

Honey leans down towards me, brushing the hair from my face. Her fingers stroke my cheek, trace the shape of my lips, slide softly down my throat to rest on my collar-bone. I close my eyes, my breathing suddenly ragged. I have never felt as lost or lonely as I do right now, and it would be good, so good, to hold someone close.

But the person I want to hold close is not Honey.

I pull back abruptly, and my ex-girlfriend laughs, tugging

60

the beanie hat I always wear down over my face, turning the whole thing into a joke.

'Hey, you can't blame a girl for trying,' she says, flopping down on to a rock a safe distance away. 'I guess you really are missing Cherry – how else could you resist me? Better tell her, Shay. Stuff the emails and texts, be direct. Paint it in three-foot-high letters along the playing-field fence at school . . . do SOMETHING!'

'Well, I wrote her a song . . .'

'Is that what you were playing before?' she asks. 'Nice one. Mopey, but nice. Why don't you put it online and send her the link? Declare your love for all to see? She'd fall for that, I bet!'

'You think?'

'I think,' Honey says. 'Play it again and I'll film it for you and email it over. You can do whatever you like with it then.'

She perches on the rock, fiddling with her mobile, while I pick up the guitar and strum some chords. Then I start to play properly, and I forget that Honey is watching, filming. I put everything into the music . . . my heart, my soul, my feelings for Cherry.

❀❀❀❀❀❀❀❀❀❀❀❀❀❀❀❀❀❀❀❀❀❀❀❀❀❀

I lose myself and find myself again.

And then the song is over, and the music lets go of me and I focus again, seeing Honey, the mobile, the empty beach, the sunset fading into darkness. Nothing is different. My life is still in ruins and my girlfriend hates me, and I am hanging out for the second time in a week with my ex, which really, seriously, cannot be a good thing.

Honey puts away her mobile, stands up.

'I'm not a total bitch, you know,' she says quietly. 'I've tried telling Cherry that nothing happened on Monday. I swore there was no funny business, but she didn't believe me. Why do people never believe me?'

I can think of a few reasons, but I say nothing. Honey is a magnet for trouble, but she has a sweet side too and right now she is trying to do something useful, something to fix up the mess the two of us have created between us.

'I'll load this on to my laptop and email it over to you,' she says. 'I hope you can patch things up. Really. And I hope your dad has a personality transplant and works out that he has two talented sons, not just one. It sucks about Wrecked Rekords.'

'It does,' I say. 'Thanks for trying to help.'

❀❀❀❀❀❀❀❀❀❀❀❀❀❀❀❀❀❀❀❀❀❀❀❀

She pauses, the wind catching her hair. 'You really love her, don't you?' she says. 'Cherry. That's cute. Really. Don't mess it up.'

She turns away, and I am almost certain I can see the glint of tears in her eyes.

7

I sleep late on Friday, and as I'm scrambling into my school clothes, my mobile rings: Finch.

'Hello, mate,' I say. 'How's life in the big city?'

'Pretty dull compared to the dramas going on down your way,' he responds coolly. 'I was speaking to Skye last night. I never had you down as a love-cheat. What are you playing at, Shay?'

I sigh. How could I forget that Finch and Skye were an item? They were practically joined at the hip all summer. Looks like I just lost another friend.

'It wasn't like that,' I tell him. 'Seriously.'

'So what was it like?'

I talk to Finch and the whole story spills out: Honey threatening to run away, Cherry calling at just the wrong moment, how trying to help turned into a disaster. I tell him about the awkward moment in the school canteen when Cherry saw her stepsister's thank-you hug and got the wrong idea, how the school grapevine took it and blew it out of all proportion, turned me into a lying love-rat.

'There was really nothing in it?' Finch checks. 'What a mess. Mate, you'd better set the record straight quick because right now you are not popular with the Tanberry-Costello family.'

'Tell me about it,' I say. 'I'm not popular with anyone lately. It sucks.'

'Gotta go, mate,' Finch says. 'School's calling, and I'm helping in the studio later. They're filming the last few studio scenes for the movie. Good luck with Cherry!'

'I'll need it!'

By the time I end the call, it's too late to even think about cycling to school. Looks like I'll be braving the bus – and if I survive that, I might try yet again to screw up my courage and talk to Cherry. Finch is right – the longer I leave it, the worse it will be. Today I will swallow my pride and tell Cherry exactly what happened, even if it means grovelling a little. Or a lot.

✿✿✿✿✿✿✿✿✿✿✿✿✿✿✿✿✿✿✿✿✿✿✿✿

I grab a quick smoothie in the kitchen while Mum, Dad and Ben sit down to a full-English. Dad is sorting through his post and passes a long white envelope across to Ben.

'Sheffield Hallam University,' he comments, looking at the postmark. 'What the heck do they want? You went to Birmingham!'

Ben takes the envelope and slices it open, unfolding the sheaves of paper inside. He scans the contents, smiles, then folds it up and puts it back again.

'Mistake, is it?' Dad presses. 'Just bin it, son. No worries.'

'It's not a mistake,' Ben says.

'Oh?'

'They do a great postgrad course at Sheffield,' Ben says carelessly. 'I can turn my degree into a teaching qualification.'

Dad pauses, a chunk of black pudding speared on his fork, hovering in mid-air.

'Why would you want to do that, Ben?' he asks quietly.

My brother shrugs. 'I'd like to teach,' he says. 'I've always enjoyed teaching the kids at the sailing centre, and it got me thinking about what I want to do with my life.'

Mum moves her chair back from the table and stands,

scraping her half-empty plate into the bin and catching my eye with an anxious expression. I don't blame her – I'm feeling anxious too.

'You already know what you're doing with your life, Ben,' Dad is saying. 'You're going to work alongside me, at the sailing centre – and take over one day. It's understood.'

'Not by me,' Ben shrugs. 'I've never actually said that was what I wanted, Dad. I've tried to tell you about this a million times – you never listen.'

'Of course I don't,' Dad snaps. 'It's nonsense. You don't need to do a postgrad course. Why would you want to be a poxy PE teacher, running round after snotty-nosed kids? I need you here – I'm happy to give you more freedom within the business, listen to your ideas – and in a year or two I'll make you the general manager.'

'I don't think so,' Ben says. 'Helping out at the sailing centre has only ever been temporary for me. I want to teach, and this course is one of the best in the country.'

Dad looks bewildered. He is used to Ben doing exactly as he suggests – I guess we all are.

'Well,' he blusters. 'We'll talk about it. Not many young men get to walk into a managerial job in the family business.

I admire your independent streak, but we're in a recession right now, son. A job means security, a future . . .'

'Dad,' Ben says patiently. 'I'm sorry. I'm going to do the postgrad course at Sheffield. It's all decided.'

'Not this year, though?' Dad argues. 'It's too late to apply now; term must be starting in a week or so.'

'I applied in January,' my brother says. 'They offered me a place and I grabbed it with both hands. I've been trying to tell you ever since . . .'

Mum steps forward with a well-timed mug of tea, aimed at calming the situation, but as she sets it down on the tabletop Dad slams his fist down, splashing tea everywhere and making his breakfast plate clatter.

'NO!' he roars at several thousand decibels. 'No, Ben, I am not going to let you do this. You'll live to regret it, and I will not let you ruin your life!'

'But, Dad,' Ben says reasonably. 'It's my life, surely? I'm not a kid any more, I'm twenty-one years old. I have thought this through long and hard, and it's what I want. I'm sorry but I am going to do it, whether you like it or not.'

'Over my dead body!' Dad roars, and his arm swipes across the tabletop, sending the breakfast plate and the mug of tea flying across the kitchen to smash into the cupboards and splatter all over the tiles.

'Go, Shay,' Mum says, stuffing my rucksack into my arms and pushing me towards the door. 'You too, Ben. Give your dad a chance to cool down . . .'

I don't need telling twice. I am out of there, grabbing my guitar and legging it out of the door. I'm running late already, and the kitchen drama hasn't helped – unless I sprint I might actually miss the school bus and earn myself a late-mark for my trouble. I am loping along the path when I hear the door slam behind me.

'Wait up, little brother,' Ben yells. 'You're cutting it a bit fine, aren't you? I'll give you a lift. C'mon . . . I could use the company!'

'OK – thanks!'

Ben's face is set, determined. He doesn't say much as we pile into his beat-up old car and drive away from the kerb, just slides the sunroof back and slots an ancient Beach Boys CD into the player and turns the volume up to max. We drive like this for ten minutes, deafened by Ben's favourite surf band churning out relentlessly happy sixties pop, before he relents and turns the volume down to bearable again.

❀❀❀❀❀❀❀❀❀❀❀❀❀❀❀❀❀❀❀❀❀

'I am going, you know,' he says eventually. 'I'm sick of him running my life for me, controlling every little thing I do. I didn't know any better when I was your age, Shay, but I'm older now – I know what I want, and it definitely isn't this.'

'Dad'll calm down,' I say. 'I think it was just a shock for him – it was for me!'

'Yeah,' Ben sighs. 'Sorry. I should have said something to you. Mum told me to . . .'

'Mum knew?' I check, surprised.

'Yeah, of course. She's totally behind me. I've tried to talk to Dad about it loads of times, but he won't listen – he just blocks me off, changes the subject. Mum was going to break it to him gently, but . . . too late now.'

'Wow.' I blink. 'I always thought you wanted to run the sailing centre. I mean, I know that you wanted to be a footballer until you had that injury, but after that I was pretty sure you were set on the sailing centre. I really had no idea!'

'That was all Dad too,' Ben says, his eyes on the road. 'I liked football, but it was his passion, not mine. I was good at footy, and Dad pushed me, so I went along with it . . .

until Southampton dropped me from the youth squad. That's when it all went pear-shaped.'

'Yeah, the accident,' I remember. 'That must have felt like the end of the world.'

Ben just laughs. 'Shay . . . there was no accident,' he says. 'No injury. Southampton dropped me from the squad because in the end I wasn't good enough.'

My head struggles to make sense of this.

'But you said . . .'

'Dad said,' Ben corrects me. 'He told everyone I'd had an injury because he couldn't bear to tell people the truth . . . that I just didn't make the grade. He was ashamed of me, Shay. I'd let him down.'

'Whoa,' I say. 'I never had a clue! I mean . . . you're Dad's blue-eyed boy, Ben! The favourite! He's always been so proud of you . . .'

'That's what I always thought too,' he shrugs. 'But Dad's such a control freak – he was only ever proud of me when I was doing what he said, and doing well at it. When things went wrong he lied to everyone to save face. How d'you think that felt?'

I'm guessing Ben felt the way Dad's always made me

❁❁❁❁❁❁❁❁❁❁❁❁❁❁❁❁❁❁❁❁❁❁❁❁

feel – a disappointment, a let-down, second best, but there is no comfort in knowing that my perfect big brother is not so perfect after all. I just feel sorry for him, and glad that he's able to get out of Kitnor and follow his own path.

I notice that Ben has driven right past the turn-off for Minehead.

'Hey – you've missed the turning!' I point out. 'Better take the next left, or I'll be late for school!'

'You're not going to school today,' Ben says. 'Lessons can wait. Dad almost ruined things for me, Shay – I'm not going to let him do the same to you. Sometimes you have to seize the moment – take the opportunities that come your way.'

'Huh?'

'Take control of your own destiny,' he says. 'Look to the future.'

'Ben, what are you talking about?'

'Wrecked Rekords,' my big brother says. 'You and I are going to London!'

8

As kidnaps go, this one is pretty cool. The morning unfolds into a road trip, with lots of brotherly bonding and advice and a long stop for Coke and chips at a greasy-spoon cafe just outside Swindon. The two of us have never talked so much before, not properly – our friendliest exchanges have always been wind-ups and jokes.

We've never been close – perhaps that was Dad's fault, or maybe it was just the age gap, but now I am getting to know my big brother and I can see he's not so very different from me. A couple of times I think of telling him about Cherry, but I don't know where to start. I want Ben's support, but not his pity.

I guess I don't need anyone else to tell me I've been an idiot. I already know.

'Dad used to play football, y'know,' he tells me. 'Small-time, Sunday league stuff. It was his dream, though. That's why he pushed me so hard – he thought he was helping me, but really it was all about him. His dream, not mine.'

'Just like the sailing centre is his thing,' I say. 'And you're turning your back on it. That takes courage, Ben – we all know Dad has a temper on him.'

'We should have stood up to him years ago,' Ben sighs as we cruise along the M4. 'Just for the record, Shay, I'm sorry about the go-cart thing. I didn't think you'd actually go and break your arm . . .'

I laugh, and as we approach the outskirts of London I take the forms that Curtis Rawlins gave me out of my rucksack, where they've been hidden for the last few days, still slightly stained and now quite crumpled too. Can Ben really sign them for me, open up the doors to possibility again? Maybe. I hope so.

Ben makes me navigate, using a dog-eared street map and his iPhone. We get lost about a dozen times before we finally pull up outside Wrecked Rekords' Camden HQ.

It's like stepping into a dream – a dark, edgy, slightly psychotic dream. The walls are papered with silver foil and a collage of iconic album covers stretching back decades. A huge, shiny mobile made entirely from CDs spins silently in the stairwell, and framed gold discs line the hallway. Even the sofas in the waiting area look like they have been borrowed from a passing spaceship.

The girl at the reception desk has fuschia-pink hair and a pierced nose, and she seems to be wearing some kind of cool fancy-dress outfit made from a checked tablecloth and a lace curtain. She looks at me doubtfully, taking in the school uniform and beanie hat, and I flush a little pink.

I push the crumpled forms across the desk towards her, and she looks at them dubiously. 'We'd like to see Curtis Rawlins, please,' I say.

'Yeah?' the girl drawls. 'Do you have an appointment?'

'No, but . . .'

'You'll need one,' she shrugs. 'No exceptions. Why not send in a CD, some demo tracks? Then you can ring in a few weeks and if Curtis and his team think you have potential we can set you up with a November appointment. Or December, maybe. Or January.'

Or never.

Stricken, I look at Ben, who rolls his eyes dramatically.

'Don't panic, little brother,' he says under his breath. 'Leave this to me. Watch and learn . . .'

Ben leans across the desk in full-on flirt mode, his sun-gold hair flopping carelessly across his tanned face, his blue eyes intent. I am not sure that his beach-hunk looks will cut the ice with the pink-haired girl, though. She looks like she'd be more impressed with tattoos and piercings and a neon-blue mohican haircut.

'Hey,' he grins. 'The thing is . . . we've driven all the way from Somerset. Four hours on the road, and all because Curtis wanted to see us. "Drop in any time," he said. So we did. I mean, I know that rules are rules, but we need to see the guy now, not next week or next month or next year . . .'

I hear the soft West Country burr in Ben's voice and I can tell that his charm offensive isn't working. I wonder why we didn't just wear dungarees, wellies and straw hats because to this girl we must seem like real country kids, clueless, crass.

'Aw, c'mon,' Ben pleads. 'You know what it's like. We've got the forms. You can sort this out for us – save our lives. I'd be grateful – very grateful! I'll buy you a drink after work if you like . . .'

❀❀❀❀❀❀❀❀❀❀❀❀❀❀❀❀❀❀❀❀❀❀❀❀

'No, thanks,' she says.

'Look, Curtis will see us, no worries,' Ben insists. 'He's been in talks with my little brother here about signing for Wrecked. Shay's going to be the Next Big Thing!'

'They all say that,' the girl says, going back to her computer screen.

'No, seriously,' Ben presses. 'Curtis came all the way to Kitnor to see him. He's already listened to the demo tracks, and seen him play live. He wanted to sign him, but there was a bit of a mix-up. Circumstances beyond our control. But we're here to fix it now, so if you'll just let us see Curtis . . .'

'Can't,' the girl yawns. 'He's gone out. Not sure when he'll be back.'

My heart sinks. Ben's attempt to save the day has backfired, failed. We've driven all this way for nothing, but looking on the bright side, at least I got to skip a day of being glared at and frozen out at school.

We are walking out through the plate-glass doors when the miracle happens. A man in a skinny suit and a red trilby hat comes towards us, and when he sees me his face lights up.

77

'Shay Fletcher!' he grins. 'Great to see you! Come in, come in . . .'

He ushers us into the foyer and the fuschia-haired girl looks up from her computer screen, raising an eyebrow.

I introduce Ben and we sit on the space-age sofas while Curtis fetches us fancy cappuccinos with chocolate sprinkles and thick wedges of shortbread.

'So,' he asks me. 'What brings you all the way to London? Has your dad changed his mind?'

'Not exactly,' I admit.

'Mum supports him, though,' Ben chips in, and this is news to me. 'She's his guardian too, right? And I'll look out for him if you need me to. He'd like to go ahead and sign up, wouldn't you, Shay?'

'Well, yeah . . . I'd love to,' I say.

Curtis smiles. 'That's great, Shay,' he says. 'So . . . you're saying that your mum would sign for you, even if it goes against your dad's wishes? Really?'

'Definitely,' Ben says. 'Maybe. Well, possibly . . .'

'No,' I admit sadly. 'I don't think she would.'

The look on Curtis Rawlins' face says it all. We are wasting his time, wasting our own. Why didn't I see that before?

❀❀❀❀❀❀❀❀❀❀❀❀❀❀❀❀❀❀❀❀❀❀❀

'Listen,' Ben cuts in. 'I'm twenty-one and I can take charge of Shay, look after him, sign for him . . . whatever you need me to do. Dad doesn't understand and Mum won't go against him, even though she'd like to . . . but I can be the responsible adult, surely? Not everybody gets offered a chance like this. I want Shay to take it!'

I have never loved my brother more than I do right now, I swear, but Curtis sighs, and I know that Ben's suggestion isn't going to change things.

'Thing is, you're not Shay's guardian,' he says sadly. 'His parents need to be on board, and . . . well, they're not.'

'He has a talent,' Ben argues. 'You said so . . . can't you take a risk on him, bend the rules, just this once? Shay loves his music. He won't let you down!'

'I'll do whatever it takes,' I promise. 'I've got a new song – it's good, really good. Shall I play it for you?'

Curtis Rawlins shakes his head.

'I'd love to hear it, Shay, but . . . it won't make any difference. There's nothing I'd like more than to sign you up . . . but your age is against us here. I've been talking to my colleagues. Your dad doesn't just have misgivings, he's actively hostile to the whole idea. Even if your mum was totally on board with all this I'd be very wary about taking things further right now. When we work with a minor, we need to know that the family are in, one hundred per cent. In your case, Shay, we couldn't rely on that, no matter how supportive your brother may be.'

'So . . . what are you saying?' Ben asks, frowning.

'I'm saying . . . there is nothing I would like more than to sign you to Wrecked, Shay, but right now I can't. Keep working – keep singing and writing. And come back and see me when you're eighteen.'

We shake hands with Curtis Rawlins and walk out of there with our heads held high, but inside I am shaking. I'm not sure I can take another knock without falling to pieces.

'Sorry, mate,' Ben says. 'That didn't go so well.'

'I'm sorry,' I sigh. 'I've wasted your time . . . all that effort for nothing.'

'It wasn't for nothing,' he grins. 'I got to spend some time out with my little brother, even if I had to practically kidnap you to do it. I've had fun. And it wasn't a waste – we know the situation now. You have something to work for, something to aim for.'

❁❁❁❁❁❁❁❁❁❁❁❁❁❁❁❁❁❁❁❁❁❁❁❁

'I guess,' I say.

'Definitely,' Ben insists. 'We tried, didn't we? If you want something badly, you go the extra mile. You don't just sit back and accept things, you do everything you can to make it happen. Maybe it didn't work out this time, but if you keep believing, keep working, then sooner or later it will. Keep the faith. We gave it our best shot. No regrets!'

I frown. Ben is talking about the record deal, of course, but he has a point.

I think about a girl with glossy, blue-black hair, shining almond eyes fringed with long, sooty lashes, the sweetest smile. Cherry is my best friend, my crush, my confidante. Without her, everything is dull and pointless. Without her, my heart is in the gutter.

I remember Honey's advice from last night, Finch's words from this morning.

I messed up the best thing I ever had, and all over a tangle of lies and misunderstandings. I need to ditch the excuses and fix it up before it's too late. I wonder if there's time to meet Finch for a pep talk before facing Cherry, seeing as we're actually in London. I pick up my mobile to message him and find it's dead, out of charge. Looks like I'm on my own with this.

What was it Ben said? If you want something badly, you go the extra mile.

9

Ben and I mooch around Camden for a while, checking out the quirky stalls and eating pitta bread and falafel down by the canal in the sunshine. I remember Honey's pipe dream of running away and starting a fashion stall here, and sigh. Ben buys a couple of T-shirts and I buy a second-hand silver chain with a cherry-motif pendant, hoping I get the chance to give it to Cherry. We both pick out mirrored sunglasses and drive out of Camden at sunset with the sunroof down and Ben's Beach Boys CD blaring.

We don't get home till midnight.

Dad appears in the doorway the minute Ben's car pulls up, the anger rolling off him in waves. I can feel my shoulders slump.

Today is the day I learnt how cool my brother really is,

and the day I found out for sure that I will not be a fifteen-year-old teen idol signed up to Wrecked Rekords. It's the day I discovered that the best things in life are worth fighting for, that if you don't like something you change it.

It was a life-changing day, but now, back home, it feels like nothing has altered at all. Dad unleashes his temper, ranting about how Ben and I have let him down, left him short-staffed, had everyone worried sick.

Yeah, right.

Following Ben down the garden path, I stop abruptly and turn, dropping my schoolbag into the flower bed and shrugging my guitar over one shoulder. I walk away, Dad yelling my name into the darkness.

For once, I just don't care.

I walk through the silent village, street-lamp spooky, and out along the dark lane that leads to Tanglewood. The sky is scattered with stars and my eyes adjust quickly to the dark, but I am scared. What if it all goes wrong, if Cherry won't see me, if Paddy and Charlotte set the dog on me or call the police?

Don't just sit back and accept things, I remember. Go the extra mile.

❀❀❀❀❀❀❀❀❀❀❀❀❀❀❀❀❀❀❀❀❀❀❀❀

What's the worst that could happen?

I push the gate open and crunch across the gravel, beneath trees hung with solar-powered fairy lights, a left-over from the summer. The house is in darkness, silent, sleeping. I hear Fred the dog barking from inside the house and Humbug the sheep bleating from his stable, but I walk on until I am positioned beneath Cherry's attic window. Picking up a handful of gravel, I throw one small pebble upwards in a swift arc and hear the satisfying clink of stone on glass.

A light goes on, but it's the wrong light. The room Skye and Summer share. Great.

The twins appear at the window, then the sash slides up and Skye leans out.

'Shay?' she whispers. 'What the . . . ?'

'Shhh,' I say. 'Please? I know what you think of me, Skye, but give me a chance – I just need Cherry to hear me out.'

'Finch rang me this afternoon,' she says softly. 'He explained. To be fair, Honey'd been saying the same thing too, but we didn't listen . . .'

'You're speaking to me?' I ask, wide-eyed. 'You believe me?'

Summer leans out of the window alongside her twin.

❁ ❁

'Of course we do,' she says. 'We've been texting you all day . . . Cherry has too!'

'She has?' I grin. 'My mobile's dead. Sorry!'

'No, we're sorry,' Summer says. 'We should have given you a chance. It's just – Cherry's cool. She's our stepsister, and she's had a rough time, and nobody – NOBODY – is allowed to hurt her.'

'I wouldn't,' I argue. 'I won't!'

'Better tell her that,' Skye laughs.

I take another piece of gravel and aim higher, but this time the pebble hits the roof and skids down the slates again with a clatter. Abruptly, the turret room lights up and Honey's window swings open.

'About time,' she calls down. 'Have I missed the big apology?'

'No,' I huff. 'Give me a chance. I wasn't counting on having an audience . . .'

'Too bad,' Honey drawls. 'You've woken us up, you'd better entertain us now.'

Another light snaps on, over to the right, and Coco's window creaks open. 'Is that you, Shay?' she wants to know.

'Who else would it be?' Skye yells across. 'We don't

usually have random teenage boys wandering about the garden in the middle of the night, do we?'

'You never know, with you lot!' Coco smirks. 'This is SO slushy! Are you serenading her, Shay? Romeo, Romeo, wherefore art thou, Romeo?'

'Cut it out,' I say. 'It's not funny!'

'It is from where I'm standing,' Honey says, and Coco pushes her window open wider, settling herself on the window sill with her violin. A whining dirge begins to swirl out into the darkness, and in the kitchen Fred the dog begins to whine along in tune. On the plus side, if the pebble-throwing doesn't wake Cherry, the violin solo definitely will. Ouch.

The downstairs lights flare into life, the kitchen door opens and Paddy and Charlotte appear on the doorstep in PJs and dressing gowns.

'What the heck is going on?' Paddy demands. 'Is this some kind of midnight garden party, or are you just casing the joint for a possible burglary? Shay?'

'I can explain,' I say, alarmed. 'If I could just talk to Cherry . . .'

'Finally,' Charlotte says. 'Can you two just make up, please? I can't take any more of the tears and moping.'

'Somebody wake Cherry, for goodness' sake,' Honey grumbles. 'We'll be here all night.'

Finally the light goes on in Cherry's attic room, and the Velux window lifts and opens and a sad, pale face framed with dark, rumpled hair appears above me.

'Say something then,' Coco says, setting down her violin at last. 'She's waiting!'

They're all waiting. I know I need to apologize, but not to the whole family, surely?

I clear my throat. 'Cherry?' I call up to her. 'I think we need to talk. I . . . I've messed up and there's a lot I need to say to you, but . . . it's hard to find the right words. So . . . well, I wrote a song. For you.'

I take a deep breath.

'Go for it, Shay,' Honey says. 'What are you waiting for?'

So I play. I try to forget that Cherry's dad and stepmum are right in front of me, that Fred the dog is sniffing around my feet, that her stepsisters are watching, that my ex-girlfriend is listening. I blank it all out and keep my eyes on Cherry, putting my heart and soul into the song.

When I finish, there is a silence and Cherry puts a hand to her mouth and ducks away from the window, out of sight.

❀❀❀❀❀❀❀❀❀❀❀❀❀❀❀❀❀❀❀❀❀

Then Skye and Summer begin to clap, and Coco whoops and whistles, and even Honey, Paddy and Charlotte join in. Fred licks my hand and wallops the blue guitar with his tail.

At last Cherry appears in the kitchen doorway and her stepsisters vanish, one by one, their lights extinguished like candles on a birthday cake.

'Don't be too late,' Paddy says, and he and Charlotte retreat too, leaving Cherry and me alone. In the shadows outside the kitchen door we are awkward, unable to look at each other.

'I'm sorry,' I blurt.

'No, I'm sorry –'

'It was all a mistake – I know I shouldn't have blanked your call – but there was honestly nothing going on . . .'

'I know,' she says. 'Honey swore the same thing. And Skye said you told Finch the whole story . . .'

'I should have told you, though,' I sigh. 'I'm an idiot.'

'I'm an idiot too, for not trusting you . . . it's just that it looked bad, and I was so upset and didn't want to listen . . . I felt so stupid!'

'No, I'm the stupid one . . .'

We move away from the house, in case well-meaning stepsisters are eavesdropping in darkened rooms. We walk down beneath the trees strewn with fairy lights and sit on the steps of the gypsy caravan, the way we used to last summer when we first met, before we were actually going out together.

'You wrote a song for me,' Cherry says. 'It's beautiful.'

'You're beautiful,' I say. 'The song doesn't even start to say what I'd like to say, but it was terrible without you . . . I'm going to make sure I don't lose you again, OK? No matter what.'

'I'm not beautiful, though,' Cherry protests. 'I'm just ordinary, really, and Honey – well, she really is gorgeous. That's why I thought . . . maybe you'd had enough of me, maybe you wanted to be with her again . . .'

'You're a million miles from ordinary, Cherry,' I sigh. 'You're the most beautiful girl in the world to me, inside and out. I never felt that way about Honey, not ever. I cared about her, sure – I still do because she's so mixed up, so unhappy. She was in pieces about the threat of being taken into care, threatening to run away again – I don't know why she came to me, but she did, and I had to at least try

❀❀❀❀❀❀❀❀❀❀❀❀❀❀❀❀❀❀❀❀❀❀

to help. I had no idea it would all turn into such a mess, or I wouldn't have bothered . . .'

'You would, though,' Cherry says. 'Because you're kind and caring and thoughtful. That's why I love you.'

When I hear those words I don't care any more about the ruined record deal or wasted trip to London or the fact that Dad will probably ground me for the rest of my life when I finally go back home. I don't even care that I've just had the worst few days of my whole entire life because I know that everything is going to be OK again. Better than OK.

Cherry leans up and kisses me, and I want the kiss to go on forever, warm lips, the taste of mint toothpaste, happiness. We pull apart and sit for a long time on the caravan steps beneath the cherry trees, arms wrapped round each other.

'We'll be OK, won't we?' I ask at last.

'We'll be fine,' Cherry says. 'Promise. But . . . will you play that song again? "Bittersweet"? Please?'

So I do.

10

I get home at daybreak, and Dad yells and roars and tells me I am grounded until Christmas, except for school and my job at the sailing centre. I shrug. Nothing he says or does can touch me now.

When I don't react, he takes away my mobile phone and bans me from the internet, even says he'll put my blue guitar on the bonfire.

'No,' Mum argues. 'Enough! I won't stand for it, Jim. That's plain cruel. You've pushed one son away – don't do the same to Shay!'

I don't remember Mum ever standing up to Dad before, certainly not to defend me. Dad looks just as shocked.

'I just want what's best for him!' he protests. 'He'll thank me, one day!'

❀❀❀❀❀❀❀❀❀❀❀❀❀❀❀❀❀❀❀❀❀

'Like Ben is thanking you?' Mum asks. 'You have two wonderful, talented sons – but you can't see that because all their lives you've been trying to bully and control them, push square pegs into round holes. You've spent years trying to turn Ben into a carbon copy of you, but you'll never do it – he's different, can't you see that?

'You've ignored Shay because you don't understand him, which is just as bad. Perhaps he is too young for the music business right now, but you can't crush his dreams just because they're different from yours. He's going to shine, with or without your help!'

Dad's face struggles between anger and irritation, finally settling on disgust.

'I didn't mean it, about the guitar,' he grates out. 'I'm not a tyrant, you know. I just want what's best for them!'

'Then let them make mistakes, and learn from them,' Mum says. 'The way we did. You have to stop this, Jim. Let them have the freedom to be whoever they want to be, and be proud of them for that.'

Dad rolls his eyes and stomps away. In the end, he leaves me with my guitar but sticks with the mobile/internet ban. Mum stops talking to him, except in front of the

❀❀❀❀❀❀❀❀❀❀❀❀❀❀❀❀❀❀❀❀❀❀❀

sailing-centre clients. She stops bringing him cups of tea, gives up ironing his shirts, abandons the morning fry-ups.

It goes on for a week.

In fifteen years, I have never known Mum to protest at all, but now she is making her feelings clear, and Dad is not impressed. You could cut the atmosphere at home with a knife.

It's actually a relief to be at school. I hang out in the music room at lunchtimes with Cherry, but the other kids are talking to me again – all is forgiven. They ask if I've signed the contract with Wrecked Rekords yet; when I tell them there is no record contract, they look disbelieving, like I am trying to hide my imminent fame and fortune from them. It's like they are expecting me to pop up on X Factor any day now.

'Love the new song,' one kid says. I can't help noticing he's wearing a beanie hat just like mine.

'Brilliant stuff,' a girl chips in.

'What are you talking about?' I frown. 'How...?'

'"Bittersweet",' the beanie-hat kid says. 'Awesome.'

'Have you been telling people about the song?' I ask my mate Chris at lunchtime. 'Kids keep asking me about it. I mean, how do they even know?'

✿✿✿✿✿✿✿✿✿✿✿✿✿✿✿✿✿✿✿✿✿

'Hard to miss, these days,' he says, grinning. 'You have a lot of support, Shay.'

'Everyone knows who you are now,' Luke cuts in. 'You've gone way up in the popularity stakes, I kid you not. All the Year Ten girls are crushing on you, and I counted seven kids wearing beanie hats in the canteen yesterday lunchtime. Jammy swine – how did you manage to get so lucky?'

'All hope of a recording contract shot down in flames,' I remind him. 'Grounded till Christmas? Mobile confiscated? Banned from the internet? How is that lucky, exactly?'

'You're obviously getting round the internet ban somehow, though,' Chris says. 'Your music page on SpiderWeb is updated every day . . .'

I frown. 'Hang on . . . I don't have a page on SpiderWeb!'

'You definitely do,' Luke insists. 'That song you wrote for Cherry is on there. "Bittersweet". Nice one!'

'The page has loads of "likes",' Luke tells me. 'People commenting and stuff. It's good!'

'But . . . I don't get it! I haven't made a music page!' I argue.

Luke takes out his iPhone and searches the net, and sure

enough up comes a page called 'Shay Fletcher Music'. There's a photo of me, a moody black-and-white snapshot of me playing guitar by a beach bonfire. I've never seen the picture before, but I know it's from the summer, from one of the beach parties we had. Who took it?

Just as Chris and Luke said, a video of 'Bittersweet' is on there; the shadowy, grainy film Honey took of me down by the shore. Someone has ramped up the contrast and chopped the editing around a bit, and the whole thing looks pretty awesome for something recorded so quickly. There's a sort of home-made cool to it, and the sound is actually pretty good.

The video has hundreds of comments, and the page itself has almost 1,200 'likes'.

'Who put all this together?' I puzzle. 'And how has it got all these followers so quickly? I don't get it! I only wrote the song last week!'

We scroll through the comments, all good; some of the names I recognize – Cherry, Skye, Summer, Alfie, Finch . . . plus lots of kids from school and even our maths teacher, Mr Farrell. Others are names I don't know at all.

'That's how the internet works,' Chris shrugs. 'Things

❀❀❀❀❀❀❀❀❀❀❀❀❀❀❀❀❀❀❀❀❀❀❀

snowball. Some musicians don't actually need a record deal to make the big time these days, you must know that!'

My head spins with questions . . . Honey took the video of me singing 'Bittersweet', but would she go to all the trouble of making a page to promote it? I'm not convinced. Cherry, maybe? Honey must have given her the video.

'I love that fanpage on SpiderWeb,' I tell her on the school bus home. 'I can't believe you'd do that for me!'

'I didn't.' She smiles mysteriously, sliding the little cherry pendant I bought her up and down on its silver chain. 'Someone's on your side, though. Someone who knows a lot about you. It's so cool . . . and you're getting loads of "likes"! Everyone I know is sharing the link!'

'OK . . . that's great! But . . . it's definitely not you?' I check.

'Not me. I thought it was Ben, maybe?'

'I don't think so . . . not really his style.'

Cherry shrugs. 'I don't suppose it matters who it is . . . It's taking off, and that's what counts! You never know just who might hear that song . . . if you know what I mean!'

'Um . . . I don't, actually,' I say.

'Never mind,' she says cryptically. 'You'll find out soon enough, if things work out the way we think . . .'

'Huh? Cherry, you can't just say stuff like that and leave me hanging!'

'Don't listen to her,' Skye says, leaning across the aisle. 'She's talking rubbish. Just trying to confuse you. It might all come to nothing . . .'

'What might?' I growl. 'You're not making any sense!'

'Be patient!' Summer chimes in. 'If it happens, it happens. If it doesn't . . . well, no harm done. Don't worry, Shay!'

The three of them giggle and whisper and nudge each other, refusing to say anything more.

The next day, my brother Ben moves out. He packs his little car up with a suitcase and a couple of boxes, scrawls his address on a scrap of paper and hands me fifty quid.

'If you can't stick it, jump on a train to Sheffield and come find me,' he says. 'I mean it, mate. I'm there for you, whenever, whatever.'

'Thanks, Ben.'

'If Dad's still being an idiot, or school sucks, or even if you just fancy another road trip . . .'

I laugh. 'I know. I'll miss you,' I grin, and my big brother hauls me in for a big bear hug. I wonder why it has taken me fifteen years to see just how amazing he really is?

'Seriously,' he says. 'Don't let the old man push you around the way he did with me. You always were better at standing up to him than I was. Be strong. Be your own person.'

'I will, promise.'

Mum hugs Ben next, wiping away tears. 'He's a silly, stubborn man,' she tells Ben. 'But he loves you very much. He'll come round.'

'I know,' Ben says. He gets into the car and starts the engine, idling a little as he looks up beyond us to the cottage. I can't imagine what he must be feeling – a jumble of emotions, good and bad, for the man who tried to live his own dreams through him.

At the very last minute Dad comes down the path, his face like stone. Ben winds down the car window. 'I hope you don't live to regret this, son,' he mutters. 'I think you're making a big mistake.'

Ben just smiles. 'It'll all work out. I wish it could be different, Dad, but . . . no regrets.'

❀❀❀❀❀❀❀❀❀❀❀❀❀❀❀❀❀❀❀❀❀❀

As the car pulls away, Dad shades his eyes with one hand, watching until the battered VW vanishes over the hill.

'Still proud of you, Ben,' he says gruffly. 'Always.'

He slings an arm round my shoulders. 'Come on, son. We've got classes to take at the sailing centre, trippers to take out. Let's get going.'

We work hard, and as the day wears on I notice a thaw between Mum and Dad. Cups of tea appear between classes, smiles are exchanged, words spoken. It's like the coming of the spring after an arctic winter, slow but sure.

We're just clearing up after the last of the punters has gone when two cars pull into the car park in a squeal of gravel. One of them is Paddy's little red minivan, the other a sleek, silver Citroën like the one Finch's mum drives. Paddy, Charlotte, Cherry, Skye, Summer and Coco pile out of the red van, and Finch and his mum Nikki spring out of the Citroën.

I stop dead just outside the shower block, mop and bucket in hand.

'What . . . is something up? What's wrong?'

'Nothing's wrong,' Cherry tells me. 'Just the opposite. We have good news!'

❀❀❀❀❀❀❀❀❀❀❀❀❀❀❀❀❀❀❀❀

'We've been talking to your parents,' Nikki explains. 'Over the last few days. And we think we have come to an agreement, but of course you'd have to be up for it too . . .'

'Up for what?' I ask.

Mum and Dad appear in the reception doorway.

'We got the final go-ahead,' Nikki tells them. 'I thought we should come and tell you in person. Tell Shay.'

'Tell me what?'

'I saw your new song on the internet,' Finch takes up the story. '"Bittersweet". It's amazing . . . totally the best thing you've done. Just full of feeling. And the more I played it the more I realized it would be absolutely perfect . . .'

'Perfect for what?' I frown.

'The film,' Nikki says. 'We've finished shooting now, so it's just a matter of editing and putting it all together. We had a few pieces of music in mind for the title sequence, but nothing as powerful as your piece, Shay. We'd like to use it – the message echoes the storyline in our film perfectly, and we'd pay you, of course!'

I blink, waiting for the news to sink in, start making sense. It doesn't.

I look at Cherry, Skye, Summer; they knew, of course. I

❀❀❀❀❀❀❀❀❀❀❀❀❀❀❀❀❀❀❀❀❀❀❀

remember the whispered hints, the giggles, the smiles. But Mum and Dad? Could they have known too? I notice the glint of pride in Dad's eye, the relief in Mum's smile. This is something they've been arguing about, perhaps for days. Somehow, miraculously, they've come to an agreement.

'I can see it could be a good opportunity, son,' Dad says. 'We'll put the money away for you, for when you're old enough to use it for something sensible.'

'No way,' I say. 'You're OK with it? Really?'

'Really,' Mum grins. 'If it's what you want, Shay?'

'It's what I want,' I blurt. 'Definitely, totally. I mean . . . whoa!'

'This won't be the same as signing to a big record label,' Nikki points out. 'It's a much gentler way to make your mark. You'll get a lot of exposure, but it'll be all about the music itself . . . not about turning you into some kind of teen pop idol. Your parents are much more comfortable with that idea.'

Dad raises an eyebrow, as if he's not too sure at all, but is doing his best to live with it. 'Might all come to nothing,' he says gruffly. 'But if you end up being famous, remember your old dad, won't you?'

He smiles cautiously, and fifteen years of mis-understandings begin to fall away. It doesn't matter, not now. With families, it is never too late to start over.

Much later, I am walking over to the storeroom den at sunset, the blue guitar slung over one shoulder, when I see a lone figure down on the shore. Honey is looking out at the horizon, her blonde choppy bob ruffling in the breeze, arms wrapped around herself in the chill evening.

'Hey,' I call, and Honey turns, snapping out of her dream. 'I just wanted to thank you.'

'Thank me? For what?'

'Well . . . I think you made that music page on Spider-Web,' I say quietly. 'And the page went a bit crazy . . .'

'Viral,' Honey supplies. 'Not me, though. I don't have time for good deeds, or the internet – I spend all my spare time studying these days.'

'Yeah, right!' I grin. 'Anyway, lots of people saw it, including Finch and his mum . . . they got the TV people to listen, and now it turns out that "Bittersweet" is going to be the opening soundtrack on that movie they were making. It fits in with the theme, apparently. You probably know all

❀❀❀❀❀❀❀❀❀❀❀❀❀❀❀❀❀❀❀❀❀❀

this . . . half your family came over to the sailing centre earlier, with Finch and Nikki, to tell me the news. The best bit is, Dad finally stopped being pig-headed and he's going to let me do it . . .'

'I knew something was going on,' Honey says. 'Your luck turned then?'

'I guess. And I have you to thank because you took the video, and I'm pretty sure you posted it online. Everyone's been talking about it but nobody seems to know who's behind it . . . Cherry and the others thought it was Ben, but he'd have said. Besides, he doesn't even have Spider-Web.'

'What does it matter who made the page?' she shrugs. 'Just leave it. One of life's great mysteries.'

'I've solved it,' I smile. 'I loved what you did with the video – very arty.'

'Thanks,' she says. 'Best if they think Ben made it, though. We don't want you getting into trouble again, do we?'

'That won't happen. Cherry and me, we're fine now – unbreakable.'

'Right,' Honey says. 'Well. That's . . . good.'

✿✿✿✿✿✿✿✿✿✿✿✿✿✿✿✿✿✿✿✿✿✿✿

I catch the bright glint of tears in her eyes and look away, embarrassed. When I glance up again there's no trace of sadness, just perfectly painted eyeliner, a glossy smile, the cool, hard look I know so well.

'Run along, Shay,' she tells me. 'You know what happens when you're seen hanging out with me. I'm bad news. Trouble. Selfish to the bone.'

'I don't believe that.'

'I know you don't,' Honey says, and the ghost of a smile flickers across her face. 'You never did, and I sometimes think you were the only one. But trust me, Shay . . . some things are better left unsaid.'

She turns and walks away along the sand, back towards Tanglewood, and she doesn't look back.

The next story in this collection is all about the adorable Alfie Anderson – and Summer, of course! The story takes place after the events of **Summer's Dream**. It was cool to write a story with a Valentine's twist . . . I think you'll like it. Curl up with your book and a little chocolate treat and enjoy!

Cathy Cassidy, xxx

1

I am never very sure if it is lucky or unlucky to have a girlfriend whose birthday falls on Valentine's Day. On the up side, you get two major celebrations over in one go; on the down side, you have to pull something pretty amazing out of the hat to show that you care. Let's just say that a packet of Love Hearts and a cheesy card won't really cut it.

Not when your girlfriend is Summer Tanberry, anyhow.

Summer is my dream girl. I have been crazy about her ever since Reception class, when she and her twin Skye were mirror-image cuties with big blue eyes and blonde pigtails. They looked identical, and even the teacher used to get them muddled up, but I knew right away how to tell them apart.

Skye spent the whole of Reception year wearing a tattered feather boa from the dressing-up box that was usually reserved for rainy days. So Summer was the one without the boa, to begin with. There was something bright and burning behind her wide blue eyes, a kind of flame, a promise of something awesome just out of reach. She always had about a million friends, and the teachers loved her too.

They didn't love me. I got told off for painting my hands blue with powder paint and making handprints on Miss Martin's skirt. I got told off for eating seven chocolate puddings and going all hyper in the lunch hall. I got told off for writing in my news book that I had a monkey as a pet, and when Miss Martin asked me if this was true I said it wasn't, only my new baby sister *looked* a lot like a monkey, and then of course I got told off again.

When I looked at Summer I saw fire and ambition; she was going places, places I could only dream of. I didn't dare imagine tagging along with her, at least not until I saw her dance. We'd been practising for the nativity play in the school hall, thirty small children disguised as shepherds, wise men, angels, camels and innkeepers, a final dress

❀❀❀❀❀❀❀❀❀❀❀❀❀❀❀❀❀❀❀❀❀❀

rehearsal before the play itself next day. We said our lines and sang carols about stars and donkeys and stables, and Miss Martin smiled through gritted teeth when Marisa McTaggart was sick all over her angel dress and had to go to the office to be cleaned up.

Miss Martin wasn't too impressed with me either. I remember her telling me off for changing the words of a carol about the three kings to include a line about them selling ladies' underwear. She frogmarched me back to the classroom at the head of the line where she could keep an eye on me, and that's when I realized I'd left my papier-mâché crown in the hall. It wasn't a very good crown, but I had made it all by myself and added jewels made of scrunched-up sweet wrappers and so much glitter the school cleaners complained the next day because they couldn't get it all out of the carpet tiles.

Miss Martin rolled her eyes and told me to go back and fetch it before the cleaners found it and put it in the bin. When I reached the hall doors, I could hear Miss Martin's CD player still playing 'Silent Night', which was a bit strange because we'd finished for the day. Was somebody in there?

✿✿✿✿✿✿✿✿✿✿✿✿✿✿✿✿✿✿✿✿✿✿✿

I pushed open the door and looked inside. Summer Tanberry was dancing to the music, her eyes closed, her tinsel halo askew. Her angel dress swirled out around her as she dipped and spun, and her skinny blonde plaits flew.

I closed the door quietly and crept back to the classroom. When Summer came in a few minutes later, there was so much chaos while everyone changed and hung up their costumes that I forgot about the papier-mâché crown. The cleaner probably did chuck it in the bin, because I never found it and I had to wear a tissue-paper one that came out of a cracker for the actual play. Miss Martin was furious and when we had our Christmas party lucky dip a few days later I got a gift-wrapped tin of baked beans while everyone else had cool stuff. I'm pretty sure that wasn't a coincidence.

All that was a long time ago, of course.

We grew up. I got into more and more trouble as the years went by . . . I developed a skill for practical jokes and acting the clown. I could make most of my classmates laugh, but Summer's eyes would slide right past me as if I was invisible. I always wished she'd notice me because she was my idea of perfect. She was clever, popular, beautiful, talented – everyone knew she was brilliant at ballet. Once,

❀❀❀❀❀❀❀❀❀❀❀❀❀❀❀❀❀❀❀❀❀❀

in Year Seven, we had to write about our hopes and dreams in class, and Summer wrote about wanting to be a ballerina, wanting to dance onstage at the Royal Opera House in a white tutu with feathers in her hair. *Swan Lake*, or something.

The English teacher made her read out the whole essay, and Summer's eyes burnt bright with determination. Her dream was so real we all believed in it. It wasn't a question of if it would happen, just when.

Summer was so far out of my league I got altitude sickness just thinking about it, but I couldn't help myself.

I talked to Skye, her twin, gathering information, planning how best to make Summer notice me. I cut back on the clowning around, rationed the practical jokes, cut my hair and tried my best to look cool and mysterious. Skye said Summer would like that better than 'clueless' and 'idiotic'.

Harsh words, but I did my best. I bought a silk flower hairclip and wrapped it, then left it in Summer's locker with a card 'from a secret admirer'. It backfired bigtime – she thought the flower was from Aaron Jones and started dating him instead. I almost gave up then, but you can't switch your feelings on and off that easily, can you?

Summer has my heart, always.

And when the fire in her eyes began to flicker and fade, and she began to fall, I was there to catch her.

Summer was lost, burnt out, pushing herself so hard she began to lose the plot. She stopped eating, stopped thinking; her eyes were dark and full of fear. It was as if she was trying to disappear, to make herself invisible, lighter than air.

I saw it early on, the way I saw everything Summer did. I saw the plates piled high with lettuce leaves, the way she'd lift a spoonful of pudding up to her mouth and laugh and start to talk as she put it down again, untouched. I noticed everything.

She was unravelling.

She ended things with Aaron Jones and one day she looked at me instead of through me, and although I knew she didn't see me as anything more than a friend, it was a start.

I had waited a very long time for her to see me at all.

So, yeah . . . you could say that Summer Tanberry has taught me to be patient, to take things slowly. It's like a

❀❀❀❀❀❀❀❀❀❀❀❀❀❀❀❀❀❀❀❀

dance, a slow, careful, perfectly choreographed one. Trouble is, I am really not a dancer. I have two left feet . . . possibly three. OK, OK, I know . . . It's just that it feels that way.

We danced past friendship and on to the handholding stage, then right on forward to kisses and promises and whispered secrets. Things are good . . . very good. I worry that the tempo will change, that I'll mess up and get the steps wrong, that I am treading on eggshells, dancing on them even. I worry that everything will fall apart.

And when Summer looks at me with her lost-girl eyes, I wonder if I'll ever see that flame again, that fire.

2

I'm working the late afternoon shift in Mum and Dad's shop, but things are quiet. The only customer in the place is an elderly bloke in socks, sandals and corduroy trousers, browsing the herbal tea section, trying to decide between liquorice and nettle.

Mum appears, her green velvet skirt jingling a little as she walks. Living above the shop, she sometimes uses it as a kind of extension to the kitchen cupboards, and now she is ransacking the shelves for lentils, soya cream and paprika.

'I'm making buckwheat pancakes for tea,' she tells me. 'It's a new recipe.'

'Wow,' I reply, as politely as I can. 'That'll be . . . um . . . amazing!'

'I know you weren't keen on the chickpea flour variety,

but buckwheat tastes totally different,' Mum says. 'Nutty. Very unusual. An acquired taste.'

It's the story of my life, but I love my hippy-dippy parents and my mad little sisters. I love the healthy food they make, even when Mum's quest for nutritional variety takes us into the darkened realms of chickpea flour and buckwheat pancakes.

'You OK on your own until then?' Mum checks. 'You'll cash up and everything?' I tell her I'm fine, that I'll most likely use the shop computer to do some homework, and that I'll cash up. She disappears back upstairs as the old guy brings his shopping to the till. He has settled on a tea called Acorn Infusion which I happen to know (from bitter experience) tastes like old socks. He has also thrown in a heart-shaped bar of vegan chocolate with a big red bow round it.

'Valentine's Day prezzie?' I ask brightly, and the old bloke tells me he's going to ask a lady at his art class out on a date for Valentine's Day, and is hoping the vegan chocolate will help.

'Can't go wrong with chocolate or flowers,' I say. 'Guaranteed to win her heart!'

❀❀❀❀❀❀❀❀❀❀❀❀❀❀❀❀❀❀❀❀❀❀❀

I wish it was that simple with Summer. When the old guy has gone, I log on to the shop computer in search of inspiration. I have been looking for the perfect present since January, trawling the shops in Minehead and coming up with nothing. Mum and Dad may be flaky, New Age types, but they pay me for the hours I put in. I worked quite a bit over Christmas and New Year, helping people to pick out their tofu turkey cutlets and advising on gluten-free mince pies, so I have some money saved.

I just don't have the inspiration. A box of chocolates is out of the question, clearly. Summer's stepdad runs a fancy chocolate business, but that's not the problem . . . it's more that she is struggling with food right now. She's been going to an eating disorders clinic in Exeter, and I think it has helped a little, but right now she sees chocolate as the work of the devil. She won't even go into Paddy's workshop, in case she inhales some calories by accident.

Not chocolates then. Flowers are the next option, but that seems so predictable. And they'd be gone in a week, leaving nothing behind but shrivelled petals and crispy leaves. I've looked at scarves, bags, earrings, lockets . . . but choosing seems impossible.

I check my watch and turn the *open* sign to *closed*. I cash up at the till, rearrange the display of organic vegetables, sweep the floor.

What would Summer like? I really don't know.

Just a couple of days ago I asked her what she'd like most in the world, and she said she wanted to get well again, properly well, and to be able to dance again. She's doing one ballet class a week these days, but she says it's all messed up, that her steps are stilted, wooden.

'I've ruined everything,' she sighed. 'Thrown it all away.'

I told her that wasn't true.

'It kind of is,' she said. 'It's like one thing goes wrong and everything else follows. I wish Honey would come back from Australia too . . . I hate it when she's not here. Sisters are supposed to be together.'

'Wish I could help, but I'm not sure my savings can stretch to an airline ticket,' I pointed out, and Summer laughed.

'You did ask,' she said with a shrug. 'It's too bad that the things I want I just can't have. I want not to be sick any more. I want to stop feeling so frozen, so lost. I want to be *me* again.'

❀❀❀❀❀❀❀❀❀❀❀❀❀❀❀❀❀❀❀❀❀❀

'You'll get there,' I said, feeling helpless.

'Will I?' Summer challenged. 'I don't know, Alfie. It never used to be this difficult. When I was a kid I was so sure of everything – my hopes and dreams were so real I thought I could just reach out and take them, like apples from a tree. I remember staying behind in the school hall one Christmas, switching on the CD player when everyone had gone and dancing like mad to "Silent Night". It was perfect.'

I blink. She's describing the day of the nativity play rehearsals, the day I peeked through the doors and saw her dancing. The day I lost my heart.

'That's what I'd like most in the world,' she said sadly. 'That magic back again. You know?'

I knew, of course, but Summer was right – those things can't be bought.

I bit my lip.

'I was thinking more of actual things,' I pointed out. 'Like . . . I dunno, a book or a bracelet or a bunch of flowers . . . for your birthday. And, y'know . . . Valentine's Day.'

I felt my cheeks colour as I said the words, but Summer shook her head.

'You don't have to get me anything for my birthday,' she said. 'Or Valentine's Day, silly. I'm not really in the mood for any of it. Just be here, Alfie, that's enough. You're the only good thing that's happened to me, these past few months, y'know?'

She put her arms round me then and I hugged her back, and it was like holding a robin in your hands, tiny, fragile, perfect. She was like something wild, something beautiful, something you want to hold on to but know you probably can't.

It made me more determined than ever.

I want to find something special, something Summer will never forget, something that will re-light the fire behind her blue eyes. I need an idea that says *I love you* without me actually having to say the words. I am not good at slushy stuff, and I have to tread carefully. I don't want to scare Summer away.

I have the girl of my dreams, but she's sick, broken. The spark has gone out of her and even dance can't put it back, so how can I hope to?

And just as suddenly as that, the seed of an idea takes

❀❀❀❀❀❀❀❀❀❀❀❀❀❀❀❀❀❀❀❀❀❀❀

hold. Summer loves dance, more than anything else in the world. She loves it so much that the pressure of trying out for a boarding ballet school got to be too much; it tipped her right over from talented perfectionist to lost little girl with an eating disorder, trying and failing to hang on to her shattered dreams.

Supposing I could tip things back again? I've heard Summer talk about her hopes and dreams often enough, though always in a sad, resigned way. What if I could help her put those dreams back together, help her find her love of dance again?

I'll give her back the magic.

It will take a bit of planning, of course, but luck is on my side as Valentine's Day falls in half-term. I call Finch, Skye's sort of long-distance boyfriend, to see if he can help – he's in London, so he'll know how to get things sorted.

'Nice idea, Alfie,' he tells me. 'It's definitely Summer's kind of thing. I can book the tickets, no problem . . . I'll get Mum to put them on her credit card, and you can settle up when I see you.'

❀❀❀❀❀❀❀❀❀❀❀❀❀❀❀❀❀❀❀❀❀❀

'Want to come along?' I ask. 'You and Skye? It could be a kind of double-date.'

Finch considers this. 'We're not as close as we were back in August,' he tells me. 'It's not easy when you live so far apart, y'know?'

'Might be exactly what you need,' I say. 'A grand gesture, something special to show you still care?'

Finch laughs. 'I was only going to send a birthday card,' he confesses. 'Trust you to go all flash on me, Alfie. If you're doing all this for Summer and I just give Skye a measly birthday card, it's going to look pretty bad, right?'

'Pretty bad,' I agree.

'OK, OK,' Finch considers. 'Maybe I will come along . . .'

'Listen,' I push, 'you're one of those arty types, aren't you? You'll be going to drama school one day, right, so just think of this as research.'

'If I hate it, I'm blaming you.'

But then Finch laughs and says what the heck, he'll do it, and promises to meet us at Victoria Coach Station to help us navigate the Tube. Between us, we get the logistics ironed out.

❀❀❀❀❀❀❀❀❀❀❀❀❀❀❀❀❀❀❀❀❀❀

'One thing,' Finch says. 'Summer *will* like all this, right? I mean . . . it won't bring back memories, make her feel . . . I dunno . . . worse? Will it?'

'Course not,' I say confidently. 'She'll love it!'

I hope.

3

I set the alarm on my mobile phone with two alarm clocks as backup, but nothing really helps when you have to drag yourself out of bed at 3.45 a.m. I ring Tanglewood to check that Skye and Summer are awake too, then shower, dress and battle with the hair gel in an attempt to get my unruly hair to calm down and look smooth and suave, and not as though I just stuck my fingers in an electric socket.

Dad is in the kitchen, glugging peppermint tea, getting ready to be our first taxi driver of the day.

'She's a nice enough girl, Summer Tanberry,' Dad says. 'But are you sure she's worth all this trouble?'

'Totally worth it,' I reply.

'Huh. Well, I hope she appreciates all your hard work to

❀❀❀❀❀❀❀❀❀❀❀❀❀❀❀❀❀❀❀❀

set this up,' he grumbles. 'And the fact that I had to get up in the middle of the night to drive you.'

When we draw up on the gravel at Tanglewood, Dad toots the horn once and Skye and Summer come outside, wrapped up against the frosty morning in coats and scarves, wide-eyed and hesitant in the yellow light from the car headlamps. They both look amazing. I told them to dress up, and Skye is in a vintage duffel coat with a print dress peeping out beneath, while Summer wears a velvet jacket over a pink floaty dress, the silk flower I gave her the Christmas before last clipped in her hair along with a little bunch of feathers. She looks awesome, and I cannot wait to see her face when she discovers where we are going.

'Did we really have to be up so early?' Skye groans, scrambling into the car. 'Where are you taking us, Outer Mongolia?'

'It feels like Outer Mongolia here,' Summer says, shivering as she scoots across the seat to snuggle up against me. 'Cold. Mind you, I always seem to be freezing lately. So . . . where are we going?'

'Exeter Bus Station,' Dad says, turning out on to the road

again. 'Can't say more than that – it's more than my life's worth!'

'Why is it all so secret?' Skye demands. 'And why am I here, anyhow? Is it so you get to look like some kind of player, Alfie, with two girls hanging off your arm?'

'Busted,' I say. 'You know me too well, Skye Tanberry.'

'I like secrets,' she says. 'Secrets are cool . . .'

'Maybe,' Summer says. 'But I think we deserve to know a bit more, Alfie. You can't just tell us to dress in our best stuff and be ready at five, and not say *why* . . .'

'Can you give us a clue?' Skye chimes in.

They take it in turns to try and tease and trick the surprise from me as we drive through the winding, early morning lanes, and by the time we finally reach the bus station I relent and reveal that we're taking a coach to London.

'I knew it!' Skye says. 'Is Finch in on all this? Because if he isn't and I'm just some kind of gooseberry, I will not be pleased. Two's company and three's a crowd, as they say . . .'

'Finch is meeting us at the other end,' I admit.

'Yay!' Summer squeals. 'That's perfect! Just like old times!'

'OK,' Skye says. 'I might have to kill him when I see him,

❀❀❀❀❀❀❀❀❀❀❀❀❀❀❀❀❀❀❀❀❀❀❀

though. He never said a thing. He hasn't been in touch for ages . . . but all the time the pair of you were planning this!'

We get to the bus station just in time, and pile on to the coach, grabbing seats along the back. Summer sits in the middle, sandwiched between me and Skye, and I break out a picnic breakfast of apples, tofu burger and bottles of fruit smoothie, all designed not to freak Summer out. Skye is less anxious about that, and adds a couple of chocolate bars into the mix. Summer doesn't eat any of those, but they don't seem to bother her either.

'Even you are all dressed up,' Summer comments as I shrug off my anorak and stow it on the luggage rack above us. 'That's your best Christmas jumper, right? What is going on?'

'Nothing,' I say. 'I just don't want us to look like country kids once we get there.'

'Are we having a sightseeing day?' Skye wants to know. 'Because I haven't done that for soooo long. We came up years ago, when Dad was still around, and went to see Buckingham Palace and the Tower of London and the Houses of Parliament. We rode around on one of those sightseeing buses that have no roof, and it started to rain, so Mum bought us umbrellas . . .'

❀❀❀❀❀❀❀❀❀❀❀❀❀❀❀❀❀❀❀❀❀❀

'With pictures of London cabs and the London Eye on,' Summer finishes for her sister. 'And Beefeaters and Scots Guards with those red jackets and big furry hats . . .'

'That's right,' Skye agrees. 'And then Mum stopped at a street stall to buy us all souvenir T-shirts, and a sandwich from a cafe because we were starving, and we missed our train and Dad had to pay extra for us to catch a later one, and they quarrelled all the way home.'

'Coco wouldn't stop crying,' Summer remembers. 'She was only about four . . .'

'Happy days,' Skye quips. 'Not.'

I frown. 'Today will be better,' I say.

'Obviously,' Skye says. 'My dad is not involved in it, so it has to be better. He wasn't good at family days out.'

'He wasn't good at families, full stop,' Summer adds, yawning and leaning her head against my shoulder. 'Don't worry, Alfie. Today will be awesome, whatever it is you've got planned.'

I hope so, I really do.

Finch meets us at Victoria Coach Station as arranged, looking effortlessly cool in an old suit jacket with the sleeves rolled up and a T-shirt advertising some indie band I've never heard of. I instantly regret my Fair Isle jumper and anorak. I was aiming at the hipster look, but suddenly panic that I look more like a middle-aged trainspotter. It's very demoralizing.

'So,' Finch says, hugging Skye and Summer in turn, 'your birthday treat awaits you! Follow me . . .'

'Follow you where?' Skye wants to know.

'To the ends of the earth,' Finch quips. 'Well, Covent Garden, anyway. I thought we could grab a birthday brunch before we unveil the Special Treat!'

'Great,' Skye says. 'I'm starving!'

Summer flicks an anxious look at me and slips her hand into mine, and we follow along as Finch cuts through the crowds and leads the way down steep escalators to the Underground. We pile on to a busy train and then pile off again at Green Park to change on to the Piccadilly line. A little while later, we emerge from the ancient lifts at Covent Garden Tube and wander out into a crazy, crowded plaza filled with tourists and entertainers and shops and stalls.

We mooch around for a little while and watch a man juggling fire and two girls doing acrobatics, and try to figure

❀❀❀❀❀❀❀❀❀❀❀❀❀❀❀❀❀❀❀❀❀❀

out how the man sprayed gold is able to sit cross-legged in mid-air with only his stick touching the floor; then Finch checks his watch and takes us to a cafe overlooking the square.

It's a good choice . . . there are lots of healthy options on the menu; Summer picks poached egg and spinach and actually manages to eat quite a bit of it.

'What's the surprise?' she asks me for the millionth time. 'Are you ever going to tell us? Or is it just being in London? Because that would be brilliant . . . but Finch did mention a Special Treat.'

Summer's eyes are hopeful, and I know she has started to put the pieces together, begun to guess.

'Be patient,' I say. 'You'll find out in a minute.'

We scrabble our money together and pay, then pull on coats and head out into the bright, cold air. I check my watch and exchange a glance with Finch.

'OK,' I say. 'Let's go. Shut your eyes . . .'

'You're joking, right?' Skye argues, but Finch puts a hand over her eyes and leads her forward, and Summer closes her eyes, her lips curving into a nervous smile. She knows. She's hoping.

I take her hand and lead her through the crowd, and the four of us stop in one corner of the plaza, a little way back from our destination. 'You can look now,' I say.

Summer opens her eyes wide, and I watch her mouth quiver into an enormous smile as she takes it all in.

'The Royal Opera House,' she says, her voice barely a whisper. '*Romeo and Juliet*! Oh, Alfie . . . I can't believe it!'

4

Finch has collected the tickets already so we check our coats into the cloakroom and go up the stairs to the auditorium. We are up in the amphitheatre bit, in the upper slips, way up high where the cheap seats are. We'll probably need a telescope to see the actual ballet, but that doesn't matter.

The place looks like a palace.

Summer moves slowly, as if in a dream, feet sinking into the thick carpet, her head held high. She walks right past our seats and glides down towards the front of the amphitheatre, looking down on the tiers below, the circle stalls, the wide sweep of stage partly hidden behind thick swathes of crimson velvet. Her eyes rake over the grand boxes where the plushest, private, priciest seats are, everything trimmed with crimson and gold.

She looks perfect in her pale pink dress, the skirt gauzy, floaty, like a dancer's. The flower and feathers in her hair catch the light as she gazes downwards, transfixed.

I walk down to stand beside her.

'Happy?' I ask.

'Happy,' she echoes. 'Alfie, this is the best surprise ever. You are the best boyfriend ever. It's awesome! I have always, always wanted to come here. It was my dream . . .'

'I know,' I say.

'It must have cost a fortune!'

'I've been saving,' I say with a shrug. 'I wanted to do something special for you.'

She turns to me and plants a light kiss on the end of my nose, then grabs my hand and dances a pirouette in front of me, laughing. I'd say every single bit of planning and effort has been worth it, just for that moment alone.

Summer stays down at the front of the balcony, watching the orchestra pit as the musicians begin to tune up. Around her, the theatre fills slowly. I shift in my seat, awkward in my Christmas jumper. I am way out of my depth, and very glad Finch and Skye are here too. I feel like a scarecrow next to the old blokes in suits and bow ties, the younger men in cord jackets and paisley-patterned scarves. As for the women, they're downright scary, especially the old ladies with their elegant faces and smart blouses with glittery brooches. I see Summer turn to watch a family take their seats, the parents smiling brightly, the two little girls in red velvet and lacy white socks and black patent leather shoes.

Does it remind her of when she was little, of when her dancing dreams first began?

Finch heads off to buy a programme, and Skye turns to talk to me.

'You care about my sister a lot, don't you?' she says as I watch my girlfriend lean against the balcony, transfixed by all the glitz and glamour. In the midst of it all, she looks beautiful, ethereal, perfect.

'Obviously,' I say to Skye. 'You know that.'

'You've put a lot of thought into this, I can see,' she says. 'It was nice of you to include me and Finch too.'

'Moral support,' I say. 'I mean, this is me, Alfie Anderson, at a ballet . . . a slushy one at that, *Romeo and Juliet*. In the poshest theatre in London. I may look calm, but inside I'm terrified!'

'Maybe,' Skye says with a shrug. 'You really are one of the good guys, Alfie.'

I laugh. 'Dunno about that,' I say. 'I try!'

She shakes her head. 'Look . . . don't take this the wrong way,' she says. 'I don't want you to get your hopes up. I know exactly what you're trying to do . . .'

I blink, baffled. 'What am I trying to do?' I ask. 'I thought I was just arranging a birthday treat for my two favourite girls?'

Skye rolls her eyes. 'You're worried about Summer, like I am. Like we all are,' she says. 'You'd do anything to make her better, make her happy again. And she loves ballet, so to see a performance here . . . well, it's an amazing thing for you to arrange. Awesome. Only . . . it could actually be quite difficult for her too. Painful. Do you know what I'm saying, Alfie?'

'Yeah, but . . . it's the thing she loves most in the world, right?' I argue. 'I know what you're saying, Skye, but . . . well, I think it'll be fine. What harm can it do?'

Skye sighs. 'The problem is that Summer's dream was to *dance* onstage at the Royal Opera House, not just to watch a ballet here,' she says. 'She wanted it so much, and now those dreams aren't going to happen.'

❀❀❀❀❀❀❀❀❀❀❀❀❀❀❀❀❀❀❀❀❀

'They could,' I argue, but Skye interrupts me.

'They won't,' she says, and I recognize the truth in her words even though I really, really don't want to.

'Don't get me wrong,' she goes on. 'I want those things for Summer almost as much as she wants them for herself. But can't you see, Alfie? She's ill. She's not well enough to go to a boarding ballet school, or to train with a professional ballet company. Not now . . . probably not ever. Maybe she'll be a dance teacher, or a choreographer perhaps; maybe she'll run a dance supplies shop and work with dancers that way, but she won't be a professional ballerina. She's too fragile for that. She'd break under the pressure.'

A wave of anger surges through my body, hot and hopeless. Skye is right, even though I don't want her to be. I hate Summer's illness with a passion – it has taken so much from her. It's not fair. I'd like to punch a fist through the ornate walls, kick a hole in the gilded balcony, smash this whole place to pieces. But that wouldn't change a thing, of course.

'You can't know all that for sure,' I say. 'She'll get better – she's getting stronger already. This might be just the thing to change it all, give her something to aim for again.'

But even as I argue, I know deep down that chasing after impossible dreams won't help Summer to get well . . . and it could push her backwards, down into the darkness of her eating disorder, all over again. Summer is walking up towards us, ready to take her seat. I can see the sadness in her eyes, the shadows.

What if Skye is right?

5

Finch comes back and Summer slips into the seat beside me, and the lights are dimmed as the orchestra launches into action. The auditorium is filled with music, and as it reaches a peak the crimson curtains swish back to reveal a busy marketplace scene. It's not my thing, obviously – men in tights and all that – but to my surprise, I can follow the story. There are young men trying to impress the girls (happens every day at Exmoor High) and even a dramatic fight between two feuding families, with swords and knives and some rich bloke wading in to break the whole thing up.

It's not as bad as I was expecting.

The dancer who plays Juliet is fair-haired and beautiful, and I imagine she's Summer and I'm Romeo, although obviously you would never catch me in tights in a million years. After a really slushy love scene between the two of them, the lights come up and there's an interval, and I am certain Skye is wrong about how Summer will react because her face is bright with the thrill of it all. She turns to me and starts explaining about Montagues and Capulets, the two feuding families, and how Juliet is only supposed to be fourteen, and how Margot Fonteyn and Rudolf Nureyev danced the roles here at the Royal Opera House in the 1960s. She flicks through the programme to tell me about today's dancers while Skye and Finch head off to queue for ice cream, and then the seats fill again and the lights dim and Act 2 begins.

This time there's a secret wedding and a murder, and Summer leans forward in her seat, lips parted, eyes wide, unable to take her eyes off any of it. During the second interval she drifts down to the balcony again, looking down at the stage and the people in the stalls below.

'Wish I'd been able to get better seats for us,' I say. 'They're all millionaires down there, I reckon.'

'I don't care,' she replies. 'I'm here with you, and that's what counts. I can't believe you did this for me, Alfie. You are the best boyfriend ever!'

❀❀❀❀❀❀❀❀❀❀❀❀❀❀❀❀❀❀❀❀❀❀

I am still glowing from the compliment when the lights dim again and we slide back into our seats for the final act. This one is crazy. There are sleeping potions, daggers, vials of poison and secret letters that don't get delivered so that everything goes horribly wrong. The music works itself into a crescendo as the drama unfolds. Mistakenly thinking Juliet is dead, Romeo drinks poison, and, awaking to find him dead, she stabs herself . . . and that's the end. Seriously. The curtain goes down on two dead bodies.

I don't know what I was expecting, but it wasn't that. I thought all stories had to have happy endings these days? Apparently not.

The whole place goes crazy with the applause, and the dancers come on for a curtain call, even Romeo and Juliet, miraculously risen from the dead. A small girl with ringlets and a lacy dress comes onstage with a bouquet of flowers almost as big as she is, presenting it to the ballerina who played Juliet. Roses, crimson and white.

When I turn to look at Summer, I see she is crying, tears rolling down her pale cheeks as if her heart will break. That wasn't in the plan.

'Um . . . you didn't tell me it was so sad,' I say. 'It's like an episode of *The Jeremy Kyle Show* mixed up with *Crime Scene Investigates*. Heavy.'

Summer just nods and bites her lip and lets her hair fall forward to hide her face.

'Are you OK?' Skye is asking. 'Summer, what's wrong?'

But Summer is sobbing uncontrollably, her body shaking, and people are looking at us oddly as they gather up their bags and scarves and programmes and file out of the theatre. Skye slips an arm round her twin, whispering softly, but Summer just shakes her head and pushes a fist against her mouth, and still the tears come.

'What should we do?' Finch asks me, looking bewildered. 'Get a cup of hot, sweet tea or something? That's supposed to help when people are upset, isn't it?'

'Dunno, Finch,' I say.

'Talk to me, Summer,' Skye is pleading.

But Summer says nothing, and Skye's eyes flash towards me, leaving a taint of blame. This is my fault. Finch warned me, Skye warned me . . . but I thought I knew best. I didn't, clearly.

'Look, can you give us some space?' I ask Skye and Finch. 'Some time alone. Yeah?'

❀❀❀❀❀❀❀❀❀❀❀❀❀❀❀❀❀❀❀❀❀❀❀

Skye looks doubtful, but the two of them head for the exits as the cleaners come in and begin to gather rubbish and vacuum the carpet. The buzz of noise offers some camouflage as I sit down next to Summer, curling my arm round her shoulder.

'I thought you'd like it,' I say quietly. 'I didn't know it was going to be so sad.'

Summer struggles to catch her breath, letting the sobs subside.

'It's not that,' she whispers eventually. 'The ballet was beautiful. Amazing. I . . . I loved it.'

I frown. 'Then how come . . .?'

She throws her head back, wiping away tears with the back of her hand.

'You don't understand,' she says. 'Nobody does. This place . . . it means so much to me. It's a part of every dream I've ever had. But . . . Alfie, those dreams will never happen now. I've ruined everything, thrown it all away.'

'Of course you haven't!' I protest. 'Don't talk like that!'

Summer squeezes my hand. 'It's true,' she says, and her blue eyes brim with tears again. 'I have, Alfie. Ballet's not a forgiving career. I messed up, blew my chance of dance

❀❀❀❀❀❀❀❀❀❀❀❀❀❀❀❀❀❀❀❀❀❀❀❀

school. Not once, but twice. You don't get third chances in a game like this. I have to face it – I'm not well enough for dance school, and I'm not strong enough to work with a professional dance company. The pressure of it is too much – I can't handle it. It makes me panic, it makes me ill. And sometimes I'm scared that this . . . this illness . . . will eat me up, every last bit of me, until there's nothing left at all.'

The thought of that makes me go cold all over.

'You'll get better,' I argue. 'This is just a blip. You'll get well again, and then . . .'

'Then it will be too late,' Summer says. 'Too late for the dream. I wanted to dance onstage at the Royal Opera House, but I might as well have asked for the moon. It's never going to happen. Not your fault, Alfie . . . I'm so happy to be here, I promise I am.'

She wipes her eyes again, holds her head high, and I look down across the empty auditorium where the cleaners are working quietly, moving around us, aware that something's going on, something sad and personal and awkward.

'Dreams can come true,' I say rashly. 'Just not always the way you imagine they will.'

'Not all dreams,' she says. 'Not mine.'

❁❁❁❁❁❁❁❁❁❁❁❁❁❁❁❁❁❁❁❁❁❁

'Do you trust me?' I ask, and Summer looks up and her blue eyes hold mine, steady, still.

'Always,' she says. 'You know that.'

It's all I need to know. I jump up, grabbing her hand, pulling her behind me along the row of seats, into the aisle, up the steps and out into the corridor. Finch and Skye are there, leaning against the wall; we fly past them, taking the stairs two at a time, heading downwards.

'What's going on?' Finch yells after us.

I look at Summer. As we run, her mouth twitches into a curve and then she's laughing, really laughing, and I'm laughing too as we tumble into the foyer outside the fancy doors that lead into the stalls.

'Dreams,' I yell back up the stairs to Finch and Skye. 'We're making dreams . . .'

6

I am about to push the doors to the lower auditorium open when they swing open anyway, releasing a small crew of cleaners in smart uniform. Three of them vanish along the corridor with their cleaning kits and Hoovers, but one turns back to lock the doors.

'You can't,' I say and the woman looks up, startled. 'I've left my mobile in there. It's very expensive – my dad'll kill me if I lose it!'

'There are no mobile phones in there,' she says. 'Everything is cleaned, everything is checked. Sorry.'

'I know exactly where it is,' I argue. 'It was silly of me, but I sort of hid it, pushed it underneath the seat in front. So if you'll just let us in . . . seriously, it will take about a minute, that's all.'

❀❀❀❀❀❀❀❀❀❀❀❀❀❀❀❀❀❀❀❀❀❀

'Please?' Summer begs. 'He'll be in so much trouble otherwise. His dad is so strict. Please?'

The woman is wavering. She almost believes us – almost decides to risk letting us in. But she's clearly the boss cleaner, the one with the keys, and that's quite a responsibility. She shakes her head.

'I can't let you in there now,' she says. 'I'm sorry, but it's more than my job's worth. You'll have to ask at the desk, report it missing. They will send someone to search. If anyone hands it in, you'll be informed.'

My heart sinks. I see Finch and Skye walking down the stairs towards us; it is time to give up, time to leave.

That's when Finch launches himself forward, shouting loud enough to bring the whole place down.

'Help! Help!' he cries. 'There's an elderly gentleman on the top floor having some kind of seizure. He's gasping for air . . . very pale . . . Quick, come with me!'

Finch has dreams of a career in acting, and now I can see why.

'I'll show you,' he is saying to the cleaner. 'But hurry, it could be a matter of life and death!'

'I can't –' the woman starts to argue, but Finch has her

❀❀❀❀❀❀❀❀❀❀❀❀❀❀❀❀❀❀❀❀❀❀❀

by the hand, pulling her up the stairs, and in that moment I push open the door and Summer and I slip into the auditorium.

It's empty, of course, quiet and dark with the lights all dimmed. We walk along the aisle and right up to the orchestra pit, deserted now. And then I see steps to one side.

I lead Summer forward, hold her hand as she walks slowly up the stairs, on to the stage.

She looks anxiously around her in case the cleaner should suddenly burst in through the doors at the back, or in case a siren might suddenly sound to tell the world that the best-behaved girl in the whole of Somerset is breaking the rules, big style.

Neither of those things happens.

'Go on,' I say quietly. 'This is it. This is your moment!'

Summer looks at me for a second. I wonder if she's going to bottle it, but after a moment she unzips her boots and throws them through the air at me, then shrugs off her cardigan and stands shivering in a pink slip dress with a floaty, gauzy skirt.

She looks uncertain, lost, and for a moment I panic. Maybe this is another mistake?

✿✿✿✿✿✿✿✿✿✿✿✿✿✿✿✿✿✿✿✿✿✿✿

Summer's eyes catch on to mine, then drift away, out to the auditorium behind me, as though scanning an invisible crowd. Her chin tilts higher, and she smiles, as if she can see and hear something I can't.

Then, as I watch, Summer rises up on to her toes and begins to dance. She is slow and soft at first, wary. She only has a thin strip of stage to work with, the narrow area in front of the theatre curtains, but as her confidence grows she takes possession of it as if she dances there every day, her skirt flying out around her, arms stretching upwards and then outwards as she begins to twirl and spin.

It's beautiful. It begins as a slow, gentle, ghost-girl dance, then builds and builds into something free, frenzied. Although there's no music I can almost hear the beat inside my head, the wild crescendo as she leaps and whirls and pirouettes, each step so sure, so strong, so perfect. There's an ache of pride and love inside me as I watch, and even in the half-light I am certain Summer is dancing better than anyone else has . . . ever. Better than Juliet, better than the Firebird in the piece she learnt for her audition, better than the white swan in her favourite ballet. She's just pure magic. She is dancing her own story, straight from the heart, and I'm feeling every emotion along with her. I think I might burst with happiness.

I am watching a dream, and I really don't want to wake up.

Without warning, a spotlight turns on. Summer doesn't falter, though. She turns her face up to the light as if it finally dawns on her that she is really here, in London, dancing onstage at the Royal Opera House. She has come a long, long way from being the little girl dancing alone in the school hall, her plaits flying out around her, but this dance has the same spirit, the same joy.

Dreams can come true.

When she sinks down into a final curtsey, I realize my own cheeks are wet with tears, but boys don't cry so I wipe them away and start to clap. The sound of clapping comes from the amphitheatre above too, and when I look up I can see Finch, Skye and a bunch of cleaners applauding from on high. There is muffled clapping from the wings, and a whistle from above as the spotlight is turned off again.

And then the most amazing thing happens.

A figure appears in the wings, a dancer in leotard and leg warmers, her fair hair pinned back into an intricate arrangement of braids, face still painted with the exaggerated stage make-up from the ballet. I recognize her at once as the dancer who played Juliet, the ballerina I thought looked like Summer. The breath catches in my throat.

Behind her, a handful of other dancers appear, smiling, clapping.

'That was wonderful,' the first dancer is saying. 'It is not every day somebody dances for us, and with such feeling. It was beautiful.'

Summer's face lights up from inside, her eyes bright. The fire I've longed to see there for so long is back.

'You were Juliet,' she says to the woman. 'You were amazing . . .'

The dancer turns back to the little group behind her and lifts a bouquet from the arms of one of them, the beautiful bouquet of crimson and white roses she was given at the end of the ballet.

'*You* were amazing,' she says to Summer. 'Really. I'd like you to have these.' She walks forward and holds the flowers out to Summer, who takes them carefully, her eyes wide with awe. The dancer enfolds Summer in a brief hug, then laughs and runs back into the wings.

153

❀❀❀❀❀❀❀❀❀❀❀❀❀❀❀❀❀❀❀❀❀❀❀

Summer is alone in the shadows once more, her arms filled with crimson and white roses, her smile a mile wide. I guess she knows that she may never dance on this stage again, never get the chance to be given a dancer's bouquet . . . but right here, right now, she's living her dream.

By the time the doors burst open as Finch, Skye and the cleaner come in, she is sitting on the edge of the steps, pulling on her boots, shrugging on her cardigan.

'We're going, we're going,' I say, bowing low to the cleaning lady as I usher Summer past. 'It was all a mistake. I think I left my mobile at home after all, but thank you . . .'

But the woman has nothing to say to me. Her eyes are fixed on Summer. She touches her arm. 'Lovely,' she says. 'Just lovely.'

And then we are out of there, collecting our coats, spilling out into the darkening afternoon. Covent Garden is bright with fairy lights but it has nothing on Summer, burning with life, her eyes sparkling with happiness.

'I take it all back, Alfie,' Skye is saying. 'You are a genius. I will never doubt you again.'

'Nice one, mate,' Finch agrees. 'That was epic.'

❀❀❀❀❀❀❀❀❀❀❀❀❀❀❀❀❀❀❀❀❀

Summer doesn't say anything at all. She just holds my hand tightly and runs out into the plaza, twirling round, dragging me with her. Finch and Skye laugh and join in, and we are still spinning and dipping and whirling around, laughing like crazy people, when Finch's mum turns up to take us to Victoria Coach Station.

On the way home, Summer cradles the bouquet of flowers, breathing in their sweet scent.

'I can honestly say these are the best Valentine's flowers I have ever had,' she tells me. 'Or ever will, come to that. So cool!'

'Top marks for your method of delivery,' Skye chips in. 'Original, Alfie. I'm impressed.'

'It was nothing,' I quip. 'What can I say? I have friends in high places.'

I can't help smiling. Sometimes, the unplanned, unexpected stuff works out a whole lot better than anything you've actually arranged.

As the coach rolls slowly out of London, Skye falls asleep with her head against the window and Summer presses her face against my neck and tells me she's had the best birthday ever, and the best Valentine's Day too. I slide an arm round her shoulders, and somehow she feels stronger, warmer than before; less fragile, and maybe a little less lost.

It crosses my mind that I am the luckiest boy alive.

'You have hidden depths, Alfie Anderson,' she whispers. 'You can make dreams come true.'

'Not guilty,' I protest. 'You did that all by yourself. I just staged a small diversion – with Finch's help, of course!'

'Still,' she says, 'you made it happen. You're the best boyfriend in the world. Guess I'd better hang on to you.'

'Guess you had,' I say.

Summer puts her head on my shoulder and I rest my cheek against her hair, and we stay like that all the way home.

This story is told from the viewpoint of Jodie, Summer's dance-school friend. The story begins just after the events of **Summer's Dream**. Finding herself at Rochelle Academy instead of Summer, Jodie is feeling out of her depth; can she push aside the guilt and let her own hopes and dreams take centre stage?

This mini-book has two new boy characters, joker Sparks and cool French heartthrob Sebastien . . . I think you'll like them!

xxx

4th September

Dear Summer,

I have started writing this letter a million times, but I don't know what to say except that I am sorry, sorry, sorry. We both had the same hopes and dreams, but I've known for a long time that you are the better dancer. I got a place at the Rochelle Academy, but that place should have been yours ... would have been yours, if you hadn't got ill.

So ... yeah, it's all kind of weird. One minute I feel like the luckiest girl alive, and the next I am swamped by a wave of guilt so huge and heavy I think it might crush the life out of me. I got what I wanted, but only because you're not well. Sometimes I lie awake at night and wonder if you'll ever forgive me.

I'm so, so sorry for how things worked out. I wish it could be different, that you were well again and we were here together because maybe then I wouldn't feel so scared.

Lots of love,
Jodie
xxx

❀❀❀❀❀❀❀❀❀❀❀❀❀❀❀❀❀❀❀❀❀❀❀

1

'So,' my room-mate Grace says to me on our first day at Rochelle Academy, as the four of us sharing this bright, baby-blue dorm room unpack our bags. 'You must be Summer Tanberry, right?'

My cheeks darken. 'No,' I reply. 'I'm actually Jodie. Jodie Rivers.'

Grace frowns. 'Oh! My letter said I'd be sharing with Naomi Prince, Olivia Mulgrave and Summer Tanberry!' she says, puzzled. 'I wonder if there's been some kind of mix up?'

'Summer couldn't take up her place in the end,' I explain, trying to stay upbeat. 'She was ill and had to drop out. I was on the reserve list.'

'Ah.' Grace exchanges glances with Naomi and Olivia. 'I see . . . the reserve list.'

I try to smile, but I know they've judged me already, these willowy girls with perfect poise and manners and perfect hair in various shades of blonde, pinned up into perfect buns. I am not like them. I am not willowy and poised, I am curvy and talkative, and my long dark hair is thick and unruly and escapes from even the most carefully constructed bun, no matter how many kirby grips or how much gel and hairspray I use.

I am a scholarship girl, one of the few students here purely on merit. So why do I feel out of my depth? I am not here just because my parents can afford the fees, although, of course, even fee-paying students have to pass a strict audition.

Grace, Naomi and Olivia smile politely and start arranging photographs on their bedside tables, folding clothes away into drawers. I roll my eyes, wondering how I am going to endure another ten minutes in this place, let alone the next six weeks until half-term. Why did I ever think this would be a good idea? I wish I was back at my old school, where everyone knew me and I didn't have to struggle to fit in. I never really allowed myself to believe I'd get a place at Rochelle Academy, not when I knew I was up against Summer. I was over the moon to be given a chance, but I guess I haven't properly prepared myself for it . . . boarding ballet school. Reality is starting to kick in now, and I'm not sure I can handle it.

My parents said their farewells and drove away an hour ago, and already I am fighting the impulse to ring and tell them to come back and fetch me. I won't, obviously. I am not a quitter, and this is my dream.

I think.

Summer would have slotted in here without a problem; she'd have taken it all in her stride, charmed everyone, made three new best friends in the blink of an eye. Well, Grace, Naomi and Olivia are all out of luck. They've ended up with me.

There's a tentative knock at the door, and the four of us exchange glances.

'Who d'you think that could be?' Olivia whispers, and I laugh because, clearly, there is only one way to find out. I whisk open the door to reveal four fellow students crowded on to the threshold outside.

❀❀❀❀❀❀❀❀❀❀❀❀❀❀❀❀❀❀❀❀❀❀❀

'Hey!' a pretty Asian girl says. 'We're your next-door neighbours! I'm Priya, and this is Annabel, Tasha and Niamh . . . can we come in? We come bearing gifts!'

A few moments later, the whole bunch of us are squashed into the room, sharing Jaffa Cakes and fruit juice, laughing, exchanging stories of where we've come from and how excited we are to be here. The ice is broken. Our neighbours are chatty, funny, friendly, making my new room-mates seem less certain, less sure of themselves; somehow less perfect than before. Perhaps they're just as nervous as I am; perhaps, after all, we will learn to get along.

Suddenly I am excited and hopeful; the fear of being second best, surplus to requirements, recedes a little. This is a new beginning; we are all starting from scratch in a brand new dance school with a world-class ballerina, Sylvie Rochelle, as our principal. Anything should be possible here.

'Our first regular lessons start in the morning,' Tasha, a slender black girl with amazing braided hair, is saying. 'I'm not looking forward to the maths and science bits, and lessons start at eight a.m. That's going to take some getting used to!'

✿✿✿✿✿✿✿✿✿✿✿✿✿✿✿✿✿✿✿✿✿✿

'But at least we get all of that stuff over with by midday,' I point out. 'Then it's lunch break, and then, just imagine – a whole afternoon of dance! Every day of the week and optional Saturdays too . . . It's a total dream come true! Bliss!'

'I'm a bit worried I won't be able to keep up,' Naomi confesses. 'I've only been doing three classes a week up until now . . .'

'Just two for me,' Annabel chips in. 'I'm scared you lot will outclass me by miles . . .'

I realize that these girls really are just as scared and nervous as I am, no matter how poised and perfect they may appear.

Even Grace is nodding her head. 'I think we all have a few doubts and worries,' she says. 'It's only natural. We're used to being the best dancers in our old ballet schools back home, aren't we? Here it could be a different story.'

I bite my lip. The trouble is, I *wasn't* the best dancer in my ballet school back home – that was Summer. Doubts flood through me all over again, but I push them away, firmly.

'The thing to remember is that we're all in this together,'

I point out, and I see my new classmates tilting their heads to listen, as though I'm saying something important, something worthwhile. 'Every one of us dreamt of a chance like this, and we've been given it, just thirty of us in our year group – how cool is that? I'm not saying it's going to be easy because I know it won't be; I think it will be really tough, and there might be times we wish we'd never auditioned at all, but . . . well, let's be glad we're here. We don't have to be competitive and we don't have to judge ourselves against others. Let's face it, ballet is pressured enough already without all that. Let's be friends, and support each other, and maybe that way we can help each other through.'

'Well said, Jodie,' Priya says. 'If we stick together, we can do just about anything, right? Boarding school might be a challenge for me. I'm going to miss my family SO much. I for one am hundreds of miles from home, so it's not like I can just nip back for the weekend!'

'It's not just family I'll miss,' Naomi admits. 'I've got a boyfriend back home. We've only been together six weeks, but still, I'll miss him. And it's going to be very strange adjusting to life with no boys around at all . . .'

✿✿✿✿✿✿✿✿✿✿✿✿✿✿✿✿✿✿✿✿✿

'I know, right?' Niamh agrees. 'No flirting, no rivalry, no annoying boys winding you up . . .'

'No distractions!' Annabel says.

'No crushes,' Priya adds, sadly.

'And we'll be the oldest in the school,' Olivia reminds us. 'Nobody to look up to, nobody to ask for advice, just twenty brand-new Year Sevens, twenty Year Eights, and thirty of us Year Nines. That's a whole bunch of us, all missing home and friends and boys. It'll take some getting used to . . .'

We descend into silence, contemplating a loveless, boy-free life of eight a.m. starts and relentless, gruelling practice, shared with a mob of hormonal teenage girls all striving for perfection. It's not a pretty picture. Naomi sniffs and blinks a few times, her eyes too bright, and I know that unless someone does something fast, this whole getting-to-know-you thing will end in tears.

I jump up, pulling Priya and Tasha to their feet alongside me. 'So,' I say. 'We should go and explore! Find out who else is here! It's a bit of an adventure, right? Like Harry Potter at Hogwarts, only with pointe shoes and leotards!'

Grace frowns, studying the welcome pack folder in her hand. 'The welcome dinner is at six o'clock,' she reads. 'In between arrival and dinner, students are advised to unpack and get to know their room-mates. Alternatively, they may meet up with their fellow students informally in the first-floor common room . . .'

'Let's do it,' I say, taking charge. I round them up and usher them out of the door. 'Forget the formal introductions, let's explore!'

We find the common room and burst in, an unruly group of giggling, chattering girls. It's huge – an airy, wood-panelled room with a parquet floor and an antique Persian rug. There are four mismatched sofas, a scattering of bean-bags and a big polished wood table by the window. On the far side of the room, a woodburning stove is smouldering gently, giving the whole room the smell of beach bonfires and possibility.

And lounging on armchairs and beanbags in front of the woodburner are four students who stand out from the crowd of slim, elegant girls I've met so far this afternoon.

They look up at us, grinning.

'Oh. My. Days,' Tasha whispers. 'Boys!'

It looks like Rochelle Academy isn't girls-only after all . . .

Dear Summer,

I hope you got my last letter. I know you're not well, and that replying might not be your number-one priority, but I hope the silence is not because you're upset about me being here at Rochelle. I'm pretty sure it's not, but . . . well, I worry. You know how it is.

I'm settling in, getting to know my classmates pretty well, but my closest friends so far are a couple of girls called Naomi and Tasha, and a boy called Sparks. Yeah, I know . . . a BOY!!! I just sort of assumed that Rochelle Academy would be girls only, but there are twenty-six girls and four boys in our year . . . Can you imagine? There's Sparks and Josh and Matt and an actual French boy called Sebastien Dubois who is Sylvie Rochelle's godson. How cool? This place is a crazy hotbed of hormonal madness, I am telling you! But Sparks . . . well, a few of the girls fancy him, but he's not interested in girls, if you catch my drift. He is SO funny and really good fun, and I think he keeps me sane . . . so, yeah. That's my news.

I'm loving the classical ballet classes but I don't

understand contemporary dance at all . . . The teacher must think I'm hopeless. It's all about 'feeling' the music and interpreting things, and I feel really out of my depth without set steps to follow. I bet you'd like it, though!

Only a couple of weeks until half-term and we can catch up properly . . . talking is easier than writing letters, I guess! Shall I ring you first or just turn up? I hope things are going well with you and that you're feeling better. Maybe you can audition next year and we can still be here together!

Love you lots,
Jodie
xxx

2

Sparks is sitting on my bed, backcombing his wavy blond hair until it sticks up at all angles, like some kind of punk porcupine. He is grumbling about his maths homework.

'Fractions and equations and square roots are kind of pointless,' he argues, blasting his hedgehog hair with a cloud of borrowed hairspray. 'I won't need any of this once I'm a famous dancer, so why torture me with it now? It's cruel. Possibly even an infringement of my human rights.'

'Rubbish,' I tell him, working through yet another page of equations. 'Maths is a basic skill. You'll need it one day to negotiate your fees when you're dancing for the Royal Ballet!'

'I wish,' Sparks says.

❁❁❁❁❁❁❁❁❁❁❁❁❁❁❁❁❁❁❁❁❁❁❁

The door opens and Grace comes in, her face registering annoyance when she sees Sparks.

'What's *he* doing here?' she asks, rudely. 'Boys aren't allowed in the girls' dorms, Jodie. You know that. I could have just been in the shower or anything! It's totally against the rules!'

'Hello?' Sparks says, waving his fingers at Grace. 'I am actually here, y'know! You can talk to me directly, like everyone else does. You weren't just in the shower, so I won't be fainting clean away at the sight of your naked ankles. And before you get your knickers in a twist, we are just chilling, and doing a bit of recreational maths homework, none of which is illegal or dangerous or threatening to the fabric of society. Don't go stirring up trouble where there is none . . .'

'Sparks is just a mate,' I say, trying to defuse things a little. 'Mates like to hang out together. It's no big deal!'

'He's a *boy*!' she huffs.

'Well, yep, last time I looked,' Sparks quips.

'You've been at my hair gel!' Grace howls, outraged. 'And my hairspray! Sparks, you spend more time here than in your own dorm. Seriously, this just isn't funny!'

❁❁❁❁❁❁❁❁❁❁❁❁❁❁❁❁❁❁❁❁❁❁❁❁

Sparks rolls his eyes and jumps off the bed, leaping effort-lessly across the room in a dramatic *grand jeté* before bowing low to Grace and blowing her a kiss.

'Thanks for the loan of the hairspray,' he says. 'I'd advise you to buy the extra-hold version next time, though. I know how you hate having even a single hair out of place . . .'

He flounces out into the corridor and I follow, biting back a giggle. Grace can be a bit moody at times, and she is a real perfectionist. Sometimes she makes me feel I'm making the dorm untidy just by being there; the fact that I occasionally dare to breathe, talk or express an opinion can be enough to send her off the deep end.

When that happens I take myself off to the common room or head outside for a trudge through the grounds to blow the cobwebs away – living 24/7 with twenty-five ballet-mad girls and four dance-crazy guys can get a little intense sometimes.

'Grace is so fussy and dull!' Sparks complains, as we flop down beside the woodburner. A few of the other students are loafing on the sofas across the room watching a DVD. They can't hear our chat over the noise of the film. 'I think she's jealous of you, Jodie. She thinks you'll land the leading role in the Christmas production, and she's all eaten up with envy.'

'Or else she just hates me,' I say, gloomily. 'She's so serious and determined . . . I bet she ends up in one of the top ballet companies. I'm not exactly a threat to her, am I? I'm not a classical-type ballerina, like most of the girls here, and I'm not really solo material . . . I don't even know why they offered me a place at all.'

Sparks rolls his eyes. 'They offered you a place because you're amazing,' he says. 'You've got natural talent oozing from every pore. Grace can see that, and it makes her nervous . . . because no amount of hard work and practice can substitute for that! Besides, why shouldn't you be a soloist? You should put yourself forward a bit more!'

'No, I'm happiest in the background,' I say, laughing. 'Thanks for the flattery, though! You're not so bad yourself, Sparks!'

'I know, right?' he teases. 'We can't help it if we stand out from the crowd. Mind you, I think there could be another reason why Grace has a problem with you . . .'

'Yeah? What's that, then?'

'One word,' Sparks whispers. 'Sebastien Dubois!'

❁❁❁❁❁❁❁❁❁❁❁❁❁❁❁❁❁❁❁❁❁❁❁❁

'That's two words,' I point out, hoping that the heat in my cheeks is not translating into a crimson blush. 'And I don't know what you're talking about!'

Sparks raises an eyebrow knowingly, and the two of us sneak a glance at the kids lounging on the sofas. Sebastien is at the centre of a gaggle of girls, seemingly oblivious to their starry-eyed glances as he watches the DVD. He has dark, unruly hair, flashing eyes and olive skin that marks him out as different, Gallic, cool. I know that when I look at him my eyes go starry too, but I was hoping nobody had noticed.

'Ooh la la,' Sparks says under his breath, jabbing me in the ribs with an elbow. 'You 'ave a bad case of zee love bug! Don't try to deny it . . . I can tell!'

'I do not!' I protest. 'I hardly know him!'

'You'd like to, though,' he teases. 'And so would Grace. I've seen her – her eyes are out on stalks every time he's around. That's why she gives you a hard time.'

'She can have him,' I declare, recklessly. 'He's way out of my league anyhow.'

Sparks shakes his head, despairing. 'Don't run yourself down,' he says. 'You do it all the time – with your dancing, your looks, everything.'

177

'Self-defence,' I tell him. 'If you don't build your hopes up, you don't get too disappointed when things knock you down . . .'

Even as I say this, I'm not certain it's true. I get hurt when things go wrong, just like everybody else. There've been a few knocks; I failed the Royal Ballet School auditions back when I was ten, and I was only offered a place here because Summer dropped out. I guess that hanging out with Summer Tanberry hasn't helped my confidence over the years. Our dance teacher, Miss Elise, was always kind and encouraging, but everyone back home knew that Summer was the star. The harder she pushed herself, the cooler I played it. Admitting how much I cared would have been asking for trouble.

When Summer was given the place at Rochelle Academy we'd both worked so hard for, I was genuinely pleased for her; she was one of my best friends, and she deserved the chance to shine. I would have been very mean to have begrudged her that. I cried myself to sleep every night for a week, but I would never have shown anyone just how gutted I felt.

And then Summer dropped out and her place was offered to me.

178

'I'm so proud of you, Jodie!' Mum had said. 'Only the very best young dancers are given this kind of opportunity!'

I smiled, but deep inside I knew I was second best to Summer, that I always would be.

'Modesty gets you nowhere in this life,' Sparks says, toasting his toes in front of the woodburner. 'You can't just switch off the passion and pretend you don't care. That's only half a life, Jodie! You have something special, you know that, don't you?'

I look across at Sebastien and he glances over at me, grinning briefly before looking back towards the DVD. I wonder if he knows I think of him in those half-dreaming moments before I sleep, before I wake? I wonder if he cares? He's a friendly boy, but I don't think he has a clue who I even am.

'I'm a realist,' I tell Sparks. 'Why reach for the moon when you don't have a skyrocket to get there?'

'I don't have a skyrocket either,' he replies. 'It's not going to stop me. Today Rochelle Academy . . . tomorrow the world!'

I wish I had half his confidence.

179

❀❀❀❀❀❀❀❀❀❀❀❀❀❀❀❀❀❀❀❀❀❀❀

Dear Summer,

I'm sorry that we didn't get to meet up at half-term.
I'm not sure if you actually got my messages? I rang
you a few times, but it all sounded kind of crazy and
hectic and you never did ring back, so maybe you
didn't get the messages at all. I hope that it's not
because you're mad at me or anything.

I spoke to Skye the last time, and she said you were
doing fine, just that you were spending a lot of time at
the clinic, and if you didn't have time to see me you
would definitely write. I hope you do, and that you're
feeling better, Summer. It's so odd to think of you
being ill - you've always been so strong.

It was weird to be back home - I've spent the last
six weeks feeling homesick, but after the first few days
home I was counting down the time until I went back to
Rochelle. It's hard to explain . . . it's the hardest I
have ever worked, but I love it. It gets under your skin.
Well, I guess you know about that. There's loads going
on in the run-up to Christmas, and this week they'll be
announcing which ballet we'll be putting on for our first

major production, and everyone is working extra hard, hoping to get picked for one of the main roles. I know I don't have much of a hope, but I'll give it a go.

Skye told me you're with Alfie now; that's a surprise! Hope it's going well. I have a bit of a crush on that French boy I told you about, Sebastien. Not sure he even knows I'm alive, but hey . . . you can't pick who you fall for, can you?

I feel a bit silly writing to you and never getting any replies, so if I don't hear from you this time I'll leave it a while and catch up with you at Christmas. I'll be thinking about you, though, promise.

Love you lots,
Jodie
xxx

3

I thought that ballet was second nature to me already, but after weeks of daily practice, it becomes as instinctive as breathing. Moves that were challenging to me a couple of months ago come easily now, but my teachers raise the bar higher ever week; they want us to push harder and harder, reach for some impossible, invisible goal. We keep pushing, keep reaching.

I can feel my body getting leaner, stronger; my muscles ache from hard work, and my toes are bruised from hours and hours of pointe work. At Rochelle Academy, you live and breathe dance. It's part of the deal.

And all of us are waiting to find out what the Christmas production will be, and whether we might have a chance of a solo. The first week after half-term, Sylvie Rochelle calls an assembly in Dance Studio One to announce that we will be working on a production of *The Nutcracker*, to be staged the week before Christmas at the theatre in nearby Plymouth. Every student at the academy will take part.

I look at Sparks, to my right, his fingers crossed, his face hopeful; Tasha, to my left, chewing her lip. A metre away, Grace is sitting rigid with anxiety, her forehead creased, her eyes bright with a mixture of fear and longing. All around the studio, the students are pensive, wound up, daring to dream that it could be them. You could cut the atmosphere with a knife.

I am careful to stay guarded, my face a mask of careless nonchalance. A girl who knows she is second best cannot afford to hope too much, or to care. I am not hoping for a solo . . . the chorus line will be good enough for me. I am not ready to be centre stage.

The leading roles go to Annabel, who'll be playing Clara, and Grace, who gets the role of the Sugar Plum Fairy. When Madame Rochelle tells us that Sparks will be playing the Nutcracker Prince, he lets loose a whoop of pure joy, hugging everyone in sight. The rest of us get smaller roles, short solos from the second act of the ballet

❀❀❀❀❀❀❀❀❀❀❀❀❀❀❀❀❀❀❀❀❀❀❀

when Clara is in the land of the sweets. I'm given the part of 'Hot Coco' who does a Spanish flamenco-style solo, and I don't know whether to be terrified or happy. Naomi, Priya, Niamh, Tasha and some of the others all land similar cameos, and then Madame Rochelle reads out the parts for the younger students who will make up the chorus, doubling up as party guests and snowflakes and mice. Relief rushes through me, joyful, intense; I have a solo, a respectable role, a part worth having. Then the doubts crowd in, sucking all the joy out of the moment. A solo. I'm not ready for this, not brave enough, not good enough. And everyone will see that.

'A-mazing,' Tasha whispers, beside me. 'We got solos! How cool?'

'Cool,' I agree.

Beside me, Sparks is fizzing with glee and Grace's face is radiant at the news that she has a major part. I know how much this means to her, and I try to be glad.

'We will begin working on the production tomorrow,' Sylvie Rochelle says. 'Well done, everybody – I know you will do your best. For now, *mes chéris*, you are dismissed!'

We stand to go, but as I file past Madame Rochelle with

Naomi, Tasha and Sparks, she reaches out and touches my arm.

'Jodie?' she says. 'I wish to speak with you a moment. You 'ave five minutes?'

My heart thumps, and my mouth is suddenly dry; is something wrong? Am I in trouble?

'Yes, of course,' I say. 'No problem . . .'

'Shall I wait?' Tasha whispers.

'No, don't worry, I'll find you,' I tell her. 'I'll be fine.'

I follow Sylvie Rochelle to the side of the studio as the last of the students leave. I have attended ballet lessons every day for six weeks with her; she is a strict and exacting teacher, but inspiring. She looks at each one of us and sees our strong and weak points. Has she seen mine?

She smoothes back her neat, greying hair, tilts her elegant chin. Her blue eyes, sharp and bright, seem to see right into my soul.

'I 'ave been watching you very carefully, Jodie,' she says. 'You show great skill and promise in classical ballet, yet all the time I feel there is something . . . missing?'

Fear closes my throat. Something missing? I am dancing for hours each day, pushing myself harder than I ever have before; if something is missing, I'm not sure it is within my power to find it. Will my stay at Rochelle Academy be over so soon?

'Jodie?' she says gently, and my name sounds alien, exotic, in her strong French accent. 'Do you understand what I am saying? At the auditions, back in August, I felt you were holding something back. That is why we did not offer you a place to begin with; I sense the same . . . how should I say, reserve . . . in the way you dance now. Technically, I cannot fault you. You do what I ask of you – work hard . . . yet somehow, still, you are holding back. I need my students to dance with their heart and soul, not just with their bodies. You 'ave to want this, Jodie. You 'ave to want it more than anything else in the world. When you do that, the magic begins.'

'I am trying my best,' I argue.

'I don't think so,' Sylvie Rochelle says. 'I think you are playing safe. I want you to take some risks, open up, show me that you have something to give!'

'Yes, Madame Rochelle,' I whisper.

I turn away, holding my shoulders back, my head high. I put every ounce of energy I have into making sure I look calm as I walk carefully out of there; I will not let her see my tears. The trouble is, in a boarding school, there is nowhere to run to if you want to be alone. I share my bedroom with three other girls, and I have never seen the common room with less than half a dozen people in it. Even the bathroom is no escape – if you're in there too long someone comes along and starts hammering on the door, I kid you not.

At Rochelle Academy, when you want some space, there is only one option.

I walk along the corridor and push through the heavy oak front door, run down the steps and out across the frost-rimed grass. There's an old summer house half hidden behind a stand of willow trees down beside the river: the doors hanging off, the paint peeling on the veranda – the wood beneath weathered to a silvery grey. Some of the other students must know about it too because inside, in the corner, there's an old wicker chair and a blanket with chocolate wrappers, banana skins and squashed-up Coke cans littered around it.

It's not my private place, I know, but I have never seen anyone else here. It's where I come when I want to be alone.

❀❀❀❀❀❀❀❀❀❀❀❀❀❀❀❀❀❀❀❀❀❀❀

I make it as far as the steps before the tears come, sliding down my cheeks, hot and salty and bitter. I sink down on to the steps and wrap my arms round my body, gasping and shaking as the sobs rack through me. Sylvie Rochelle thinks I am holding back. That's crazy – why would I hold back? I am giving everything I have, and still it's not enough.

The truth is that Sylvie Rochelle has seen through me, seen that I am second best, not good enough.

It's only as the tears begin to subside that I realize I am still dressed in leotard, tights, leg warmers, wraparound cardi and pointe shoes, and that I'm achingly cold.

Could it get any worse?

It could. It really, really could.

'Hey,' a voice says behind me, and someone drapes a jacket round my shoulders, thick and warm and heavy.

A boy sits down beside me on the ramshackle steps, dark hair falling across his face.

Sebastien.

4

I drag the sleeve of my cardi across my eyes to blot away the tears. My sleeve comes away damp and streaked with eyeliner. I bury my head against my knees. If I count to ten, will Sebastien go away?

Apparently not.

When I look up, he's still there, his face kind and concerned, his corduroy jacket with the badges all over one lapel still hanging round my shoulders.

'How long have you been there?' I ask, my voice still wobbly and thick with tears.

'Long enough,' he says. 'I came out here after Sylvie announced the cast list. Well done on the solo, by the way. I am playing the Mouse King. Lucky me!'

'It's not a bad part,' I say.

✿✿✿✿✿✿✿✿✿✿✿✿✿✿✿✿✿✿✿✿✿✿✿

'It's OK,' he says with a Gallic shrug. 'I guess it proves that I do not get, what do you say – *special treatment* for being Sylvie's godson, as some of the students may think. She is scrupulously fair and honest, no?'

'Too honest, sometimes,' I blurt out, suddenly angry. 'She just told me I am holding something back, not giving enough to my dancing. What more does she want? Blood?'

The minute I say the words, I wish I could take them back. I don't even know this boy, yet I've shown him how hopeless, how insecure I am. Worse still, I have criticized Sylvie Rochelle – a world-class ballerina, principal of our dance school . . . and, oh yes . . . Sebastien's godmother.

I wish the ground would open and swallow me up.

Sebastien laughs. 'This is what has upset you? Ah, Jodie, Sylvie will push you hard. She sees something in you, something special, and she will not rest until everybody else sees it too!'

'I don't mean to be negative about your godmother,' I say. 'She's amazing, obviously. An awesome teacher. But to be totally honest, I don't think she actually sees anything in me. I think she's sorry she gave me a place here.'

❀❀❀❀❀❀❀❀❀❀❀❀❀❀❀❀❀❀❀❀❀❀

The French boy frowns. 'No . . . I do not think so. My godmother, she does not make mistakes.'

'She made one with me,' I tell him. 'I auditioned with a friend from my old dance school, a really gifted dancer. She was given this place, but then she got sick and couldn't take it. Sylvie Rochelle didn't choose me, not really; I'm second choice.'

If there is one way to make an impression on the boy you've been crushing on, it's to spill your guts and show him how needy, how insecure you are. That and the tear-stained face should do it. What is wrong with me? Why can't I keep my big mouth shut?

It's too late, of course; the floodgates have opened, and all my doubts and fears have come tumbling out, stark, ugly, embarrassing.

Sebastien frowns. 'You carry this doubt with you all the time?' he asks. 'This fear that you are not supposed to be here? Trust me, Jodie, my godmother does not take "second best" dancers; this I can promise you.'

I pull the jacket a little closer, shivering.

'She didn't choose me,' I repeat. 'I was a last-minute substitute. How do you think that makes me feel?'

❀❀❀❀❀❀❀❀❀❀❀❀❀❀❀❀❀❀❀❀❀❀❀

He raises an eyebrow. 'Not good,' he guesses. 'This is how I feel too – I would not be here if Sylvie was not my godmother. I am a good dancer, good enough to make the grade, but Sylvie felt – and I agreed – I might be better studying at home in Paris. There was a dance school specializing in contemporary dance I would have loved to go to. Do you think I wanted to leave my home, my friends, to move to another country? This was not my choice, nor Sylvie's – it was my mother's.'

I look sideways at Sebastien; suddenly he looks less self-assured, less confident. Something vulnerable, uncertain, flickers behind his dark blue eyes.

'How come?' I ask.

He shrugs. 'It suits my mother to get me out of the way for a while. She is divorced, and lately she has been seeing a new man. Having a teenage son around all the time did not suit her, so I am here, out of the way.'

'But . . . you don't want to be here?'

'I am not stupid,' he says. 'Sylvie is one of the best teachers in Europe. Training with her will open doors for me one day. And Sylvie has a soft heart and believes that a good dancer can become a brilliant dancer if he – or she – is willing to give his heart and soul. I'm here because I am lucky enough to have Sylvie as a godmother, and perhaps I should be ashamed of that, but I am not – just the opposite. I will work and work until I make her proud that she took a chance on me! I will prove that I am worth taking a risk for!'

I blink. One or two of the more gossipy students have speculated that Sebastien was here because of his family connections, but you would never guess it to see him dance. He is good, as good as anyone – and he works really hard. Maybe that's why – because he has something to prove?

Our eyes meet, and a spark of connection flares between us. I am aware of my smudged eyeliner, my eyes pink from crying, my hair coming adrift from its bun and hanging down around my face in unruly ringlets. Sebastien looks right back at me, taking all of this in. I find myself wondering what it would be like to stretch out my fingers, trace the contours of his perfect cheekbones, and then I blush crimson at the very thought.

I drag my eyes away, try to focus on what he's just told me.

'I'm sorry . . . I didn't realize!'

He frowns and looks out through the canopy of willows,

across the frosted grass towards the golden stonework of the academy.

'It is not so bad,' he tells me. 'My mother – she loves me, and she believes she is doing this for the best. It's just that it has turned out to be the best for her, not for me. I do not talk about this to anyone at the dance school, Jodie, you understand?'

'I won't say anything,' I promise.

'It is not so bad,' he says. 'I enjoy the contemporary dance lessons very much. Joe Nash is an amazing teacher.'

'I know,' I agree. 'He's cool. I'm a bit out of my depth in his classes, though!'

'It is new to you . . . that is to be expected,' he says.

We sit for a while in silence; me huddled in the corduroy jacket, Sebastien leaning back on the old steps, thoughtful.

'I think it is it true, what Sylvie said,' he says at last. 'You hold back, a little, with your dancing. What are you afraid of?'

'Nothing!' I protest.

But I'm not sure this is the truth. I am afraid of rejection, for starters – I have been knocked back before, first at the Royal Ballet School auditions when I was ten, and then here. In between I have lived with the casual assumption of everyone back home that Summer was the star, the one destined for the top. Having such a talented friend is hard. I was glad for her, always, and very proud; but sometimes I wished people could see past her dazzle, and maybe, just maybe, notice me.

'Maybe I do keep a little bit of myself back,' I admit. 'It's not a crime, is it? I'm not really one of life's risk-takers!'

'Perhaps you should be,' he says. 'It is fun! I think you can be a risk-taker, Jodie. Like me.'

I shake my head. 'My friend Summer – the girl who got ill – she was the kind of dancer who took risks, gave everything. Look what happened to her! She burnt out, got eaten up by it all . . .'

'What kind of ill?' he wants to know, and I tell him, even though I've never told the details to anyone before, not Sparks, not Naomi, not Tasha, not even my parents back home. I don't know why it feels OK to tell Sebastien, but it does, somehow. It feels right. I explain how the pressure pushed Summer over the edge and into the arms of an eating disorder, how she ended up losing herself, losing her love of ballet, losing her whole future.

❀❀❀❀❀❀❀❀❀❀❀❀❀❀❀❀❀❀❀❀❀

'Scary,' he says. 'I hope your friend gets well again, but what happened – it wasn't your fault, Jodie. You got this place because you are good. My godmother offered you a scholarship place. She thinks you have something special . . . and she wants to see it in your dancing.'

'She's asking too much,' I say. 'Lots of dancers work hard and focus on skills and technique. Can't that be enough? Why does Sylvie want more from me?'

'Because she *sees* more in you,' Sebastien says, simply. 'I know she does because I see it too . . . there is so much hidden with you, Jodie Rivers. So much going on beneath the surface.'

He stands abruptly, shivering without his jacket in the cold, reaching out a hand to pull me to my feet.

I like the feel of his hand in mine, and I think he likes it too. We stay that way all the way back to the school, and by then I don't think I will ever want to let go.

Dear Jodie,

I know this isn't quite what you wanted, but I happened to find one of your letters to Summer a while ago and I wanted to get in touch. I know she hasn't written to you, but your letters mean the world to her, I promise. She reads and re-reads them, then folds them away and stores them in her desk. I think those little glimpses into life at dance school are like gold dust for her.

Summer is OK . . . wobbling a little right now, I think, but the doctors say that the run up to Christmas is often a difficult time for someone who has anorexia. In case you are wondering, I did pass on your message when you called at half-term, but things were a little hectic here (as usual) and Summer felt a bit anxious about meeting up. I don't know if you've heard, but Honey has messed up one time too many and the fallout here has been pretty full-on. Honey's gone to stay with Dad in Sydney for a while, and that's upset Summer loads, as you can imagine.

So, yeah . . . all a bit chaotic here. A bit sad too. Still, we're getting ready for Christmas and that's cool, and Summer says she'd love to see you while you're home, if you'd like to. I hope you can. I bet you'll be able to cheer her up better than anybody.

Anyhow, hope you don't mind me writing . . . just wanted to fill you in on what's happening with Summer. Let me know when you're home, and when you might be free to meet up!

See you soon,
Skye
oxox

5

The Mad Hatter Cafe is bright with tinsel and fairy lights, a glittering oasis in the quiet dark of Kitnor High Street. There's a bite of cold in the air, the threat of snow to come. My dad drops me off with a promise to return in an hour, and I watch his car drive away with a sinking feeling. Will meeting up with Summer really cheer her up, as Skye hopes, or will it make things worse? It can't be easy, catching up with your old friend to listen to stories of the dance school life you were supposed to be leading, can it?

I push open the door to the cafe and step into the warmth, and right away I see Summer and Skye sitting at a table in the corner. I wave and walk across to join them, slipping into a seat opposite Summer. The twins have drinks already, a diet Coke for Summer, a hot chocolate with whipped cream and marshmallows for Skye. The waitress comes over and I order a hot chocolate and a cupcake iced to look like a reindeer's face, complete with red-nose cherry.

'I'm not staying,' Skye says, scooping up a spoonful of melted marshmallows. 'I'm helping out with the costumes for the village pantomime . . . I need to be there in five minutes. I just wanted to say hi, that's all . . .'

'Hi,' I say. 'The costumes thing sounds great!'

'It is,' Skye says, draining her hot chocolate. 'Look, I'd better go – have fun, you two!'

She stands up, shrugging on a red wool coat with a black velvet collar, and sweeps out of the cafe with a grin and a wave. Suddenly, the easy chat is replaced by silence, shyness. I notice how frail Summer is looking, her skin so pale it looks translucent, blue shadows streaked beneath her eyes.

'It's good to see you,' I say. 'I've missed you like mad.'

Summer smiles, but it's a sad smile.

'Sorry I haven't written,' she says. 'I love your letters. They almost make me feel like I'm there . . . and then I remember that I'm not, and it makes me feel so sad.'

I bite my lip. 'I can imagine. It must be really hard. I wish you were there too; it'd be amazing! You'd absolutely love the place . . . It's so pretty, a real Victorian mansion. The dorms are really cute. They're all painted different pastel colours . . . Ours is baby blue, but Grace hates it and she's campaigning to be allowed to paint it pink . . .'

I am gabbling, I know, but I feel anxious, awkward, keen to fill the silence with something, anything. Summer reaches out and touches my hand.

'It's OK, y'know,' she tells me. 'I'm not mad at you, Jodie. I'm glad you're at the academy. I wish I could have gone, but I couldn't, and knowing you're there is the next best thing. Tell me all about it . . . everything! Is Sylvie Rochelle very strict? How was the Christmas production? Do you love it, Jodie? Tell me everything . . . and what's all this about boys?'

I laugh, and the tension lifts as I explain all about the dance classes: the classical ballet, the character classes, the contemporary dance classes, which I am starting to love more and more. I tell her about dancing my short solo in *The Nutcracker*, about Naomi and Tasha and Sparks and how Grace drives me nuts sometimes with her fussing and her fretting and the shelf full of soft toys she has above her bed.

'So . . . Sparks is just a friend?' Summer checks.

'Definitely,' I insist. 'He's funny and outrageous and hugely talented. He'll be famous one day, I'm sure of it . . .'

'No romance, then?'

'Well . . . there is Sebastien,' I confess. 'The French boy I told you about, Sylvie Rochelle's godson. He's really good-looking and he has the coolest accent I have ever heard in my life, and . . . well, I like him. We're sort of going out . . .'

I flick open my phone and find a few Instagram pictures of Sebastien looking cool and French and moody.

'Wow,' Summer says. 'He's gorgeous!'

'He really is,' I say. 'I don't know what he sees in me at all!'

Summer rolls her eyes. 'Silly,' she pronounces. 'He sees a sweet, clever, kind girl who doesn't have a clue how beautiful she is, or how talented. I'm so happy for you. Don't you see, Jodie? You were meant to go to Rochelle Academy so you'd meet Sebastien; and I was meant to stay here, so I could be with Alfie . . .'

'Alfie Anderson?' I check. 'You're still together?'

'Sure we are,' she says. 'He keeps me sane. Well, sane-ish.

❀❀❀❀❀❀❀❀❀❀❀❀❀❀❀❀❀❀❀❀❀

I am glad for you, Jodie, honestly; you deserve to meet a nice boy, and you deserve to be at Rochelle Academy.'

I pick at my reindeer-face cupcake, unable to meet her eye.

'Hey,' she says. 'You're not still feeling guilty, are you? Because I'm happy for you, I truly am . . .'

I should just smile and nod and pretend it's all OK, but the truth seeps out in spite of my good intentions. 'You don't understand,' I whisper. 'It's hard, really hard. You don't know what it's like to be second best the whole time, to know you're not anybody's first choice . . .'

'No, no, you mustn't think that way!' Summer argues. 'It's fate, a chance to grab your dream, Jodie. Give it all you've got!'

I shake my head. 'Madame Rochelle thinks I am holding back,' I tell her. 'Keeping something back from my dancing. Sebastien thinks so too, and maybe I am, I don't know. I'm scared, Summer. What if I do put everything I have into this and it's still not enough?'

Summer shrugs. 'What if it IS enough? What are you actually scared of, Jodie? Failing? Or . . . well, maybe the opposite?'

I frown. 'What do you mean?'

She sips her diet Coke. 'It's just that . . . well, ever since I've known you, you've held back a little. You always let me take the lead, have the limelight, even if it meant stepping back a little yourself. I used to wonder if you just quite liked being on the sidelines. You've always been so sensible, so relaxed about it all, like you didn't really mind one way or another whether you got a leading role or a place at Rochelle Academy. I didn't really question it, but . . . well, it was self-defence, wasn't it? If you didn't put yourself on the line, you couldn't feel too bad if things didn't work out.'

'Maybe,' I say. 'I'm just the cautious type, right?'

'Or maybe you just take the easy way out,' Summer says, and I flinch at her words because there's truth in them, whether I want to admit it or not. 'Thing is, Jodie, if you mess up and waste this opportunity I don't know if I can ever forgive you. It's what we've both dreamt of for as long as I can remember. I've blown it, but you haven't – you still have everything to play for. Don't wimp out, OK? Give it all you've got. Heart and soul.'

Relief floods through me, hope taking hold again after the longest time. I can't stop smiling. It will be New Year's

Eve in just over a week, and I know already what my reso-
lution will be.

Heart and soul – that simple, that life-changing.

And, just as simply, my friendship with Summer patches
itself up, good as new. All the awkwardness and tension
that crowded in when she began to get ill, the guilt that
swamped me when I was given a place at the academy, the
polite, one-way letters – all of that is wiped away.

Outside, fat white flakes of snow are beginning to fall
. . . a white Christmas.

We exchange prezzies; a glittery pink scarf for Summer,
a silver heart charm bracelet for me. It's getting late by now,
the waitress quietly stacking chairs and wiping tabletops.
Outside, I see the glow of headlights as Dad's car draws
up to the kerb.

We stand, pulling on our coats, paying our bill, and head
for the door. Outside in the snowy street we cling together
in a lingering hug, and even through her coat I can feel
how thin Summer is, just skin and bone, a wisp of a girl
who might blow away in the blizzard.

I no longer feel like I've stolen her dreams, her future.
Instead, I promise myself I will do everything I can to make

❀❀❀❀❀❀❀❀❀❀❀❀❀❀❀❀❀❀❀❀❀❀❀❀

the most of the chance I've been given. I'll do it for both of us.

'I'm glad we got to catch up,' I whisper. 'You're amazing, Summer. Get well, OK?'

'I'm trying,' Summer promises. 'I'll write. And remember – heart and soul.'

I watch her walk along the street, alone in the streetlights, slender, bird-like, picking her way carefully through the freshly fallen snow. We are on different paths these days, Summer and I, but I think our friendship will survive whatever lies ahead.

5th March

Dear Summer,

Thanks for your last letter. I was so glad to hear that
Honey's home, and that you're starting to feel better.
Your Valentine's Day surprise with Alfie sounded
amazing! Sebastien and I had a candlelit picnic in
this derelict summer house we know; not quite as cool
as your day out, but still pretty awesome.

Anyway, you asked how things were going and the
answer is that, finally, things are going great.

Heart and soul . . . that's my new mantra these
days. Madame Rochelle says it's like having a
different person in class, and my contemporary dance
tutor, Joe Nash, says I have a rare quality,
an intuitive, instinctive talent. Me, Jodie Rivers . . . who
knew? All this time I've been pushing and pushing with
the classical ballet, but I honestly think contemporary
dance might be my thing. I am loving it so, so much!

It's all been kind of crazy here and I never seem
to have a minute to myself. I don't mind, though - it's
brilliant. I'm starting to feel like I actually fit in.
And last week something really exciting happened . . .

We're putting on a contemporary dance production called 'Spring Awakening' that we've created and choreographed ourselves with lots of improvised scenes and dances, and Sebastien and I have the leading roles. I am having to pinch myself every five minutes to remind myself it's true!

Me, finally, centre stage!

Love you lots,
Jodie
xxx

Dear Jodie

Dear Summer

Dear Summer

Dear Summer

6

How do you open up and let your feelings show when you've spent a whole lifetime hiding them away? It doesn't happen overnight. It's about learning to trust, learning to let go of the fear that people will laugh or frown or turn away if they see what lies behind the mask of friendly politeness.

Love, fear, anger, sorrow . . . they're not so scary any more, not now I have stopped burying them and begun to dance them free.

Music is the key, of course. It connects with a place much deeper than my mind – heart and soul, I guess.

And now I am listening to the music properly, I dance with everything I have. Even Grace has started to look at me with a new kind of respect.

✿✿✿✿✿✿✿✿✿✿✿✿✿✿✿✿✿✿✿✿✿✿✿✿

In contemporary dance class, I finally understand what I am supposed to be doing; it's all about feeling the music, reacting, responding, expressing, interpreting. It makes sense now, and I wonder how I ever managed all these years without making the connection. It's like I have been dancing in my sleep, just going through the motions.

'Excellent, excellent,' Sylvie Rochelle says, a few weeks into the new term. 'You have woken up at last! I knew you could do it, Jodie!'

Joe Nash is even happier. 'Yes!' he yells as I partner Sebastien in an improvised dance about waking up from a long winter sleep. 'Let your body tell the story . . . it's your musical instrument, your paint and canvas! Forget about traditional dance moves, forget what they've taught you in classical ballet; feel it, live it . . . Fantastic, Jodie!'

It's easy enough to dance a story about waking up from a long sleep, of course, because it's exactly how I feel. As I dance, I can feel the wonder of it all right down to my fingertips. It's there in every heartbeat, in every breath I take, and that knowledge is exhilarating.

'Why didn't you tell me?' I ask Sebastien, after class. 'Why didn't you say I was doing it all wrong? I've wasted years

❀❀❀❀❀❀❀❀❀❀❀❀❀❀❀❀❀❀❀❀❀❀❀

hiding in the shadows, going through the motions, thinking that was enough. Why didn't somebody TELL me?'

'You weren't ready to hear,' Sebastien says.

Of course, Sebastien had told me, and Sylvie, and even Summer; and in the end I understood. It's not just true for dance, either. Whatever you care about in life, you have to give it everything – heart and soul.

Joe Nash is working with our class to create a whole story around the theme of coming back to life, and so our *Spring Awakening* performance is born, with Sebastien and me taking the main roles. Joe is steering the storyline, choosing the music and helping us to create responses that work well, but much of the work is down to us. The result is far less structured than any classical ballet might be; it's like creating an expressive, abstract painting as opposed to painting by numbers.

It's all about freedom, letting go, but instead of making me feel weaker, more vulnerable, it makes me feel stronger than before. It makes me feel like *me*.

On the afternoon of the performance, I sit in the communal dressing room at the theatre in Plymouth, dressed in a green tutu with a skirt of layered chiffon, green footless tights and a ragged white velvet cloak hung with ribbons of icy blue satin. Tasha is dabbing my face and arms with a base of soft spring green, then painting on curving tendrils of emerald that spiral round my arms and snake up round my neck to flower on my cheeks.

'You're a work of art,' Tasha says. 'Awesome!'

I look in the mirror, shaking my hair free from its ponytail. There will be no tightly wound ballerina bun for this production. Naomi backcombs my hair to make it bigger, wilder, and Niamh threads it with green ribbons and tiny flowers.

It feels strange to be the focus of so much attention; for years I have been a shadow girl, waiting in the wings, keeping out of the limelight. Today, that will change. Today, I will be centre stage.

The thought pours icy water over my confidence, makes my belly curdle with fear. Is this why I held back for so long? Did I know that fear would unravel me at the last minute? Even my hands are shaking.

'I can't,' I whisper, but Tasha just laughs and Naomi rolls her eyes and everyone else is too busy putting last minute touches to their own costumes. Panic floods through me, and my mind goes blank; I cannot remember what I am

❀❀❀❀❀❀❀❀❀❀❀❀❀❀❀❀❀❀❀❀❀

supposed to do, and this time there are no classical ballet moves to fall back on, to help me through.

Someone is behind me suddenly, strong hands resting lightly on my waist, warm breath on my neck.

'OK, Jodie?' Sebastien asks. 'Not long now!'

I turn into his arms. 'Not OK,' I whisper. 'I can't do it, Sebastien . . . I'm frightened. I'll mess up, forget my moves, fall, fail . . .'

'No,' he says into my hair. 'No, Jodie, you won't. This is just nerves . . . it will pass. You will be perfect, as always, I promise.'

'Five minutes to curtain!' Joe Nash calls, sweeping through the changing room, checking everyone is ready. 'Prepare to be brilliant, guys! Sebastien, what are you doing here? You need to be onstage, ready for your cue; chorus girls, you need to be in position now too – we're almost ready for curtain-up. Come on, come on, this way!'

He ushers everyone out and I am left all alone except for Sylvie Rochelle, watching me quietly from across the dressing room.

'Nerves?' she asks, and I nod because my mouth is dry and I cannot trust myself to speak.

❀❀❀❀❀❀❀❀❀❀❀❀❀❀❀❀❀❀❀❀❀❀❀

'It is natural,' Sylvie tells me. 'The adrenalin, this small flutter of fear, it is what we need to keep us sharp . . .'

I shake my head. 'No, no, it's more than that,' I whisper. 'I just can't do it . . . I can't! This is why I held back before. I understand now. I never wanted this!'

Sylvie walks towards me, takes my hands in hers. Somehow, the shaking stops and I feel myself standing a little taller.

'You do want this,' she tells me. 'You have wanted it all your life, Jodie, to be centre stage, and now it is happening. You are ready for this!'

'But . . . I'm scared!' I argue.

'So? You think I have never been scared before a performance?' she challenges me. 'Every single time, Jodie. It is part of it all. Perhaps you are scared, but once that curtain opens you will forget everything but the dance. Trust me. Be scared, if you must; but dance anyway.'

She is steering me towards the curtain at stage right, ready for my entrance, and suddenly the orchestra begins to play and I see the thick curtains sweeping back to reveal my classmates, curled as if sleeping, scattered across the stage. The performance has begun.

❀❀❀❀❀❀❀❀❀❀❀❀❀❀❀❀❀❀❀❀

'No,' I protest again. 'Madame Rochelle, I mean it, I really don't think . . .'

'Don't think,' she hisses. 'Just dance. Yes?'

I hear the swell of violin music that heralds my entrance and I move forward, running barefoot on to the stage. I catch sight of the audience, rows and rows of people sitting in the darkened auditorium, and I think I might falter. Instead I turn away, beginning my first solo. The music takes me by the hand, leading me out of danger, and soon I am lost in it all, heart and soul, loving every moment as I whirl about the stage, swishing my wintry cloak before finally discarding it as the music warms and works its way to a crescendo. I am springtime, the pulse of green running through me, wakening the chorus girls one by one from their winter sleep until all of us are dancing together.

The music slows and the chorus girls move back, kneeling in a semicircle. A golden spotlight picks out Sebastien, curled up tight at the back of the stage, slowly stretching and standing tall, dressed in shades of orange and ochre to represent the sun. He walks towards me, takes my hand and pulls me close, and the two of us use every bit of space to dance out the joy of the music. As our duet finishes the first act with a swooping lift and an embrace that sinks down on to the floor, the audience is whooping and cheering and clapping for so long I think I must be dreaming.

By the end of the third act, as spring fades gently away to a riot of summer colour from the chorus girls, I am exhausted, exhilarated, ecstatic. Behind the curtain we listen as the audience goes crazy, and then the lights come up and we run onstage again for a final bow. When I look up I can see my mum and dad and my little brothers in the front row of the theatre, and just behind them, Summer, Skye and Alfie with Charlotte and Paddy cheering louder than anyone else.

I drop into another curtsy, my eyes wet with tears of happiness.

The evening is crazy; that backstage buzz lasts right through a makeshift after-party in the theatre cafe, through hugs and praise and kind words from Mum and Dad and Summer, from Sylvie and Joe, from total strangers. The

❀❀❀❀❀❀❀❀❀❀❀❀❀❀❀❀❀❀❀❀❀❀

local newspaper takes photographs and promises a review, and I watch wide-eyed as the reporter scrawls 'Jodie Rivers: exciting new talent' in her notebook.

'You were awesome,' Summer tells me, and I hold her tight and tell her I did it for her too, for both of us, heart and soul.

'I know,' she whispers back, her eyes bright. 'I know you did.'

When everyone has gone, we travel back to Rochelle Academy in a couple of coaches, talking non-stop, laughing at the remnants of stage make-up still on our faces, outlandish false eyelashes, streaks of green around our hairlines, ribbons and flowers in our hair.

'Epic stuff,' Sparks declares. 'We blew them away back there! With a little help from Jodie and Sebastien, of course . . .'

'You were incredible,' Tasha tells me.

'Fantastic,' Naomi agrees.

Grace smiles and leans across the aisle. 'I never really understood contemporary dance until tonight,' she says. 'You made it come to life, Jodie. You were great!'

That is my favourite compliment of all.

Back at the academy, the cooks have laid on a celebration buffet; we eat quiche and salad and cake while Sylvie and Joe tell us we were all amazing. We are even given an extended curfew because it's clear that none of us will be in bed by ten-thirty, not on a night like this.

Things are starting to break up by half eleven, and I am trying to sneak away quietly when Sylvie catches me by the wrist.

'You see?' she teases. 'Centre stage is not such a scary place to be. Some of us were born to it, Jodie Rivers. And you cannot hide from your destiny.'

I smile at her, and wonder how she seems to know me better than I know myself. 'Thank you,' I say. 'For giving me a chance!'

'I was always willing to give you a chance,' Sylvie replies. 'You just had to find the courage to take it!'

'How about me?' Sebastien asks, coming up behind me. 'Was I OK?'

'You were excellent,' Sylvie tells him. 'Just as I knew you would be.'

And then we are out of there, just the two of us, slipping

down the empty corridors, grabbing jackets and sliding silently out of the kitchen door, the one that nobody ever remembers to lock. We walk across the moonlit grass, hand in hand, under the willow trees wearing their fresh green ribbons of leaves, down to the ruined summer house.

And now we are sitting on the ramshackle steps together, just as we did in November, all those months ago.

Sebastien's mum did not come to the performance; it's a long way, of course, from Paris, and he knew she wouldn't make it, but I think he is sad all the same. When term finishes Mum and Dad have said he can come home to Minehead to stay with us. Who knows, maybe one day I will get to stay with him in Paris.

I lean my head against Sebastien's shoulder and he wraps his arms round me, and I know without any trace of a doubt that today has been the best day of my life. I danced centre stage, the star of the show, and I found reserves of courage I didn't know I had. I danced better than I ever have before, heart and soul, and I loved every single second of it. Now, finally, I am here, in my favourite place, with my favourite person.

The last minutes of the day slide through our fingers like

❀❀❀❀❀❀❀❀❀❀❀❀❀❀❀❀❀❀❀❀❀❀❀

sand, but it doesn't matter; I have learnt so much today about courage and friendship and trust. I have learnt how to step out of the shadows and into the spotlight, and I won't be going back.

Lots of readers have been asking for a story from Jamie Finch's point of view . . . this mysterious dream boy who first appeared in Marshmallow Skye has a lot of fans! When I began thinking about his story, I realized it might turn out a little differently to the way my readers imagined, but that seemed even more exciting somehow!

Finch's story takes place almost a year on from the events of **Coco Caramel**  It has a few twists and turns and a little bit of mystery too . . . I think you'll like it! Finch is a bit of a charmer . . . but in 'Moon and Stars' he has a real dilemma. There's even a little Halloween magic mixed into the story . . .

Cathy Cassidy ♥ xxx

1

After a few warm-up exercises, Fitz gets us all to sit in a circle while he gives us some background on the character study he wants us to work on. It's an improvisation, a two-person piece with one of us acting the part of a polite but exasperated shopkeeper, the other an angry customer with a grudge against the world.

'If you are playing the role of the customer, I want you to get under his or her skin,' Fitz is saying. 'Imagine that life has dealt you some very bad cards . . . and now you always expect the worst. Your outlook on life is grim and grey and dismal. Be gloomy, be grumpy . . . imagine your life is a disaster, like you have your own personal raincloud following you around . . .'

Fitz moves on to the other character in his improvisation

set-up, but I've stopped listening. My gaze drifts up to the ceiling, as if a passing raincloud might be somehow visible, but all I can see are the fancy drama-studio stage lights pointing over towards the stage area. No rainclouds, and even if there was one, I bet I'd be able to find a silver lining.

Or at least – the old Finch would have. Once upon a time my world outlook was rainbow bright. I always thought I was the luckiest boy alive.

Some people see a glass as half full, some half empty; I usually feel like the glass is overflowing, full of fizz and fun. I look on the bright side and good stuff happens, and my life is mostly pretty awesome. I live in a tall Victorian terraced house in Islington, London, and my mum is a TV producer, which means we get to mix with some pretty cool people and do some pretty cool things. I have two older sisters, Talia and Lara, who are both at uni, and although my dad doesn't live with us any more he is still a brilliant dad, and he and my mum get on great.

I go to a good school, get good grades and have a whole bunch of amazing friends, and the summer before last I had a bit part in a TV film and fell head-over-heels with the coolest, cutest girl in the whole of Somerset.

❀❀❀❀❀❀❀❀❀❀❀❀❀❀❀❀❀❀❀❀❀❀❀

See what I mean? Luckiest boy alive.

It drives my mates crazy.

They think I lead a charmed life. 'It's uncanny. I swear, Jamie Finch,' one said just last week, 'if you fell right off the top of the London Eye you'd probably land on a feather mattress that just happened to be being driven past on the back of a flatbed truck. Being driven by . . . I dunno, Taylor Swift or someone. And she'd fall for you and the two of you would run off to Hollywood and you'd end up with a new career as a movie stuntman. You just always land on your feet. Lucky, lucky, lucky.'

I'd laugh and roll my eyes, but I liked being lucky. I'd got used to it. I actually thought it might last forever.

Then something happened, a small thing, an accidental thing . . . three or four months ago now.

It was a mistake, and anyone can make a mistake, right? I didn't plan it, I didn't mean it, but I could tell right away that it was one of those things there is no going back from, one of those things that changes everything.

And that's a problem, because I don't want things to change. I've been trying my hardest to pretend that nothing happened, that life's just the way it's always been, but I

❀❀❀❀❀❀❀❀❀❀❀❀❀❀❀❀❀❀❀❀❀❀❀

can't do it. Like the imaginary character in Fitz's drama scenario, nowadays my own personal raincloud is never far away, threatening to rain on my parade.

I go to school, I go to drama club, I chill out with friends and go to parties and watch the new bands that play in the Camden clubs. I do the things I've always done, but all the time it feels like the raincloud is just waiting, and when the time is right it will pour down its icy cold rain all over me, drenching me to the skin.

'Are you OK?' the girl next to me asks, nudging me in the ribs. 'Are you even listening?'

'Of course I am,' I say. 'Just thinking about . . . stuff. Y'know. Nothing much.'

She rolls her eyes. Her name is Ellie Powell and she is one of those infuriatingly enthusiastic, dedicated girls who expects everyone else to be just about as perfect as she is. I used to be enthusiastic and dedicated too, about my drama class at any rate, but that was before my raincloud appeared, squeezing the joy out of everything. Lately, I am just going through the motions, and Ellie has noticed.

'Want to partner up?' she asks. 'I can fill you in on what you missed, because I know you weren't listening. You never

❀❀❀❀❀❀❀❀❀❀❀❀❀❀❀❀❀❀❀❀❀❀❀

do these days. It kind of lets the whole team down when you obviously don't care, Jamie.'

I grit my teeth. 'I do care,' I insist. 'I just have a lot on my mind.'

'So, partner up?'

'No thanks, Ellie,' I say, casting my eyes around for another option. Any other option. I spot a small Year Seven boy who usually does the scenery painting, and breathe a sigh of relief. 'I'm going to work with Kevin here. I'm going to be the mild-mannered shopkeeper and he's going to be the raging customer. Right, Kev?'

'It's Kenneth, actually,' the Year Seven boy scowls.

See what I mean? I cannot get anything right lately. I drag the unwilling Kenneth off to plan our drama piece, leaving Ellie laughing at my discomfort. I do not like Ellie Powell at all. She has a way of looking at me as though she knows exactly what's going on behind the confident, self-assured mask I show to the world. Ellie's dark green eyes seem to have X-ray vision; the ability to sear right through several layers of skin and scrutinize what's going on inside.

It's not a quality I admire.

229

❀❀❀❀❀❀❀❀❀❀❀❀❀❀❀❀❀❀❀❀❀❀

In the end, Kenneth and I manage a reasonable improvisation piece, but only because he insists on being the mild-mannered shopkeeper. I pretend he is Ellie Powell and blast him with all of the bottled-up anger I have been holding in for the last few months.

Fitz, watching from the sidelines, comes over to intervene just at the point where I grab Kenneth by the collar and pretend to shove him up against the wall, growling a long litany of abuse right into his face. Kenneth is actually shaking. Maybe his acting skills are better than I thought?

'Enough!' Fitz says. 'Drop him! Are you OK, Kenneth?'

'Sure,' the kid says, but it comes out kind of strangled and sad.

'I was acting,' I argue, but a little bit of me knows that I took things too far. 'I . . . maybe I got carried away. Sorry, Kenneth. Sorry, Fitz.'

I can sense Ellie Powell watching from the other side of the drama studio, where she'd just done a brilliant improv with Fitz's little sister, who wasn't a drama student at all but just came along to help out and make hot chocolate after the session. I bristle with annoyance at Ellie's glance, my fists clenching.

✿✿✿✿✿✿✿✿✿✿✿✿✿✿✿✿✿✿✿✿✿✿

'Are you even listening to me?' Fitz is saying, and I know I've tuned out again and missed his sermon on why it's not a good plan to grab a small, scene-painting student by the scruff of the neck during drama club.

'Sorry, Fitz,' I mumble.

'Finch, your heart's just not in this right now,' he says. 'I need to find out why. See me after the class, OK? We need to talk.'

After class, Fitz asks me if there's anything bothering me; if anything's wrong at home. My acting has been way off for weeks, he says.

'You have masses of potential,' he tells me. 'But you're an instinctive actor. If stuff is going on in your life, you need to get it sorted or it will spill over into your acting. I may have to rethink our casting for the end-of-year play unless you can get yourself on an even keel. I can't have a lead actor who's distracted and moody all the time.'

The drama club is putting on a musical production of *Bugsy Malone* later in the year, and though the cast list hasn't yet gone up, Fitz has mentioned a few times that I'd make a great Bugsy. Now he's backtracking. I don't even have to look up to glimpse my raincloud . . . it's blotting out every bit of light right now.

'I'm fine,' I insist. 'I'll get it sorted, Fitz, I swear I will. It's a blip.'

'Hope so,' he says. 'I can't cast you as Bugsy if your heart's not in it. I need someone reliable.'

'I know, I know. Leave it with me.'

I used to be reliable; the most reliable kid in class. Not any more. I can feel Fitz's disappointment soaking through me, but I don't know how to find my way back to the boy I used to be.

I promise myself I will try.

Everybody's gone by the time I walk out of the studio; everyone but Ellie. She's sitting on the wall in the fading light, swinging her legs and sipping an iced mango smoothie from the coffee shop along the road.

My jaw sets; I'm angry all over again.

'What did Fitz say?' she wants to know. 'He mentioned last week that you were off your game – losing the plot. He kind of hinted that he wasn't sure you'd be the right choice for the lead role in *Bugsy*.'

'Thanks,' I say. 'That makes me feel a whole lot better.'

'I'm not trying to make you feel better,' she says. 'Just get a grip. Sort your life out!'

❀❀❀❀❀❀❀❀❀❀❀❀❀❀❀❀❀❀❀❀❀

I cannot think of one single polite answer to that, so I turn round and stalk off along the street, leaving her behind.

Ellie Powell is everything I despise in a girl. She seems harmless enough, but that chirpy, enthusiastic exterior hides a deeply irritating personality; Ellie is like a bouncy puppy that never gives up, even when all the signs are clear that nobody wants them around. As a last resort, she will turn her dark green eyes on you, piercing, pleading, and you'll end up feeling like you're somehow the one in the wrong.

'We could go out sometime,' Ellie said to me once, a while ago. 'You and me, we'd be good together.'

She's wrong about that, of course. We'd be bad together; all kinds of bad.

My girlfriend, Skye Tanberry, is nothing like Ellie. She's sweet, kind, daydreamy, a country girl who dresses in vintage cool. She has blonde ringlet-waves and blue-grey eyes a boy could drown in. Skye is my perfect match in every way, except for one thing: she lives in Somerset and I live in London.

Still, we have managed OK since last year with scribbled postcards, text messages, SpiderWeb posts and occasional phone calls. On Valentine's Day, we had a day out at the ballet in Covent Garden, although I admit my mate Alfie (one of the kids I met in Somerset) was the mastermind behind that. He's dating Skye's twin sister, and he set up the whole thing as a joint Valentine's/birthday treat.

I am not the kind of boy who is good at grand gestures, but I do my best. Sometimes, alas, it's not good enough.

I am halfway along the street by the time Ellie catches up with me. She's ditched her smoothie and her cheeks are pink from running, her chestnut hair mussed up. I want to stretch out a hand to smooth it down, but I don't. Ellie's eyes are still filled with exasperation, challenge, fire.

'Don't give me a hard time, Ellie,' I tell her. 'I am not in the mood for this right now, OK?'

She pulls her jacket round her in the fading light.

'What are you in the mood for, Jamie Finch?' she asks.

I hate myself, I really do, but I can't seem to help it. I snake an arm round her waist and pull her close, and then we're kissing, and her lips taste of mango smoothie and danger, and I don't even care.

2

I walk Ellie home and we don't talk about how impossible it all is; we don't talk about anything at all. We just walk slowly through the London streets and kiss for one last time in a pool of lamplight at the end of her street, and I wonder how anything so wrong can possibly feel so right.

It does, though. When I kiss Ellie Powell, the rest of the world disappears and nothing matters at all except that she's here, now, in my arms.

And then we say goodnight and I walk home, and the guilt floods in again, the raincloud hovering right at my shoulder, ready to pour its scorn all over me.

Guilt? Scorn? That's the very least I deserve.

I have a girlfriend already, the perfect girlfriend. And I also have Ellie.

❀❀❀❀❀❀❀❀❀❀❀❀❀❀❀❀❀❀❀❀❀❀❀

Long-distance romance . . . it's not easy, obviously. I remember my mates joking about it right at the start, telling me I could have the best of both worlds; an adoring girlfriend in Somerset and a free run here in London to flirt with anyone I please. Or more than flirt, in fact.

I told them that wasn't my style, but maybe they'd been right all along.

'A girlfriend in Somerset?' Ellie huffed when I first told her about Skye. 'That's hundreds of miles away. Bad planning, Jamie.'

'Bad planning indeed,' I agreed.

'Most people let go of holiday romances,' she pointed out. 'They're not supposed to be forever.'

'You don't understand,' I told her.

Ellie had laughed and rolled her eyes, and I knew that she did understand, better than I did. Things were over with Skye, whether I wanted to admit it or not.

To be honest, I'd known things were cooling off even before Alfie's London trip, way before I'd even met Ellie. I'd been getting lazy, calling less, forgetting to reply to texts. The shine had gone off it all, but even so, that didn't seem like a reason to finish. We'd planned for me to head down to Somerset for a week in the holidays; I was pretty sure some sunshine and a beach party or two would revive the flagging romance.

Then I met Ellie.

She joined my drama group after Easter, and right away her personality started to grate on me. She tried too hard, caused too much trouble, said what she thought even if it wasn't what people wanted to hear. I thought she was annoying. Then one day in July, Fitz put us on set-painting duty, finishing a piece of scenery that was meant to represent a forested hillside, and I was stuck with her. Ellie started telling me that I wasn't quite convincing enough when I was acting, as if I was always aware that there was someone watching, an invisible audience I wanted to impress.

Was that a bad thing? The barb stung.

'You never quite get into character because you're always hamming it up, flashing a cheesy grin at your adoring fans,' she said. 'You need to forget who's watching and lose yourself in the role.'

'Says who?' I'd argued. 'Fitz doesn't have a problem with the way I work, and he's the expert, right?'

❀❀❀❀❀❀❀❀❀❀❀❀❀❀❀❀❀❀❀❀❀

'Just trying to help,' Ellie shrugged.

'Well, don't,' I snapped.

'You're too theatrical,' she said, as though she was doing me a favour. 'Too full of fire and passion.'

And then she kissed me, without warning, and I was full of fire and passion then all right. By the time we managed to pull apart, she had green paint smudged across her nose and her dark hair was all mussed up and I couldn't find the words to be angry. I was already lost.

I've been lost ever since, and my life has gone from sunshiny to dark. I'm stuck in the shadows, wandering around with no map.

I didn't think the thing with Ellie would last, but it would have felt all wrong turning up at Tanglewood when I was sort of seeing someone in London. I took a summer job as a runner for the TV company Mum works for and told Skye I just couldn't get away; the coward's way out. I should have finished things there and then, but admitting you're a two-timing worm is not easy. I didn't see myself that way, and I didn't want to hurt Skye over something I was pretty sure was no more than a fling.

Besides, Skye had a lot on her plate; her twin sister

238

Summer is fighting an eating disorder, her big sister Honey lurches from one disaster to the next, and her mum and stepdad are working seven-day weeks to try to make a go of their luxury chocolate business and keep the whole family afloat. I rang a few times over the summer with the idea of breaking up, but the timing was never right. Summer was going through a wobbly patch, or Honey was in a major meltdown, or everyone was working flat out in the chocolate workshop on some important order.

It was all kind of stressful. How could I add to Skye's troubles by ditching her long distance? I decided to wait until I could do it face to face, and that's a problem because it could be ages before I get to see her again. I will be patient. I have to wait for the right moment, tread carefully, find the right words. If there are any 'right words' for a thing like that, which I doubt.

'So, Jamie Finch, tell me,' Ellie asked again, back at the start. 'If things are so serious with Skye, how come you're hanging out with me?'

I had no answer for that. No answer at all.

At least I can use my acting skills to pretend everything's fine. I smile and laugh and joke around with my friends,

❀❀❀❀❀❀❀❀❀❀❀❀❀❀❀❀❀❀❀❀❀❀❀

and nobody knows what's going through my mind. Nobody knows what a bad person I am, what a cheat, a loser. Not Mum, not Dad, definitely not Talia or Lara. My friends wouldn't understand; they'd just tease me and tell me I'm a player when actually I am a lowlife worm.

I am a better actor than Fitz thinks, though, because nobody watching Ellie and me together would ever imagine we were seeing each other. They might even think we hated each other, based on the way we act.

I actually do hate Ellie a lot of the time, but not nearly as much as I hate myself.

3

On Sunday morning I check my SpiderWeb page to find that Alfie has posted a photo of a beach party at Tanglewood to my wall with the status, 'Wish you were here.' I look at the photo, at Skye's laughing face beneath a wide-brimmed hat, at Summer and Alfie holding hands, at Coco and Honey and a bunch of tanned village kids toasting marshmallows in the firelight, and I do wish I was there because in that picture everything seems so simple, so easy, so cool.

Downstairs, the house fills up with people. This often happens on a Sunday; Mum works hard right through the week, but on Sundays she loves to have friends over. Her Sunday lunch 'open house' afternoons are legendary.

My sisters are here, along with their boyfriends, Tim and Kai. There's one of Mum's researcher friends from work,

Peter, plus a presenter, Adele; a cameraman, Mozz; and Mum's friend Della, a single mum from along the road, with her two kids, Lola and Kenzie. The kids are at the kitchen table making Play-Doh monsters and everyone else is preparing food or reading newspapers, sipping white wine and talking about a million things. There seems to be an uprising in South America and a war in the Middle East; the government have done something else ridiculous and wicked, and my sisters are debating whether it is possible to make vegan tiramisu or whether Tim, the vegan boyfriend, will be OK with a dish of fruit salad instead.

'There you are, Jamie,' Mum says, ruffling my hair in a way that would infuriate me if anyone else dared to try it. From Mum, though, it's OK, and I grin and chase the Play-Doh kids out for a quick ball game in the back garden so I can start setting the table for twelve people. A clean tablecloth, cutlery, glasses, mismatched vintage china, a few jugs of iced water . . . I can negotiate the Sunday lunch rules in my sleep.

Moments later, my sisters are setting out steaming dishes of stuffed peppers, risotto, some sort of baked fish and a vat of simple pasta and pesto all along the centre of the table.

Everybody sits down and the process of serving the food begins. After an initial lull of contented silence, the chat begins again; happy chat, the kind that goes with good food and good friends and lazy Sunday afternoons with the French windows open and a gentle autumn breeze wafting in.

I am half listening as Tim explains why a vegan diet is the way of the future when I hear Mum mention Charlotte Tanberry, Skye's mother. I snap to attention.

'They really would be perfect for the show, Peter,' she says. 'I'll give Charlotte a call in the morning and see what she says, but I think she and Paddy would be totally up for it; they have a business to build and this could be just the boost they're looking for. They really are the nicest people, and they have five gorgeous daughters between them. Add a big Victorian country house beside the sea into the mix and you've got TV gold . . .'

'We'd need a bit of drama,' Peter says. 'A story with no ups and downs is no story at all.'

Mum laughs. 'Trust me, the Tanberry-Costello family have more ups and downs than a roller coaster,' she says. 'They've had a bit of a rough time of it, to be honest . . . One daughter has an eating disorder, and the eldest has a few behavioural issues . . . though I'm not sure they'd actually want any of that made public. Let's just say that there's never a dull moment at Tanglewood. The girls are lovely . . . four blonde beauties and one stunning half-Japanese girl. And their friends and boyfriends would be great to include too . . . There's a boy called Shay, a singer-songwriter . . . we could work him into it somehow . . .'

'Mum?' I interrupt. 'What are you talking about? What do Skye's family have to do with anything?'

She raises an eyebrow. 'Peter and Adele want to pitch a new reality TV show – something upbeat and inspirational – about a family business. Peter was thinking a restaurant or a B&B might make good entertainment, but I thought of Charlotte and Paddy right away. Behind the scenes at the chocolate factory . . .'

'I'd like to meet them,' Adele says. 'They sound amazing. The chocolate strand of the story combined with the whole dysfunctional family aspect . . .'

My fork clatters down on to the tablecloth.

'Skye's family are not dysfunctional!' I protest. 'Mum!'

'No, of course not!' Mum agrees. 'Adele didn't mean that . . . They're just . . . very modern. With all the issues and

❀❀❀❀❀❀❀❀❀❀❀❀❀❀❀❀❀❀❀❀❀

worries of a modern family, and of course viewers will love that. They'd really empathize and connect. But don't worry, Jamie. I would never ask Charlotte and Paddy to do something they're not totally comfortable with!'

Adele holds up her hands in surrender. 'My fault,' she says. 'I didn't choose the best words there, but your mum is right – we need a family who would be good value TV-wise. The plan is *not* to show them in a bad light, nor to exploit them in any way . . . We just want to chart their challenges and cheer them on in their triumphs. It would be an uplifting, feel-good series.'

'You need a few bumps in the road with any story before you get to the happy ending,' Peter chips in. 'That's how reality TV works.'

I frown, uncertain. I've seen from my summer job at the TV studios that reality TV footage can be edited in any way you want. The same pieces of film can be chopped and changed, edited to look positive or negative, dramatic or serene. Still, I trust Mum's judgement. I know she wouldn't suggest Skye's family for the show unless she thought it would help them in some way, or that at least they might enjoy it.

❀❀❀❀❀❀❀❀❀❀❀❀❀❀❀❀❀❀❀❀❀❀

'Do you think they'll be interested?' Adele asks, a glint in her eye.

Mum shrugs and starts to clear the table, bringing out the puddings.

'Like I said, I'll call in the morning,' she says. 'If they're interested in hearing more, we can arrange a visit to Tanglewood so you can see what you all think, and answer any questions they might have.'

'Somerset, didn't you say?' Peter muses. 'Has to be worth a visit. It could be amazing, visually. And the family sound great . . . like you said, TV gold.'

Mum laughs. 'You researchers . . . always looking for a free trip! Well, we'll see what they say. Although if they are interested in finding out more, I bet I know someone who'd be up for a weekend trip to Tanglewood – hey, Jamie?'

I struggle to look careless and cool, but the two spots of colour that seep into my cheeks tell a very different story. A trip to Tanglewood? A chance to see Skye, to talk to her face to face? Isn't that exactly what I've wanted all along?

My half-baked plans to finish things with Ellie are shelved instantly. Better to see Skye and tell her everything. Long-distance romance is seriously hard work . . . Skye's own texts and messages have tailed off lately, so surely she'll understand? I might not even have to tell her about Ellie . . .Perhaps I can just say things don't seem to be working out, that we're drifting apart?

'Of course he'd like a weekend trip to Tanglewood,' Talia tells the rest of the table. 'To see the beautiful Skye! That's his girlfriend, by the way. They met the last time Mum was down that way filming. Romantic, huh? Long-distance love still going strong over a year along the line . . . How's that for your family-interest story, Adele?'

'Awww,' Peter says. 'No wonder you're looking out for them! Sweet! But don't worry, we'd make sure it was all handled with sensitivity . . .'

'Right,' Mozz agrees. 'Any more of that tiramisu?'

Adele narrows her eyes, watching me carefully over the top of her wine glass. 'You know, Jamie, there might even be a cameo part in the series for you,' she says. 'Teen lovers reunited! Great story. What do you think?'

I rest my head in my hands. 'Perfect,' I echo. 'Just . . . perfect.'

4

Just as Mum predicted, Charlotte and Paddy say they'd like to hear more about the idea of a reality TV series based on their business. Who wouldn't? Mum arranges that we'll head down to Tanglewood next Saturday with Adele, Peter and Mozz and an armload of plans and proposals for the projected show.

'It's all at such an early stage, I'm sure Charlotte and Paddy can call the shots and tweak things to suit them,' she says. 'I'll advise them to ask to be involved at every stage, to have the right to veto footage if they wish. It should be an amazing opportunity for the Chocolate Box business, Jamie.'

'I guess,' I say.

'Are you nervous?' Mum teases. 'Seeing Skye again after all this time?'

✿✿✿✿✿✿✿✿✿✿✿✿✿✿✿✿✿✿✿✿✿✿✿✿

'Course not,' I lie. 'It's no big deal.'

'Charlotte says we can stay all weekend,' she says, 'It'll give Peter and Mozz some time to check out the locations, and Adele can get to know everybody properly. You and Skye will have plenty of time to hang out. I know what you teenagers are like!'

'Mum!' I protest. 'Don't, OK?'

She just smiles as if she knows much better than me, as if she's given me the perfect weekend on a platter instead of the biggest headache ever. I want time with Skye, sure, but I can't help wondering how to finish things without wrecking the weekend for everyone. I punch out a brief text message to Skye, light and chirpy and cheery, but hinting that we must have a big catch-up chat.

Cool, she texts back. *A catch-up sounds good . . . I have so much to tell you . . . you've been sooooo quiet over the summer!*

Guilt floods though me and I wonder all over again just how I've managed to get myself into this mess. I think of the photo Alfie posted on SpiderWeb, of everyone having fun on the beach without me, and the guilt turns to anger.

I tap out another text message, this time to Ellie, and the answer comes back almost at once.

See you in ten minutes!

I grab my jacket and head for the park.

I'm sitting on the kids' roundabout in the playground when Ellie comes along the path. There is something magical about a children's playground at night; by day, we'd be chased away from swings and slide and roundabout by tired parents and sticky-faced toddlers, but after dark we get to reclaim those things. I don't think you can ever be too old for swings and slides and roundabouts, seriously.

Ellie pulls at a fringy scarf wrapped round her against the cold. It's October now, and although the days are bright and sunny, the evenings are chilly. October . . . four months since I first met Ellie. Four months of deception and lies.

'This has to stop,' I say, the minute she is within earshot. 'We can't keep seeing each other, OK?'

'OK,' Ellie says, as if she doesn't care at all. 'Bit of a relief, actually. You're the most bad-tempered boy I have ever met. No idea what I see in you.'

'Works both ways,' I snap. 'You're the most annoying girl in the entire universe. You argue about everything. Apart from this . . . So, you're OK with us breaking up?'

To be honest, I feel a little let down that after four

250

months of torturing myself and feeling like a heel every single day, Ellie actually doesn't care if she sees me or not. Typical.

'Totally OK with it,' Ellie confirms. 'We're not a good match at all. We clash all the time. You're not my type . . . you're way too vain and self-absorbed, and you can't take criticism. Face it, we are polar opposites . . .'

'I can take criticism!' I argue. 'Just not total character assassination . . .'

Ellie rolls her eyes. 'I hate your style too,' she goes on. 'That jacket . . . yuk! It looks like somebody died in it!'

'It's vintage!' I howl, outraged. 'A genuine army jacket from World War Two! It cost fifty quid at Camden Market!'

'They saw you coming,' Ellie says. 'Sorry, Jamie, I think we are better off apart. Stick with your country girlfriend . . . she's perfect for you.'

'Maybe she is,' I growl. 'Maybe all this . . . with us . . . is just one massive mistake.'

Ellie just shrugs and pushes against the ground with the tip of one toe, stirring the roundabout into creaky action. We spin slowly for a while as the light fades, not talking.

'I suppose I can't help wondering why you're still trying

251

to be loyal to a girl you haven't seen since February,' Ellie says at last. 'Not that you're doing a good job with the whole loyalty thing, clearly, but . . . is she really that special, your Skye?'

I sigh. 'She's great,' I say. 'You'd like her.'

'I doubt that,' Ellie corrects me. 'I've hated her ever since you told me she existed. She sounds too good to be true. How can I compete with that? I may not be perfect but I do have feelings, y'know.'

I reach out a hand to hold hers, but Ellie snatches her fingers away.

'So, anyway, you decided,' she says. 'Skye wins, I lose. Too bad.'

Her voice has lost the careless tone it had before; the fierce anger has faded, leaving nothing but sadness. I bite my lip.

'It's just that we're going down to Tanglewood this weekend,' I explain. 'I have to make a decision. I was pretty sure that the right thing was to finish things with Skye, and then I saw you and I got muddled and angry and guilty all over again . . .'

'. . . so you finished with me instead.'

❀❀❀❀❀❀❀❀❀❀❀❀❀❀❀❀❀❀❀❀❀❀

'Not really. Look, Ellie, it's such a mess,' I say. 'I don't know what to do. I wish I'd broken things off with Skye ages ago, only it's complicated . . .'

She laughs out loud. 'Don't give me that! Complicated? How complicated can a relationship between two fourteen-year-olds be? Finch, you are such a coward!'

I hear the accusation and swallow it down. Ellie's right – I am a coward.

'It is complicated, though,' I insist. 'Before we met, Skye had these dreams about a boy . . . and there was a bird, a kind of finch, in the dreams. Then we came to the village because Mum was producing a TV movie there, and I met Skye, and it was . . . well, we liked each other. We had a holiday romance, I suppose, but Skye thought it was some-thing more, because of the dreams . . . she thought we were meant to be together.'

'True love,' Ellie says.

'Not exactly,' I admit. 'It was a summer thing, that's all, but we tried to keep it going over the winter and it seemed to work for Skye, but I guess the magic just kind of fizzled for me. And then I met you.'

'Unlucky,' Ellie quips.

❀❀❀❀❀❀❀❀❀❀❀❀❀❀❀❀❀❀❀❀❀

'I don't think so,' I say, and I realize that I genuinely don't. Meeting Ellie has been one of the most amazing things that has happened to me, even though I haven't handled it so well. The truth is, she's good for me; her straight-talking honesty cuts right through the layers of arrogance and charm I sometimes hide behind. Skye never calls me out on that, never challenges me, but Ellie does. She sees the real me, not a rose-tinted dream version; and while it was nice to be somebody's dream boy for a while, it has never quite felt real.

Ellie sits on the roundabout, her long legs curled beneath her, green eyes unreadable. I can't believe I have been such an idiot. Skye and Ellie are both awesome, but Skye isn't right for me; I've known that for a while. I have to tell her, because unless I do I'll lose Ellie too . . . and that can't happen.

I reach for her hand again, but she slides out of my grasp, jumping down from the roundabout and heading for the slide.

'I got it wrong, again,' I call to Ellie as she climbs the steps of the slide. 'A spooky dream doesn't seem like such a good reason to keep a relationship going. I've been kidding myself . . . Things with Skye are over. I just need to find the guts to tell her that.'

'Call me when you're single,' Ellie yells back at me. 'I'm fed up with all this messing around. Finish with Skye, then maybe we have a chance of making something together. Maybe.'

'Don't be like that,' I say, walking over to the slide. Ellie sits at the top ready to let go, her face a pale slice of beauty in the dusk.

'Like what?' she challenges. 'You just told me we should break up, Jamie Finch, and I agreed. It's the smartest thing you've said in all the time I've known you. Makes perfect sense to me . . .'

'Not to me,' I protest. 'I was wrong. I need to finish with Skye. I *will* finish with Skye. This weekend.'

'Like I said: call me when you're single and maybe we can work something out,' Ellie says. 'I'm sick of being second best.'

'You're not!' I argue, but she's sliding down towards me, her hair ruffled in the breeze, her fringy scarf flying out behind her.

I open my arms to catch her but she's gone before I get

❀❀❀❀❀❀❀❀❀❀❀❀❀❀❀❀❀❀❀❀❀

the chance, running away from me across the grass towards the orange streetlight glow of civilization.

'Ellie!' I yell, but she doesn't look back.

5

Going back to Tanglewood is like going back in time. We drive down on Saturday morning: three cars heading west for inspiration and research and, in my case, certain doom. I'm determined, though. I've been rehearsing my break-up speech for days, picking out the perfect combination of words for minimum pain and awkwardness. And yes, OK, I'm still dreading it.

We reach Tanglewood just after lunch; the house is still beautiful, chaotic, welcoming. Fred the dog runs around the cars as we pull up, barking a greeting, and a freckle-faced Coco appears from the stables with Humbug the sheep and Caramel the pony trailing after her.

'They're here!' she shouts, and Paddy comes out of the chocolate workshop, his white apron streaked with chocolate,

❀❀❀❀❀❀❀❀❀❀❀❀❀❀❀❀❀❀❀❀❀❀❀

while Charlotte, Cherry, Summer and Honey pile out of the house, laughing, shaking hands, hugging, talking all at once, pulling Mum's TV friends inside, making everyone welcome. Skye waits quietly, a little behind everyone else, looking very cool in a black minidress, white tights and op art pixie boots. Her fair hair is parted in the middle, sixties style, so that it falls in loose ringlets around her shoulders and her eyes are rimmed with black eyeliner.

She's gorgeous; if I passed her in the street I'd turn my head to look at her. Any boy would.

'Hey,' I say. 'Long time no see . . .'

'Hey,' she replies. 'The holidays weren't the same this year without you.'

I try to grin, but the smile doesn't get very far. 'Yeah . . . I kept thinking I'd have time to pop down for a weekend,' I say. 'But it was pretty full-on. Sorry!'

'It's OK,' Skye shrugs. 'I understand.'

I wish she didn't understand. I wish she got cross and impatient and bad-tempered sometimes. I wish she'd got plainer and grumpier and less stylish in my absence instead of prettier, cuter. I wish I still felt the way I used to feel about her, but the fizz of excitement I used to get when we were together just isn't there. Can she feel the difference too?

For a whole week, Ellie has blanked my texts and calls. She didn't turn up at drama group and she hasn't answered my messages on SpiderWeb. It looks like she really has dumped me. I've lost the girl I care about most in the world, all because trying so hard to be the 'good guy' has turned me into a cheat and a liar.

'Call me when you're single,' Ellie had said, and I straighten my shoulders at the memory.

Skye is watching me; half shy, half expectant. In the past I'd have kissed her by now, hugged her tight, lifted her up and whirled her around. That enthusiasm has seeped away, invisibly, like air from a punctured tyre. Everything feels flat. I lean in to give Skye the expected hug, but it's awkward and stiff, like I'm greeting a crusty great-aunt I haven't seen in a decade and not my girlfriend. Skye smells of lemon shower gel, fresh and familiar. I pull away quickly, flustered and guilty.

'We should talk,' I say, biting the bullet. 'We have . . . a lot to catch up on . . .'

'We do,' Skye says. 'Only, tonight might not be the best time for it, what with the Halloween party and all . . .'

❀❀❀❀❀❀❀❀❀❀❀❀❀❀❀❀❀❀❀❀❀❀❀❀❀

My heart sinks. 'Halloween party?' I echo. 'Right. I totally forgot it was the thirty-first . . . I've had a few things on my mind. Trust us to turn up right in the middle of your celebrations; Mum probably didn't think . . . Sorry about that.'

'Not a problem,' Skye says. 'We don't mind, and your mum thought it might be quite good for her colleagues to see Tanglewood at its chaotic best and meet some of the locals. She said it'd give them a taste of the kind of human interest stories they might find if they decide to use us for the series . . .'

I sigh. My mum is awesome, but she always has an eye on the story.

'Are you OK with the idea of the reality TV series?' I ask, and Skye shrugs.

'Mum and Paddy think it could be good publicity for the Chocolate Box business, but they want to know how it would be handled,' she admits. 'They don't want too much focus on Summer's problems or what happened to Honey. But apart from that . . . well, they're pretty keen. And news travels fast here, so half the village may well turn up to the party later, hoping for their fifteen minutes of fame. Your mum and her friends may think we're a bit too crazy for TV!'

'I bet they love it,' I say. 'So . . . we have a party to organ-ize?'

'We do,' Skye confirms. 'Alfie and Shay are coming up later; there's loads to do . . . maybe you can be on decorat-ing duties – and bonfire building, of course. And right now, we have ten pumpkins to carve. Mum got a job lot at the supermarket this morning because they were on special offer!'

I find myself sitting with the sisters around the kitchen table creating pumpkin lanterns while Skye's mum Char-lotte gives Mum, Peter, Adele and Mozz a guided tour of the house, the workshops, the gardens and the beach. Meanwhile, we scoop the orange flesh and seeds out of giant pumpkins; the flesh is chopped and thrown into a huge pan to make soup for later, and the seeds are washed and spread on tea towels to dry for the little kids to string into bracelets and necklaces at the party. It's up to us to carve spooky designs into the pumpkin skin. Mine is quite simple – a crescent moon and stars – but the sisters have clearly got this down to a fine art, with swirls and spirals and witches on broomsticks. Honey produces an amazing intricate cut-out of a slinky cat with a curlicue tail and 'Happy Halloween' written in swirly script, before switching tasks and frying up some onions to make a start on the soup.

It's impossible to stay awkward with the Tanberry sisters mucking around and having a laugh at the kitchen table. The chat is easy and friendly; nobody asks where I've been the last few months or questions my sudden reappearance. They just accept me, and the minute I finish one pumpkin I'm given another, and then Shay and Alfie arrive and things escalate from busy to full-on chaos.

We split into two groups. Alfie, Summer, Skye and Honey focus on making food; the list of tasks covers everything from making pumpkin soup to ghostly white chocolate cake and spider web cupcakes, as well as something called Blood-bath Trifle. I am relieved to be roped into the outside group with Shay, Cherry and Coco. We make jam-jar lanterns, looping wire round the jars with pliers and twisting it into hanging loops. Soon we have a crate full of them, each with its own tea light candle, waiting to be lit and hung from the trees at dusk.

Next we build the bonfire, hauling armfuls of driftwood from the beach and mixing it with a couple of broken pallets to create a giant, towering structure at the foot of the garden. Shay sets up some outdoor speakers while the rest of us string fairy lights through the trees.

It doesn't take long to fall under the spell of Tanglewood again . . . at least it wouldn't, if I could just get Ellie out of my mind.

After a while, Charlotte calls us and we crowd around the kitchen table on mismatched chairs, eating a buffet of pizza, dips and wedges to keep us going until the party starts. I sit beside Skye, but I can't think of a single thing to say to her.

It sounds as though the negotiations and discussions about the reality TV series are going well, though. Peter, Adele and Mozz are buzzing with questions and ideas, and Charlotte and Paddy chip in brightly with their own suggestions. Mum is making loads of notes and Mozz stops eating at random intervals to take a photograph of Fred the dog, or of the Aga cooker piled high with party food for later, or even the 'Happy Halloween' pumpkin Honey's placed on the kitchen windowsill.

❀❀❀❀❀❀❀❀❀❀❀❀❀❀❀❀❀❀❀❀❀❀❀❀❀❀

Charlotte turns to me, suddenly, smiling. 'Jamie . . .' she says. 'We're a little short on space this weekend – we've converted one of the old guest bedrooms into an office for the Chocolate Box business. I was going to put you in a twin room with your mum, but Skye reminded me that the gypsy caravan is free so we've got that ready for you.'

'Best bedroom in the whole of Tanglewood,' Summer says.

'Totally,' Cherry agrees.

Alfie grins. 'We can do the ghost stories thing like we did the year before last . . . that was fun!'

'It can be our hideaway,' Shay says. 'We can have a party-within-a-party!'

'Ignore them,' Charlotte tells me. 'Have fun by all means, but don't let them rope you into any all-night parties! The caravan is *your* space. Sound OK?'

'Perfect,' I say. 'Thank you!'

I fight the urge to run out to the caravan right now, to flop on the bunk and pull the quilt over my head and hide until tomorrow afternoon. Beside me, Skye looks just as awkward. Can she tell what I'm thinking? How I'm feeling?

I wish I'd had the guts to finish things between us a long

time ago. With hindsight, it was the only thing to do . . . Dragging things out had nothing to do with being kind or trying not to hurt Skye's feelings; it was pure cowardice. I don't like myself right now, not one bit. I desperately want to end things, get it over and done with, but I can't ruin the party for everyone by causing a big drama and upsetting Skye. That would be just plain cruel.

'C'mon, guys,' Honey is saying. 'Let's get ready . . . I've got face paints upstairs! Let's get this party started!'

I grit my teeth, then catch myself and turn on a grin at the last minute, but Skye sees my grimace, and her blue eyes brim with sadness.

6

The party is epic. There is a flurry of last-minute activity; the jam-jar lanterns are hung from the trees, the fairy lights lit, the carved pumpkins positioned around the house and beside the front door. The kitchen table is piled high with quiche and sausage rolls and baked potatoes, and the pumpkin soup is warming on the Aga next to a stack of dishes and spoons.

Paddy and Charlotte have been at the face paints, transforming themselves into white-faced zombies with painted-on cuts and shadowed eyes, dressed in white and trailing 'blood-stained' bandages. Skye and Summer are both witches, in matching black sixties dresses worn with huge fake eyelashes and black lipstick; Honey is a ghost, in a gauzy white dress with fake bones tied into her hair, and Coco is a black cat with whiskers and fun fur ears. Shay, Alfie and I submit to green face paint and end up as monsters, Frankenstein style, but when the visitors start to arrive my eyes are popping. There are aliens, corpse brides, vampires, wizards, mummies, trolls, goblins, elves, werewolves and every kind of ghost or ghoul or witch imaginable.

A bunch of old-fashioned party games have been set out in what used to be the breakfast room of the B&B, and the place is swarming with little kids bobbing for apples or battling, blindfold, to take a bite from apples that hang on strings from one of the beams. The little ones are high on toffee apples and monkey nuts, the teens on Coke and cake, the adults on some green-tinged fizzy punch that Paddy has concocted. Seeing all the kids I knew last year again is kind of weird, and I'm relieved when Skye, Summer, Tia, Millie and their friends head out into the dark to gossip and tell spooky stories. At least, left with Alfie Anderson, I feel less out of my depth.

We hover for a while in the living room, where Mum and her colleagues are holding court to the interested villagers. Mum is wearing cat ears and a fake tail from someone's old dressing-up box, but Peter, Adele and Mozz have gone

❁❁❁❁❁❁❁❁❁❁❁❁❁❁❁❁❁❁❁❁❁❁❁❁❁

wild with the face paints and painted themselves varying shades of white, grey, blue and green before putting on tattered costumes. They move easily among the locals, chatting, eating, making notes, telling everyone more about the proposed TV show. I think everyone in the village offers to take part . . . It's like a ghoulish version of *X Factor*, with one elderly man dressed in wizard's robes bursting into song in the middle of the kitchen in the hope of being offered a bit part in the series.

'Crazy,' Alfie tells me. 'If this series happens, the media frenzy could be too much for a sleepy place like Kitnor. First the film last summer, now this . . . They'll be setting up a Hollywood sign at the end of the drive any minute now . . .'

'I know,' I agree. 'Paddy and Charlotte don't know quite what they're getting into!'

'I wonder what they'll call it?' Alfie muses. 'Paddy and the Chocolate Factory? Truffle and Strife? Village of the Damned?'

He tries to keep a straight face as a middle-aged woman dressed as some kind of zombie fortune teller bears down on us, eating a bowl of the Bloodbath Trifle. She is wearing

❀❀❀❀❀❀❀❀❀❀❀❀❀❀❀❀❀❀❀❀❀❀❀

a spotted headscarf and gold hoop earrings with a tiered gypsy dress.

'Terrific party!' she says, beaming at us between mouthfuls of trifle. 'The psychic powers are always strong at this time of year! The spirits are watching us, mark my words!'

'Are they, Mrs Lee?' Alfie replies. 'As long as they stay away from the sausage rolls, I don't really mind!'

'Ever the sceptic,' Mrs Lee huffs, turning to me. 'Ah . . . I don't know you, do I?'

'Meet Jamie Finch,' Alfie says, helpfully. 'Skye's boyfriend.'

Mrs Lee frowns. 'Skye? No, no, I don't think so,' she says. 'I read Skye's palm just a few weeks ago, and you're nothing like the boy I saw in store for her there. I am never wrong about these things!'

'But you told Skye last year that you saw a bird – a finch – in her future,' Alfie recalls, teasingly. 'And then she met Finch just a little while later. Are you saying you were wrong?'

'I'm never wrong,' Mrs Lee says. 'But life changes, Alfie Anderson. And a finch can be here one minute and gone the next, so if I saw you in Skye's palm, young man, I'm afraid it wasn't for long . . .'

She grabs my palm and squints at it while I squirm in horror, wondering what she might see. Lies? Deceit? Disaster?

'As I thought,' Mrs Lee declares. 'You have a true love already. A stormy relationship, sometimes hidden, but a true one. That's just as well, isn't it, seeing as you're not in Skye's future! Ooh, is that Paddy with the Halloween punch? I must just get a refill . . .'

My cheeks are burning at her words, but under a thick layer of green face paint this isn't visible to Alfie. I dredge up my acting skills and pretend to be offended and confused. 'What was that all about?' I ask.

'Forget it,' Alfie says. 'Mrs Lee is nuts. She's harmless, but she reckons she's part gypsy and that she can see the future. She works in the post office, and trust me, she can't even see the small print on a special delivery sticker without her reading glasses. She doesn't mean any harm. I mean, I know it's Halloween and all that, but who actually believes in ghosts and ghouls and premonitions? Load of old rubbish!'

'Totally,' I say, looking at the palm Mrs Lee had examined. It looks the same as always, a criss-cross web of lines and creases. How can it show hints of a stormy, hidden relationship? It's just not possible.

I shake off the very idea.

'Bonfire, Finch?' Alfie is asking. 'I think the others headed out that way. Shay said he'd play his guitar . . .'

Later, when it's long past midnight and Alfie, Shay, Millie, Tia and the others have gone, Skye and I walk slowly up to the caravan beneath the trees strung with fairy lights. I feel like I ought to hold her hand, but that is clearly a very bad idea.

'Great party,' I say into the darkness, because it totally was. I had forgotten how good a Tanglewood party could be.

'I can't actually believe you're here,' she replies. 'I haven't seen you in forever, and then when we do get together it has to be at a party where Mum's invited half the village . . .'

'Looked like the whole village to me,' I tease.

'Whatever. It's just that I thought we'd never get to be alone together . . .'

Alone together? I grit my teeth and look up through the

canopy of trees at the velvet black darkness, studded with stars, a crescent moon hanging above it all. This could be the perfect moment to talk to Skye, to finish things once and for all.

We get to the caravan. Someone has placed my moon and stars pumpkin on the steps, and it glows faintly orange in the darkness.

'So . . .' I say. Before I get any further it occurs to me that I'm trying to have a deep and meaningful talk with a sixties-style witch while my own face is painted green. I find a tissue in my jacket pocket and try wiping the face paint away, but without soap and water it is a hopeless task.

Skye smiles. 'I love that you still have that old army jacket, Finch. It was one of the first things I noticed about you. It used to be too big for you then, but it's a perfect fit now . . .'

'I don't really like it any more,' I say, surprising myself. 'I'm not so into vintage these days. Guess I've moved on.'

'Right,' Skye says sadly. 'That's a shame. With vintage stuff, you always feel there's a story to tell . . . a history. If clothes could talk . . .'

'They can't,' I say. 'Not even on Halloween. The past is

over with. We can't reach it, no matter how much we want to.'

I wish I could go back to the summer I met Skye and work out how to stop things falling apart, but I can't. It's over.

'Probably just as well,' Skye says. 'I have an overactive imagination as it is . . .'

I bite my lip. 'Skye?' I say. 'Didn't you once tell me you'd had dreams of the past, and I was in them? That you knew we'd be together because you recognized me from the dreams?'

She laughs, but it's a sad laugh. 'Did I say that?' she questions. 'No . . . I was having some weird dreams, sure, and I thought I was the girl in the dreams, but I wasn't in the end. Like I said, overactive imagination.'

'Was I the boy in the dreams?' I ask.

Skye hangs her head. 'I thought at the time you were, but . . . well, I don't think so. I just freaked out a little and got things muddled. Like you say, the past is over with. We have to accept that . . . let it go.'

My heart thumps. Is Skye telling me things are over between us, or is that just wishful thinking?

273

Before I can say any more, she turns away and runs across the grass towards Tanglewood, and I'm left alone on the caravan steps beneath the moon and stars.

7

I know it's a dream because, even though it feels so real, I know deep down that it can't be. I am a shape shifter, a time traveller, an invisible witness; the past unfolds before me . . .

I can see the crowded platform of a small town railway station. People are waiting for a train: men in uniform – some no more than boys – with kitbags, anxious faces, newly cropped hair. Their families crowd around them, talking too fast, hugging too tight, promising letters and prayers and that 'it'll all be over by Christmas'.

I focus on one young man; no more than eighteen, his eyes bright with adventure, his uniform still stiff and creased as if barely worn. It looks just like my jacket might have done when it was brand new. Beside him stands a girl in a blue dress; Sunday best, her brown hair swept up into a victory roll, her dark green eyes blurred with tears. She reminds me of someone, yet I know I've never seen her before.

✿✿✿✿✿✿✿✿✿✿✿✿✿✿✿✿✿✿✿✿✿✿✿

Suddenly the platform fills with noise and a thick fug of steam and smoke as the train arrives. The green-eyed girl throws her arms round the young man, hanging on tight as if she will never let go.

'James, don't go,' she whispers. 'Please don't! I'm scared!'

'It's all right, Ellie,' he says. 'I'll be back soon . . . I promise! And I'll write!'

The train begins to plough forward again and the young man jumps on just in time, dragging his kitbag behind him, leaning out through an open window to wave until the train carries him far from sight. The girl waves her handkerchief until there is nothing left to wave at. Turning away at last, she finds herself alone now on the platform except for a small brown bird that swoops around her, diving and soaring through the air. She stops to watch the bird as it flutters around her, smiling through a haze of tears, reaching up her hands towards it. I watch, my heart filled with sadness, as the finch hops on to her palms, fluffing up its feathers, stretching out its wings.

I wake up late to the sound of a gentle knock on the caravan door.

'Finch?' Skye's voice is uncertain. 'Are you awake?'

I roll out of the bunk, still wearing last night's jeans and T-shirt, taking the army jacket down from its peg as I open the door. I am trying to make sense of the dream from last night; it was so real, so vivid. I feel choked with sorrow, as though I'm still inside the dream, as though something painful, something terrible has happened. What kind of dream can do that? Was it stress-related? Did somebody spike my drink? Was it a Halloween happening, a once-in-a-lifetime glimpse into the past? Or just my freaked-out imagination going extra crazy?

'Hey,' I say, smiling sadly as I see Skye at the foot of the caravan steps. I go down to sit beside her, letting my bare feet rest on the cool, dew-damp grass. 'Think I might have slept in.'

Skye hands me an apple and a slightly mangled spider web cupcake. 'Breakfast,' she says. 'There wasn't a lot of choice . . . it's carnage in that kitchen. Mum, Paddy, your mum and the TV lot have gone down to the Mad Hatter for a full English. Looks like they're all agreed on pitching the idea for the series to the BBC. Scary, huh?'

'Cool,' I say. 'It might never happen, but if it does . . . well, Mum would make sure it was done in a good way.'

I bite into the apple and remember the dream again, the little brown bird flying high. Gradually the sadness ebbs

❀❀❀❀❀❀❀❀❀❀❀❀❀❀❀❀❀❀❀❀❀❀❀❀

away until there's a feeling of hope and freedom, a kind of lightness inside me that I haven't felt in months.

'I had a very weird dream last night,' I tell Skye. 'Kind of spooky. It felt . . . like a glimpse into the past. Does that make sense?'

'Tell me,' she says.

So I do. I tell her about the railway station, about the soldier and the green-eyed girl who didn't want her boyfriend to go to war.

'Do you think he came home?' Skye asks. 'Did they have a happy ending?'

'I don't know,' I admit. 'I think . . . I felt . . . maybe not. There was a bird in the dream too, a little brown finch . . .'

'Trust you to put yourself in the dream,' Skye says, laughing. 'What happened to the bird?'

I remember the girl holding out her hands so that the finch could fly on to them, but I say nothing.

'Skye?' I say. 'We had the best summer ever last year, didn't we? I'd never met anyone like you. It was . . . magic, almost. Unforgettable.'

'It was,' she agrees.

I force myself to go on. 'But . . . this long distance thing

❀❀❀❀❀❀❀❀❀❀❀❀❀❀❀❀❀❀❀❀❀❀❀

isn't easy, right? I'm not good at phone calls or answering texts. I get easily distracted. I sometimes wonder . . .'

Skye puts her hand in mine as we sit beside each other on the caravan steps. 'What do you wonder?'

I take a deep breath. 'I met your crazy neighbour last night,' I say. 'Mrs Lee – the post office lady, right? She read my palm and told me I wasn't a part of your future.'

Skye's hand squeezes mine softly.

'I think we both know that,' she says.

'We do?'

'I've known for a while now that things weren't the same between us,' Skye says. 'You stopped writing, stopped messaging, stopped texting and calling. You didn't want to come down to Tanglewood this summer, and . . . well, I wondered if you'd met someone new.'

Can I say it out loud? Do I dare?

'There is someone,' I say. 'We didn't plan it . . . not at all . . . but yeah. I care about her. Her name's Ellie. I'm sorry. I've been trying to tell you; I just didn't know how . . . but I think we have to break up, Skye.'

'I think so too,' Skye says. 'Thanks for telling me, Finch. The thing is . . . I've met someone too. We're not seeing

❀❀❀❀❀❀❀❀❀❀❀❀❀❀❀❀❀❀❀❀❀❀❀

each other . . . not yet. But I think we maybe will, sometime soon, now things are finished between the two of us.'

I blink and frown and try to make sense of this, and then I start to laugh at the absurdity of it all and Skye is laughing too, and all the awkwardness and guilt falls away and what is left is friendship, strong and pure and lasting.

'I've been an idiot,' I tell Skye. 'I should have told you right from the start.'

'I kind of knew,' she shrugs. 'It's OK. Things have a way of working out . . .'

'I hope so,' I reply.

Back in London that evening, I text Ellie. *Guess what? I'm single. Want to go out sometime?*

She texts back a few minutes later. *See you at the playground.*

I'm there ten minutes early, my hair combed and ruffled, wearing my best black jeans and a pair of red Converse. I sit on the roundabout and push it round with one toe, and when Ellie appears in the distance I try to imagine her with her hair in a victory roll, wearing a blue 1940s dress and waving a handkerchief at the horizon. I try to imagine her hands, holding the little brown bird, keeping it safe.

280

280

'Hey,' she says, jumping up on to the roundabout. 'You did it, then? You broke up with her?'

'I did it,' I confirm. 'I should have done it months ago . . .' I pause. 'Ellie . . . this is going to sound weird. But what's your grandmother's name?'

'Sarah,' she replies. 'Well, that's Dad's mum. Mum's mum is called Louise.'

My shoulders slump. 'Great-grandmother?' I try. 'She was a teenager in the war. Her sweetheart went off to fight . . .'

'And never came back,' Ellie says. 'Yeah, that was my great-gran. Her name was Eleanor . . . I was named after her. Who told you about her?'

'Nobody, really,' I say. 'I think you might have mentioned it a while back . . .'

Ellie frowns. 'Did I . . . ?'

I think of the dream, of the girl with dark green eyes and the young man going to war, and I wonder if love can reach across the years and find a second chance, or if it's just that hanging out at Tanglewood has made my imagination go into overdrive. I'll probably never know.

Ellie nudges me. 'You're still wearing that horrible jacket . . .'

✿✿✿✿✿✿✿✿✿✿✿✿✿✿✿✿✿✿✿✿✿✿✿

'It's my favourite jacket,' I say firmly. 'I love it. It's got history . . . happy stuff, sad stuff, forgotten stuff.'

Ellie shrugs. 'I quite like it too,' she says. 'It looks cool. I just don't want you to get too big-headed, that's all . . .'

'Big-headed? Me?' I argue, and Ellie laughs. I remember how much I love the sound. I push the roundabout some more, making it spin, and I slide an arm round Ellie's shoulders.

'I've made a total mess of things the last few months,' I confess. 'I haven't been fair to you, but things will be different now, I promise. I've worked out what matters to me, and *you* matter to me, Ellie. Can we start over?'

'Sure,' she says. 'Without the guilt, without the rows, without the lies.'

She leans in to kiss me, and it's just like a first kiss should be, gentle and sweet and full of promise. I think briefly of Skye, and I hope that her new boy is everything she wants him to be, that he will make her as happy as Ellie makes me.

Above us, the moon and stars glint bright above the dull orange glow of the city sky.

Snowflakes & WISHES

'Snowflakes and Wishes' is a wintry tale that tells Lawrie's story, and is set on New Year's Eve, before the events in **Fortune Cookie**. Lawrie's family are back at Tanglewood for a party, and returning to Somerset reminds them all how much they've missed it. When one of the animals goes missing in the middle of the night, Lawrie and Coco find themselves on another rescue mission. They end up with a LOT more than they bargain for . . . and in the middle of a snowstorm, they begin to realize how much they've missed each other too . . .

Cathy Cassidy, xxx

1

We are an hour's drive from Tanglewood when the sky darkens to the colour of an especially nasty bruise, all blotchy purple with mustard yellow patches showing through. It feels as though the clouds are lowering, hanging just inches above us, like a curtain about to come down on a long and very boring play. We've been driving for four hours already; Mum, my little sister Jasmine and me.

'It's gone all dark,' Jas says from the back seat, leaning forward to offer me a chocolate coin left over from her Christmas stocking. 'What time is it, Lawrie? Will we be late for the party?'

'It's only just gone two in the afternoon,' I say, peeling the gold foil away from the chocolate coin. 'Relax; we've got bags of time, but I think some kind of a storm is brewing.'

'The weather forecast said heavy snowfalls in the west,' Mum says, frowning as she drives. 'Don't worry, we'll be there soon . . .'

'Snowfalls!' Jasmine breathes. 'Oh, I hope it's proper snow, the kind you can sledge on and make snowballs with. Maybe we'll get stranded and have to stay at Tanglewood forever.'

I laugh. My little sister is so transparent; she hasn't really settled back into her old school in Kendal. Some of the kids tease her a bit and although she is tougher than she looks I don't want my little sister to have to handle that kind of stuff. She's seen enough bullying to last her a lifetime.

Jasmine loved a lot of things about living in Somerset, but she'd lost a bit of confidence too, living with a psycho like James Seddon . . . I suppose we all did. He was Mum's boyfriend, and although he seemed fine to start with, it turned out he had a vicious streak. He was cruel to his animals, cold with his friends and a total bully with us. We were supposed to be his family, but he never stopped telling us that we were dirt, rubbish, scum.

He made me feel so angry, so helpless, so bad. He made all of us feel that way.

288

Seddon doesn't live in Somerset any more; Coco messaged me a while back to say he'd sold up and gone to live with his brother in Canada, and although I'd rather he was in prison (which is what he deserves for the way he treated us, not to mention the animals) I am also a little bit glad. I am glad because now there's an ocean between us and because I can breathe a little more easily now that I'm not breathing the same air as him. My mind drifts, and suddenly I am back there . . .

I'm on my knees in the mud, fumbling with the rope round Sheba's neck, tugging at the knot while the skinny, scrawny dog whimpers and yelps.

'Hurry, Lawrie!' Coco whispers. 'Quick!'

And then a flashlight flares and a shot rings out. Coco steps back into the shadows, leading the rescued ponies with her, and I see Seddon, shotgun in hand, striding towards me through the darkness.

'Lawrie?' he yells. 'Is that you, you useless boy? I've told you before to leave that dog alone – she's not a pet, she's a guard dog!'

I manage to get Sheba's collar off and the two of us duck away from Seddon . . . but not quickly enough. He grabs my arm and throws me to the ground. I can hear Mum and Jas up by the house, calling me, but when I scramble up Seddon comes for me again, shoving me back against the outbuilding. Pain sears through my arm like fire. I don't actually see Seddon hit my mum; I just hear the harsh slap of his palm against her cheek in the darkness . . .

I shudder, remembering the last time I saw James Seddon; good riddance to bad rubbish. He was a bully and conman extraordinaire. He'd come into our lives with smiles and promises and to start with we'd thought he was great . . . By the time we'd found out what he was really like, it was too late.

Sheba is cuddled up in a blanket on the back seat with Jasmine, trying to snuffle her way into the net of foil-wrapped chocolate coins. She's our dog now; Mum, Jas and I took her north to Kendal when we went back to live with Gran, and now she's well fed, with a sleek, shiny coat and the waggiest tail in the northern hemisphere. Seeing her now, you'd never believe she'd been so ill-treated. She should be in a travel crate or have some kind of dog seat-belt, but she's scared of crates and kennels and hates any kind of harness, and we haven't the heart to force her.

'Mum?' Jas pipes up. 'Are we nearly there? I want to see Caramel before it gets dark!'

❁❁❁❁❁❁❁❁❁❁❁❁❁❁❁❁❁❁❁❁❁❁

'Not too far now, I promise . . .' Mum says. 'We'll be there about four, just in time for tea. And yes, of course you'll see Caramel!'

Caramel was Jasmine's pony – a birthday present from Seddon – but really the pony had just been an excuse for him to bully and control both Jasmine and Caramel. He'd been on a power trip; he'd wanted to break Caramel's spirit and had tried to do the same to us. I'd tried to look out for the ponies, but it had been Coco who'd taken matters into her own hands and rescued them, hiding them away from Seddon. That was how I'd got to know Coco really, because before that I'd always thought she was kind of bossy and annoying . . . when actually she'd turned out to be pretty amazing.

She's my best friend; or at least she was before we moved back to Kendal last year. I have missed Coco. I ended up with a bit of a crush on her in the end, after that whole pony rescue thing; and now more than a year has gone by and I can't help wondering if I will still feel that way when I see her again.

And if I do, what then? I am not exactly known for my wit, charm or smooth chat-up lines. Coco will probably

❀❀❀❀❀❀❀❀❀❀❀❀❀❀❀❀❀❀❀❀❀❀

swat me away like some annoying insect and go on being awesome in her own sweet way.

Anyway, there'd been no way we could've turned up at Gran's house with an Exmoor pony and a half-starved dog; seriously . . . Gran doesn't even have a front garden. She'd let us keep Sheba, but Caramel had to be left behind. I love my gran, but I can't help thinking she'd be just a tiny bit relieved if Mum found a job that allowed her to move out and rent a little flat for us all. She'd never say that though, and it's not possible anyway because we are barely scraping by as it is on the wages Mum earns at the cafe.

So Coco has been looking after Caramel and sending Jas occasional picture updates, but my little sister is desperate to see her pony again. Right now, she looks like she'll explode with excitement any minute.

'I can see the sea!' she yells suddenly, and everyone sits up as the rugged Somerset coast appears to the right of us. The sea is dark grey and brooding under a gloomy sky. Minutes later we turn into a narrow, twisty lane that climbs uphill and at last we come to the rickety gate that marks the driveway to Tanglewood. It's a rambling, slightly shambolic Victorian house, complete with turret and leaded glass windows, now lit up with fairy lights and stick-on paper snowflakes. This place was our home too, for a little while the autumn before last, after we'd got away from Seddon.

The car slows, crunching along the drive, and as Mum parks beside the house the kitchen door bursts open, spilling a mad gaggle of sisters who rush across the gravel to greet us. We get out of the car, creaky from sitting still for so long, stretching, laughing. Jasmine is shy suddenly, hiding behind me, but the sisters – Cherry, Skye, Summer, Honey and Coco – wrap her in hugs and take her hands and pull her forward, and her face lights up in a way I haven't seen for a very long time.

I shoot a shy glance at Coco; she'll be thirteen now, like me, and even in her usual uniform of baggy sweater and skinny jeans she looks older, cooler, more aloof.

'Sandy, Lawrie, Jasmine . . . you made it!'

Charlotte, Coco's mum, hugs Mum, welcoming us all. 'How was the drive? It's such a long way, but we're thrilled you're here! We've got some soup on the Aga if you're hungry . . .'

Coco's stepdad Paddy appears in the doorway of the chocolate workshop, grinning, and we start moving towards

❀❀❀❀❀❀❀❀❀❀❀❀❀❀❀❀❀❀❀❀❀❀❀❀

the house because it's way too cold to be standing around outside on 31 December.

'Hey,' Coco says, falling into step beside me. 'Great to see you, Lawrie! It's been ages!'

'Too right,' I say gruffly. 'Thought you might have forgotten what I look like . . .'

'As if,' Coco laughs. 'Looks like those two remember each other too.'

Sheba is bouncing about on the driveway, skidding from person to person until she finds Fred, and then the two dogs go into a mad frenzy of tail-wagging delight.

I can feel a weight lifting from my shoulders, a weight I hadn't even realized was there. It's good to be back in Somerset; good to be with Coco. We went through a lot together, but so much has happened since. I wasn't sure how it would be when I saw her again. It might have been awkward or embarrassing, but I don't think it's going to be either of those things. It's going to be cool.

And then the first flakes of snow begin to fall out of the darkening clouds, and I catch Coco's eye and the two of us laugh out loud, turning our faces up to the sky.

2

We sit round the scrubbed pine table at Tanglewood, eating
hot soup and crusty bread fresh from the Aga.

It feels like time is peeling away, like the last year never
happened and we're still living here, a part of the kind,
crazy chaos that is Coco's family. We'd only stayed at
Tanglewood for two weeks, but it had been the happiest
time we'd had in Somerset. Mum had just left Seddon in
the aftermath of the pony kidnap drama and we'd been
technically homeless. Coco and her family had made us
welcome, treated us as family.

Mum had worked for a while in Charlotte and Paddy's
chocolate business, helping them with a big order, and Jas
and I had just let ourselves relax. Fun, mayhem, hard work,

evenings draped across the blue velvet sofas watching DVDs . . . those are the things I remember about our time living at Tanglewood. That and Coco sitting in the branches of the old oak tree practising her violin, in her duffel coat and fingerless gloves. She never seemed to get any better, but I never tired of listening. By then, I thought everything Coco did was cool.

'If everyone's finished their soup I'll make hot chocolate,' Coco's eldest sister Honey says. 'With squirty cream and marshmallows – that's the way you like it, Jasmine, right?'

Jasmine's face lights up. 'Oh yes! With extra chocolate sprinkles on top?'

'Obviously,' Honey promises. She pours milk into a saucepan and stirs in grated chocolate from the chocolate workshop's reject batches.

'We should patent Honey's hot chocolate recipe,' Charlotte comments. 'It's amazing. And once we're all warmed up, we have a party to organize . . .'

'Mum's invited half the village, as usual!' Coco says with a grin. 'But you're the guests of honour – I can't believe you're really here!'

'Nor me!' I say, grinning. 'Feels kinda weird!'

❀❀❀❀❀❀❀❀❀❀❀❀❀❀❀❀❀❀❀❀❀❀

'But good weird,' Jasmine says, her face shining. 'Can I see Caramel now? D'you think she'll remember me?'

'I know she will,' Coco says. 'I remind her all the time . . . We'll go the minute we've finished the hot chocolate.'

'And tomorrow you can go for a ride, perhaps,' Charlotte says. 'Caramel is much calmer than she used to be. We'll see what the weather is like . . .'

We all look towards the window, where the snow is swirling.

'It's settling,' I comment. 'I hope it doesn't spoil the party . . .'

'It'd take more than a bit of snow to stop people coming to one of our New Year parties,' Skye declares. 'They're legendary. And we live in the country, remember? A bit of snow is nothing!'

'We're walking distance from the village,' Paddy reminds me. 'People will come, snow or no snow! Even if they don't, you guys are here, and that's a party in itself . . . We're all so glad you could make it. We've missed you, you know!'

'We've missed you too,' Mum says. 'We often think of you and wonder how you're all getting on. They stock the Chocolate Box truffles in one of the fancy delis in town now. Things seem to be going well for you!'

297

Paddy nods. 'Very well,' he agrees. 'One of the big department stores is stocking them in all their branches, and lots of delis and luxury food shops are taking them too. We're actually in profit now, which is quite something.'

'Wow,' Mum says. 'That's terrific!'

Coco hands round the steaming hot chocolate, and there is silence for a few moments while we spoon up the melting marshmallows and sip the rich, creamy chocolate.

'And we're going to be on TV!' Coco blurts. 'Aren't we? A whole reality TV series about us!'

'Finch's mum set it up for us,' Skye chips in. 'It sounds pretty cool . . .'

'A TV show, huh?' I tease. 'You're famous now!'

'Not famous, exactly,' Coco says. 'Well, not *yet*!'

'Will Caramel be in the programme?' Jasmine wants to know. 'She might be famous too!'

'She'll be the star of the show,' Coco says. 'C'mon, let's go see her – you too, Lawrie. She'll remember you; you helped me save her, after all!'

We grab our coats and slip outside, the three of us crunching across the drive through a thin covering of freshly fallen snow.

298

❀❀❀❀❀❀❀❀❀❀❀❀❀❀❀❀❀❀❀❀❀❀❀

'It's going to be chaos now in the house . . . getting everything ready for the party,' Coco says, pushing open the stable door. 'We won't be missing much, trust me!'

As my eyes adjust to the darkness I see Caramel watching us from the far corner; small, solid, steady. The stable smells of fresh hay and warm pony with a faint scent of saddle oil. There's a sudden bleating noise, and a small, insistent shove against my legs.

'Humbug!' I say, laughing out loud. 'I forgot about you!'

The light flicks on and I see Humbug, Coco's pet sheep, pushing her head against my hand to be stroked, and Caramel the Exmoor pony, stocky and rough-coated; the pony that brought Coco and me together, the pony that started everything. She gazes at us from soft brown eyes, ambling forward to nudge at Jasmine and me with her mealy-pale nose, soft as velvet.

'She remembers!' Jasmine cries, flinging her arms round Caramel's neck.

I look at Coco and grin, and I remember too.

3

Jasmine is in heaven. Coco shows her how to brush Caramel and groom her mane. My little sister shows no signs of getting bored with the task, moving on to plait Caramel's mane with painstaking care.

'I haven't been all that good at keeping in touch,' Coco says. 'I meant to – it's just that there never seems to be time . . .'

I laugh. 'You've got the world to save, right?' I quip.

Coco sent a letter just after we moved and she posts and messages now and then on SpiderWeb, but neither of us is good at that kind of stuff. When I think of Coco I always imagine her riding Caramel across the moors or holding a placard about saving the whales . . . She is not really a letter-writing kind of girl.

'It's OK,' I shrug. 'I've been a bit rubbish too. Still, we're here now, I guess . . .'

Coco flops down on to a hay bale, leaving Jas to fuss over Caramel. An awkward silence descends and I run lines in my head, wondering how to break it. I can't say that Coco looks older, prettier; it just sounds too cheesy, too stupid, even though it's true. And now, in the half-light, my confidence has ebbed away and I can't find anything to say at all. I sink down a few hay bales along, pink-cheeked.

Coco catches my eye, and I hope the dim lighting doesn't show my discomfort. 'You've got taller,' she says, as direct as ever. 'And you got your hair cut! I think I liked it better before . . .'

'The head at our school is super-strict,' I reply. 'I'm going to grow it again . . .'

'Have you settled in OK back in Kendal? No thoughts of . . . well, coming back to Somerset, maybe?'

'I think we'd all love that,' I admit. 'Now that Seddon's gone. We do miss Somerset, Jas especially – but Kendal is OK. Or it would be, if Mum could get a better job and we had a place of our own instead of squashing in with Gran and Granddad. School's OK, though. I've got friends . . .'

❀❀❀❀❀❀❀❀❀❀❀❀❀❀❀❀❀❀❀❀❀❀❀❀

'Anyone . . . special?' Coco blurts out. 'Like . . . maybe . . . a girl or something?'

I am momentarily speechless. I once told Coco that I liked her a lot, back when we were staying at Tanglewood; she told me she wasn't ready for a boyfriend. Now she seems very curious about my love life . . . or, to be more precise, the lack of one.

'No girls,' I say, as carelessly as I can manage. 'No time for all that . . .'

'Same here,' Coco agrees. 'You know me, I am going to dedicate my life to saving the giant panda and the Siberian white tiger. No room for romance.'

Silence descends again, empty and awkward. Was Coco trying to tell me, in a roundabout way, that her views on romance have changed? If so, I have put my foot in it big style. How on earth do people ever manage to tell each other they're smitten? It's a nightmare, like picking your way through a minefield blindfolded.

'So you'll probably just stay in Kendal, then?' Coco asks.

'Probably,' I say. 'There are more jobs for Mum there, even if a lot of them are seasonal and poorly paid. I mean . . . I do miss Somerset. I even miss you, actually; there's nobody in Kendal who teases me or winds me up like you used to . . .'

'Obviously,' Coco grins. 'I'm unique.'

I lower my voice, watching my little sister combing and plaiting Caramel's mane. 'Jas is finding it harder than the rest of us,' I whisper. 'She hasn't settled at school. Some of the kids are teasing her a bit . . . and I'm at the secondary, obviously, so I can't do much to help.'

Coco frowns. 'Ouch. Does your mum know?'

'Jas won't let me say anything in case it makes things worse. It sucks.'

'Look, I'll talk to her,' Coco says. 'Tomorrow, maybe. Don't worry, Lawrie . . . look at her now; she's totally blissed out!'

'She loves Caramel,' I agree. 'This break will be good for her, and if you can have a word with her too . . . that'd be great.'

Coco grins. 'Well, it's New Year, isn't it?' she says, quietly. 'A time for new starts for all of you. Anything is possible, right?'

I sigh. I am a lot more practical than Coco, and I cannot see things improving for us any time soon. Still, I like Coco's optimism. The stable is silent for a moment, apart from the sound of Jasmine whispering to Caramel; and then a voice rings out though the darkness. Paddy is calling us from the house.

'Kids, where are you?' he yells. 'Coco? Lawrie? Jasmine? Come on back to the house – it's almost party time!'

In the house, Mum is in her element; she seems to have taken charge of things, the way she did when she worked briefly for Paddy and Charlotte. She thrives on chaos, and a transformation has taken place. The main lights have been switched off, replaced by fairy lights and jam-jar candles, and swathes of holly and ivy are draped everywhere. In the conservatory, tables have been pushed together, covered in festive tablecloths and piled high with party food; potato salad, coleslaw, hummus and crusty bread jostle for space with trifle, yule log and trays of iced mince pies and cupcakes. Pizzas, quiches and sausage rolls are lined up in the kitchen waiting to be cooked, while jacket potatoes are baking in the Aga and more soup is simmering on the stove top.

Honey is creating a non-alcoholic punch with bottles of lemonade, orange juice and tons of chopped fresh fruit and ice; Paddy is stirring mulled wine on the Aga, and the whole house smells of oranges and spices.

You can almost taste Christmas in the air, or New Year, anyway. It's a kind of magic. At Gran and Granddad's, Christmas is about thickly iced fruit cake and cold turkey sandwiches and Quality Street toffees and an endless menu of TV Christmas Specials. At Tanglewood, things are different.

'What about the dogs?' I ask Coco. 'Will they be OK?'

'Fred's fine with big groups of people,' she says with a shrug. 'Sheba should take her lead from him, but if she's looking stressed just tell me and we'll take the two of them upstairs for some peace and quiet.'

Cherry and her boyfriend Shay are testing out the party playlist, an eclectic mixture of teen music and retro stuff that Paddy and Charlotte like. Alfie, Summer's boyfriend, has arrived too, and before long we're all clowning about to the music as we set out paper cups and last-minute bowls of nuts and crisps and nibbles.

And then a car draws up outside and the first proper guests arrive, stomping the snow from their boots and handing coats to Alfie who stores them carefully in an upstairs

❀❀❀❀❀❀❀❀❀❀❀❀❀❀❀❀❀❀❀❀❀❀❀

bedroom. By the time the first drinks have been poured, the door opens again and a tribe of villagers comes tumbling in, and then another car draws up and the stream of incoming partygoers becomes constant. Shay turns up the volume and Summer and Skye duck through the crowd with trays of food, and people are slapping me on the back and asking me how life in Kendal is going and I surrender myself to the chaos, to the party.

4

I remember looking at the kitchen clock at about nine thirty, and gathering up an armful of coats from another band of newly arrived guests. I remember seeing Jas playing with Alfie's little sisters, watching the three of them weaving through the crowds, smiling because I haven't seen her so relaxed for ages. I'm keeping an eye on Sheba too, but she just pads around after Fred, looking for scraps and galloping up the stairs to the landing whenever she needs chill-out time.

As for Mum, she's in the thick of it: chatting to Mrs Lee from the post office about fortunes and futures, to Alfie's parents about the trials of raising a teenage boy, and even discussing the perils of Internet dating for the middle aged with Shay's Uncle Matt. Internet dating? I'd have thought she'd have had enough of romance to last a lifetime after dodgy James Seddon, but I guess you never can tell. You'd think that people would give up on all that mushy stuff once they're over the age of thirty and officially ancient, but apparently not.

I end up offering round plates of warm mince pies with Coco – the two of us wearing reindeer antlers, chatting to Shay about music and to Honey about her stay in Sydney, Australia, as well as having a long talk with Joe, the farmer who owns the land next to Tanglewood, about how awesome shire horses and Clydesdales are. Time slides by without me noticing and the next thing I know it is almost midnight and Skye and Summer are wandering about with paper snowflakes, asking everyone to write their wishes for the New Year on them in silver pen.

'We used to write wishes on a Chinese lantern and let it go at midnight,' Skye tells me as I scribble my wish. 'Then Coco found out they're not eco for some reason. Maybe sheep eat them, or they set fire to trees or something; anyway, we had to come up with a new idea.'

'We're going to throw the snowflakes into the sea tomorrow morning,' Summer adds. 'At high tide. When the tide turns, it will take the snowflake wishes out to sea.'

✿✿✿✿✿✿✿✿✿✿✿✿✿✿✿✿✿✿✿✿✿✿

'And our wishes will come true,' Skye finishes. 'Maybe . . .'

'Yeah, right,' I tell her. 'If only it were that easy!'

I write my wish anyway; a garbled plea for a flat of our own, a job for Mum, for Jas to be happy at school.

'Make a wish for yourself too,' Summer says, glancing at what I've written. 'You worry a lot about other people, but you're allowed some dreams too.'

'I'm fine,' I say. 'I don't need much to be happy . . .'

My eyes scan the room and I catch sight of Coco, still wearing her reindeer antlers, and I am almost certain she is talking about Greenpeace or giant pandas or climate change. That makes me smile.

Suddenly the music is switched off and Paddy is yelling that's it's almost midnight, and that we have to go outside.

'Outside?' I echo. 'What? In the snow? We'll freeze!'

'Tradition,' Skye says. 'Come on, Lawrie, grab your coat . . . you'll see!'

There's chaos then as the party moves slowly outside, Alfie and Shay handing out coats and scarves and jackets at the door. The snow has stopped and the night is still and silent as we gather on the driveway. Paddy is counting down from ten, then everyone shouts 'Happy New Year!' The minute midnight passes, people are crossing their arms and linking hands and Coco appears suddenly to my left and says this is a Scottish tradition, and that ever since Paddy and Cherry came down from Glasgow to join the family this is what they do every New Year's Eve. Everyone sings 'Auld Lang Syne' and although we don't all get the words right it doesn't seem to matter. There is much swinging of arms and shuffling about, but it feels like a nice thing to do, even though the bloke on my right is tone deaf and keeps treading on my foot with his snow boots.

When everyone breaks apart there is a terrifying moment when everyone seems to be kissing everyone else, which is not my thing at all. I'm wishing I was a million miles away when Coco appears from the darkness, flings her arms round me in a hug and kisses my ear clumsily. I panic; am I supposed to kiss her back? If so, do I aim for cheek or ear or . . . well, lips? My heart thumps and I'm still trying to work it out as Coco spins away from me and I have to make do with a hug from Mum and a sugary kiss from Jas, who skids in and then hares off again with Alfie's sisters.

I notice that Sheba, at my side, is shivering in the snow.

'Coco?' I touch her sleeve. 'Shall we go back in?'

Coco nods her head. 'Sure,' she says. 'It's freezing.'

As she speaks, a firework goes off: a plume of white that shoots high into the air before exploding into a fountain of red, blue and green sparks as the gathered partygoers whoop and sigh. More fireworks follow in quick succession, and I can feel Sheba shaking, pressing against my leg.

'Sheba's terrified of fireworks,' I say. 'I need to get her inside.'

'Fred's legged it back to the house already,' Coco says. 'He hates fireworks. For goodness' sake – whose idea was this? We never have fireworks. I should have made sure the dogs were shut inside! Come on . . .'

We are halfway to the house, my hand on Sheba's collar, when the sky explodes in a series of ear-splitting bangs that fade into screeching howls. The crowd cheer and whistle, but Sheba freaks completely, ducking backwards, sliding right out of her collar. She bolts away, running along the drive and out towards the lane.

'Sheba!' I yell, but the words are drowned out by the noise of the fireworks. '*Sheba!* Come back!'

I break into a run, skidding on the snow, but Sheba has vanished. 'Sheba!' I yell again. '*Sheba!*'

❀❀❀❀❀❀❀❀❀❀❀❀❀❀❀❀❀❀❀❀❀❀❀

Coco runs up behind me. 'At least we can see her prints in the snow.'

'I think she'll be looking for shelter,' I say. 'Somewhere quiet, somewhere safe . . .'

Coco takes my hand and we start to run again through the snow.

5

'Sheba!' Coco shouts into the darkness. 'Where are you? *Sheba!*'

'We have to find her,' I say. 'This isn't her home; she'll never be able to find her way back, and if we lost her, Jas would be devastated . . .'

I would be devastated too. We run on up the hill, slower now, feet slipping in the powdery snow. And then the prints disappear into a stand of trees and my heart sinks.

'She's gone into the woods,' I say. 'We'll never find her now!'

'Of course we will,' Coco says, confidently. 'It looks like those stupid fireworks are over . . . Sheba will calm down now. We'll get her, Lawrie.'

We cross the ditch and step into the woods. There's only

a light covering of snow under the trees, but we can't run because the ground is too rough and uneven. Coco uses the torch app on her smartphone to help us follow Sheba's prints. And then the snow disappears completely as the woods get more dense, and there are no more prints to follow.

'Where are we?' I ask, my breath gathering in the air before me like a cloud.

'No idea,' Coco whispers. 'The woods stretch along the coast for miles. If you walk far enough, you get to the cliffs above the Smugglers' Caves. Not the ideal place to go walking in the dark . . .'

I clench my fists. 'Too bad. I'm not turning back; I can't. This is all my fault . . . and now she's gone . . .'

'Rubbish,' Coco says. 'It's nobody's fault, Lawrie . . . even the idiots responsible for the fireworks didn't mean this to happen. I have a feeling it was Alfie's dad and uncle . . . They were definitely planning something. They probably thought it would be a cool surprise; they wouldn't have been thinking about the dogs . . .'

'I know,' I mutter, but right now it doesn't matter what Coco says; I feel sick with guilt, furious with myself.

❀❀❀❀❀❀❀❀❀❀❀❀❀❀❀❀❀❀❀❀❀❀❀

And then the torch app dies suddenly, and we are left in darkness.

Coco swears beneath her breath. 'Phone's out of charge,' she says. 'Have you got yours?'

'Left it in my rucksack,' I admit. 'Back at the house. It doesn't have a torch app anyway; it's just a cheap pay as you go . . .'

'We should've rung home,' Coco says. 'Mum and Paddy and your mum would know what to do. The party people will be leaving now and they'll wonder where we are. They'll be worried . . .'

'I'm not giving up,' I blurt out. 'I can't!'

'I'm not either.'

I look at Coco in the moonlight and see that she's shivering, her face pale and shadowed with blue. My hands are numb with cold and my teeth are chattering, and I know that staggering around blindly in the dark in a wood that edges on to clifftops is crazy and quite possibly dangerous.

'Sheba!' I shout into the stillness. 'Where are you?'

We stumble on, breathless, numb; feet slipping in the snow, tripping on roots. Sheba could be anywhere in the

woods, running scared in the darkness towards the dangerous cliff edge. My fault, my fault, my fault.

'Lawrie?' Coco says in a small voice. 'I'm not being funny,
but I think we're lost. Should we stop a minute, try to get
our bearings?'

'I'm not going back without her,' I say.

'I know,' Coco says. 'Nor me. But we need to think, or
we're going to end up frozen stiff and stuck out here all
night.'

Flakes of snow are drifting down on us through the trees,
softly at first and then faster. I feel like crying, but that
wouldn't achieve anything; and boys don't cry.

'*Sheba!*' I roar with all the breath in my body, and this
time, in the silence, comes the sound of twigs cracking,
leaves rustling. My heart begins to pound and hope unfurls
inside me, and at last Sheba bursts into the clearing, shaking and panting.

'Sheba, hey!'

I drop to my knees on the woodland floor and throw
my arms round her; Sheba pushes her face into my hair,
my neck, and I ruffle her coat and laugh out loud with
relief. Coco is on the ground beside me, stroking Sheba's

bedraggled coat, whispering soft words to her. Our eyes meet and I know I'm grinning like an idiot, ridiculously happy.

I catch Coco's hand and hold it tight.

'We did it!' I say. 'Another adventure . . . and everything's worked out. Team work, right?'

We get to our feet awkwardly, laughing, Sheba still whimpering softly at our feet. 'Team work!' Coco agrees.

And then suddenly, without warning, a piercing, unearthly scream splits the night in half.

It sends a shiver down my spine, and my heart is thumping so hard I think it must be audible a mile away. Coco's eyes are wide with terror. Even Sheba is pressed against me, hackles up, frozen with fear.

The scream cuts through the night again, louder and more haunting, more agonizing than anything I have ever heard in my life.

6

'What *is* that?' Coco breathes, her voice less than a whisper. 'Lawrie?'

'Someone's in trouble,' I say. 'Someone's hurt . . .'

'It could be a murder!' she whispers. 'Something bad's happening, Lawrie. I'm scared!'

'Maybe someone's fallen, hurt themselves,' I reason. 'Let's get a closer look.'

'No!' Coco argues. 'That scream was full of fear as well as pain . . . We can't handle this on our own, Lawrie. We could be walking into anything. Look, Sheba's just as scared as we are . . .'

The dog is shaking, pressing hard against my leg, but in spite of my fear I step forward, towards where the scream seemed to come from.

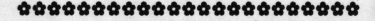

'Let's go back,' Coco pleads. 'Tell Paddy, call the police, get help! Lawrie, please!'

But I'm running now, ducking beneath branches, skidding slightly on patches of snow, lurching onwards. The scream rings out again, guttural, desperate, and I'm vaguely aware of Sheba running at my side, of Coco's footsteps stumbling along behind me.

We blunder towards the noise, coming to a halt in a small clearing where just a moment before the screams seemed to be coming from.

'Where is she?' Coco asks, breathless, scanning the dark shapes looming around us. 'She sounded so close . . .'

'Hello?' I yell into the silence. '*Hello?* Are you OK? We want to help you!'

And then the noise comes again, mewling and pitiful, no longer human-sounding but animal, agonized.

'Hello?' I call out, moving forward through the trees. 'Where are you? Hello?'

'Not a person,' Coco breathes. 'I don't think it's a human scream after all . . .'

And then I see it: the glint of silver wire on snow, reflecting the moonlight that streams through the trees. A clump

❀❀❀❀❀❀❀❀❀❀❀❀❀❀❀❀❀❀❀❀❀❀❀❀

of dead bracken, a wooden peg, tightening wire, crimson blood pooling out across the snow, a ragged twist of russet fur.

'Sheesh . . .' I whisper. 'Coco . . . it's a fox! She's caught in a snare!'

I don't know whether to feel relieved or dismayed. I remember now how other-worldly, how piercing a fox's cries can be. We would hear them sometimes in the hills around Seddon's farmhouse when we lived in Somerset before. They'd sounded like a woman's screams, sharp and shrill enough to curdle the blood.

'No, no, nooooo . . .' Coco croons, dropping to her knees in the snow. 'I can't bear it, Lawrie! We have to help her!'

'We will,' I promise, without a clue as to how I can keep that promise. 'We will . . .'

I am on my knees beside Coco, straining to see in the moonlight. Sheba is beside me, whimpering softly.

The fox's right leg is caught in a slender twist of wire secured to a peg driven into the ground a short way away. The snare is fixed so that every time the fox tries to pull away the wire tightens. You can see where the fur has been cut away by the wire to expose raw flesh and muscle and bone; worse, it looks as though the fox has tried to gnaw at the trapped leg just above the snare, in an attempt to get free. Crimson blood has seeped into the snow, and her teeth are flecked with red.

The fox has stopped screaming now; her eyes are glazed. I think she must be almost spent, her spirit fading fast. Tears sting my eyes and I don't care any more whether boys are supposed to cry. I want to help, but I think we're too late.

This was not the way I wanted my new year to start.

I reach out, fingers shaking, but the minute I touch the fox's leg she jerks and yelps, convulsing with pain, and this just pulls the snare tighter than ever. I can barely see the wire at all now; it is hidden by matted fur and clotted blood.

'The peg,' Coco whispers. 'Dig up the wooden peg!'

I kneel up straighter. Coco is right – if we can dig up the peg anchoring the snare to the ground, the pressure will ease. Perhaps then we can pick up the fox and bring her to safety.

I start scraping at the snow with my bare hands, but the ground beneath is half frozen and my fingers are like blocks of ice. Coco joins in, but it's only when Sheba begins to dig – gleeful, enthusiastic – that we make some progress. The skinny dog's paws scrabble frantically at the hard ground, sending showers of snow and soil flying. It's as if she knows what we need her to do, and she works steadily, scratching, scraping, until the wooden peg is exposed enough to loosen and, finally, pull up.

'Yessss!' I breathe, but when I look at the fox again I see that her eyes are half closed now in the moonlight, her lips drawn back from her teeth in a terrible rictus grin.

'She's still alive,' Coco whispers. 'Just. We have to try, right?'

'Right.'

I take off my coat – a thick woollen jacket – and spread it out on the snow. Moving as quickly and gently as I can, I scoop up the fox and wrap her in the jacket, tucking the trailing wire and wooden peg in too. When I take my hands away they are sticky with blood, stinking of fox. I lift up the whole bundle in my arms. The fox whimpers, but it's a tiny sound, a whisper.

'Let's go,' I say. 'We need to find the road, and fast. Before it's too late . . .'

Coco frowns. 'I don't know for sure, but if we veer to the left, I think we'll hit the road eventually. And it'll be easier to walk once we're out of the woods.'

At last the trees thin out again and the snow-covered lane comes into view. I am beyond frozen by then; my body shaking, my feet numb with cold. My arms ache from carrying the fox bundle and I don't know how much further I can go.

'OK,' Coco says as we stand in the road in the swirling snow. 'We've come out on the main road; we must have gone further than I thought. It's quite a way back to Tanglewood from here, but if we go in the other direction . . .'

'The other direction?'

'It's a risk, because she might not even be here,' Coco is saying. 'She might be away for New Year, visiting family or something, but maybe – just maybe – we'll be in luck. There's a vet who lives along this way, and she's really nice: Sharon Denny. I did some work experience with her back in the summer, just for a couple of days, and she was really cool. Her surgery is in Minehead, but still, she might know what to do, who to call . . .'

'Is it far?'

'Not far,' Coco promises. 'We can do it. Keep going!'

We trudge on through the silent dark and finally a cottage

❀❀❀❀❀❀❀❀❀❀❀❀❀❀❀❀❀❀❀❀❀❀❀❀

looms out of nowhere, a small sandstone place with fairy lights twinkling in the window and a holly wreath hanging on the red-painted door. A silver four-by-four sits in the driveway, muffled beneath a thick layer of snow.

'Let's hope that means she's home,' Coco says.

She leans on the doorbell and the buzz of it crackles out into the night.

7

Sharon Denny takes it all in her stride, as if half-frozen teenagers accompanied by dogs and foxes turn up on her doorstep regularly in the middle of a New Year blizzard. Well, maybe they do.

'Coco,' she says, rubbing her eyes, sleepily. 'What the . . .?'

'Please help us,' Coco says. 'This is my friend Lawrie, and it's a long story, but we were lost in the woods and we found a fox. She was caught in a snare . . .'

'Show me,' the vet says.

I lay my coat on the kitchen floor and open it to reveal the mangled russet-red body inside. For a moment I am sure the fox is dead, and then she writhes and jerks and thrashes, and relief floods through me because this means she still has a chance.

'OK,' the vet says. 'We are very, very lucky that the snare just caught her leg. Often it's the belly or the neck . . .'

She reaches for a leather bag and takes out a syringe, a bottle.

'I'm going to sedate her a little so I can check her properly and stop the bleeding . . .'

The needle slips into matted fur and the fox slumps abruptly. She's not giving up the fight but relaxing, allowing us to fight for her; the vet is looking at the damaged leg now, cleaning it up, stemming the blood.

'I thought snares were illegal,' I say.

'Not illegal,' Coco tells me. 'They should be, though. And I've never seen an animal caught in one before . . .'

It could have been Sheba, I think. It could even have been a child.

'I've seen it a few times, sadly,' Sharon says. 'Where did you find her? Some of the local farmers use snares to keep the fox population down. It's not something I approve of, but it happens.'

❀❀❀❀❀❀❀❀❀❀❀❀❀❀❀❀❀❀❀❀❀❀❀❀

'Not Joe Wallace,' Coco says. 'He farms the land next to Tanglewood. He wouldn't do this . . .'

'Not Joe,' Sharon agrees. 'But some of the others; they see foxes as vermin. I don't, but we have a bit of a dilemma here. She's clearly been in that snare for a while. She's lost a lot of blood and tried to bite through her leg to get free . . . I don't think we can save that leg. And a three-legged fox is not going to survive in the wild, Coco. I'm sorry.'

'She *has* to survive!' Coco argues. 'You have to help her! Please?'

The vet sighs. 'Sometimes, an injection that lets the injured animal slip away quietly is the best and kindest thing you can do,' she explains. 'Wild animals live a very harsh life out there; red in tooth and claw, as they say. She can't go back into the wild; she'd never survive with this kind of disability . . . You have to think of the animal.'

'But foxes are dogs, really, aren't they?' I argue. 'Just wilder. Surely she could be tamed? Live alongside people? We can't just let her go. I've carried her for miles through the snow . . .'

'I know you have,' the vet says. 'You've done all you could to help her, but what about her future? Even if you tried to keep her as a pet, she'd never really be reliably tame. It would be a huge challenge . . .'

'Please save her,' I say, and my voice sounds choked up and shaky and I don't even care. 'Please?'

'Are you sure?' the woman asks again. 'You can give her a home? Quality of life?'

I want to slam my fist against the wall, yell and swear and smash things. How can I give an injured fox a home when my family doesn't have a home of our own to begin with?

'I can,' Coco cuts in. 'Mum and Paddy won't mind; you know they won't. And they'd pay for the operation or whatever treatment she needs. We can convert one of the stables, make an outdoor run . . . She'll be safe. Please, Sharon? Please?'

The vet rolls her eyes. 'I must be crazy,' she says. 'Whatever. I'll do my best to save her, I promise you, but I think she'll lose the leg: that doesn't look good at all. Don't worry, OK? You're good kids . . . there ought to be more like you.'

Things happen fast after that. A call is made to the emergency vet in Minehead, and Sharon Denny says that she'll drive the fox straight there so that the leg can be operated on at once.

'No charge,' she says, shaking her head as she shrugs on a jacket and drags a comb through her hair. 'Let's just call it me getting in my good deed for the year early . . .'

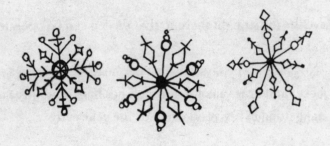

8

Later on New Year's Day, we walk down to the beach beside Tanglewood, the whole gang of us; the Tanberry-Costello girls, Jasmine and me. We bring the paper snowflakes from the party, each one carrying wishes and dreams, and throw them on to the turning tide to be carried out to sea.

I have added a new wish: for the injured fox to survive and, somehow, stay with us.

'I don't believe in wishes,' I say gruffly, watching the white snowflake shapes drifting out to sea, being tugged under by the current.

'You don't have to believe,' Coco says. 'Not with your mind, anyway. It's what your heart believes that matters.'

I roll my eyes and shake my head, but still, I can't stop

smiling. I am on the beach on New Year's Day with the girl I like best in the whole wide world. So what if we live at different ends of the country? I don't care any more, and I don't think Coco does either. We understand each other; I think we always will.

It turns out that Coco is right too. Mum, Jas and I have wished for difficult things, unlikely things, impossible things: a home of our own, a steady job, a new school with friends, a three-legged fox. And it turns out that these things are not impossible after all.

'There's something we wanted to ask you,' Paddy says to Mum as we sit down later that day to a New Year feast. 'It's a big thing, and it may not be what you want at all, but we have to ask . . .'

'It's part of the reason we asked you down to the party,' Charlotte adds. 'I mean, no pressure, Sandy, it was just something we've been thinking about and it may not be right for you . . .'

'What?' Mum asks. 'What did you want to ask?'

Paddy rakes a hand through his hair.

'The business is in profit, and we want to take on a full-

❀❀❀❀❀❀❀❀❀❀❀❀❀❀❀❀❀❀❀❀❀❀❀❀

time office manager,' he explains. 'Someone organized; someone who works well under pressure and has a flair for the publicity and press side of things too. Sandy, we've had other part-time workers over the last year or so, but nobody has been as good as you . . . We wanted to ask you first, before we put the vacancy out there. There really is nobody we'd rather have on board.'

Mum's eyes widen. I can see she's having a hard time making sense of Paddy's offer. 'Work for you?' she echoes. 'Here? At the Chocolate Box? Oh . . . you know I'd love to . . . I enjoyed every minute. It was my dream job, and I felt like I really was making a difference. But – I don't see how?'

Charlotte and Paddy start talking details then, including a salary that knocks the wages Mum has been earning in Kendal into the shadows.

'It would be official,' Paddy explains. 'Nothing temporary or cash-in-hand. You'd have security . . .'

'But where would we live?'

Charlotte shrugs. 'There are a couple of properties for rent in the village just now,' she says. 'I'd say you could pick and choose . . .'

Mum is looking overwhelmed. 'I have to admit, being back in Somerset has got me thinking. I loved it here – we all did – to begin with anyway. And then that whole thing with James spoiled it and sent us running back to Kendal. I have sometimes wondered if that was the right move; if we couldn't have found a way to stay . . .'

'Think about it,' Charlotte says. 'It's a big thing, I know . . .'

Mum laughs. 'It's too good to be true! I'd have to check . . . look into things . . . see what the kids think . . .'

'We think you should do it,' I say, glancing at Jasmine's shining face. 'It's a steady job, isn't it? Doing something you love.'

'But the upheaval!' she protests. 'Moving to the other end of the country again! Disrupting your schooling, you and Jasmine . . .'

'I don't care,' I shrug.

'Jasmine?' Mum asks. 'What do you think?'

My little sister looks like she might explode with happiness. A move away from the school where she is being picked on, a fresh start in a small village school, with Alfie's sisters already halfway to being good friends . . . and living just down the lane from her pony Caramel? Jasmine's eyes are wide with hope.

'Say yes, Mum,' she whispers. 'Please, please, say *yes*!'

The wishes come true, one after another. A job, a house, a future . . . and a three-legged fox.

Three days later, Coco and I are on the bus coming back from Minehead, where we've been to see the fox, now named Bracken after the patch of undergrowth we found her in. She lost the damaged leg, but she is recovering well from her surgery in the wild animal wing of the vet hospital.

Sharon Denny has agreed to come and talk to Paddy and Charlotte about converting the stable and looking after a wild animal; it looks like Bracken really will get a new lease of life. And once Mum, Jas and I have settled into our new cottage, maybe Bracken can come to live with us? Who knows. She'll never be a pet like a dog or a cat, but in time a bond of sorts could perhaps be made.

When I looked at her amber eyes, clear and shining, in the vet hospital today, I was pretty sure that bond was already forming.

'She's going to be OK,' Coco says to me, reading my

❀❀❀❀❀❀❀❀❀❀❀❀❀❀❀❀❀❀❀❀❀❀

mind. 'Bracken, I mean. We'll look after her for you until you move back and settle in . . . and then maybe we can build a run for her at your new place and she can be with you.'

'Hope so,' I say. 'If we can just find a cottage with a fox run attached . . . that'd be cool!'

Today should be Mum's first day back at work, but she rang to tell them she was stuck in Somerset due to heavy snowfall. Later today, we'll be looking at some places to live in the village and making a decision; it will be based on which of the landlords will accept animals. I don't think we will mention that one of the animals in question is a three-legged fox.

Tomorrow we will drive back to Kendal so Mum can give in her notice and work her last few weeks. We'll pack our stuff and say our goodbyes and move into our new home in February, if all goes well.

The bus stops in Kitnor High Street and we jump off, our boots crunching through snow as we walk up the lane to Tanglewood hand in hand. I remember the day I said goodbye to Coco last time around, sitting together in the big oak tree. I remember leaning across to kiss her, and how the kiss had just startled and scared her, and how we'd agreed to be best friends forever.

If I tried again now, it might be the same; but maybe, just maybe, it would be different?

We stop at the end of the drive and I turn Coco round, holding her hands tight. 'This has been the best New Year ever,' I tell her. 'The best.'

And before I can lean over to kiss her, Coco stands up on her tiptoes and flings her arms round me, her lips pressing softly against mine. Her lips are warm and taste faintly of chocolate, and we bump noses and Coco laughs, but it is still the best and most perfect kiss in the world.

'Sorry,' she says, grinning, when we come up for air. 'I guess we can practise . . .'

'I guess we can . . .'

So yeah . . . New Year's wishes. Maybe I'd better start believing in them after all because it looks like they believe in me.

The snow keeps falling, softly swirling, as we walk on up to Tanglewood.

HEARTS
♥ AND ♥
Sunsets

Ash has been a bit of a mystery character in **Sweet Honey** and **Fortune Cookie** . . . I just couldn't resist the opportunity to give him a story of his own and see just what makes him tick! The timing of this story takes place after the book **Fortune Cookie** . . . and Ash has some big decisions to make. Will Honey be a part of his future or not?

Cathy Cassidy xxx

1

The night train to Paris is only half full, and I have room to stretch my legs, lean back, dream. My rucksack sits on the seat beside me, looking tatty and worn now after nine months of adventures. I am probably looking tatty and worn myself.

I reach into a side pocket of the rucksack and pull out an orange – an orange picked straight from a tree in a side street on the outskirts of Madrid just a few hours ago. Picking your own oranges right from the tree might be seen as a little bit cheeky as a rule, but this particular tree was in the grounds of the backpackers' hostel where I'd been staying and I reckoned it was fair game.

I dig a thumb into the thick dimpled skin and begin to peel it away, releasing the sharp, sweet citrus aroma. The minute I bite into the first segment, memories flood my mind – not memories of Madrid, not memories of Spain at all, but of Tanglewood.

I am running out of the sea, the salt water starring my body with droplets of silver. The beach is deserted except for a girl, a long-limbed beautiful girl, fair-haired and laughing as she watches me run up and fling myself down on to the striped picnic blanket. I snake my arms round her and she wriggles free, still laughing.

'Ash, no! You're all wet!'

She shoves a towel into my arms and I wipe the water from my skin and drag it over my hair before dropping back on to the blanket to let the sun finish the job of drying me off.

Then I smell citrus and the girl wafts a slice of orange under my nose; I grab it and eat it, letting the sweet juice slide across my tongue. The girl flops down beside me and I turn to look at her just inches away from me on the blanket: her tanned cheeks crusted with golden sand, her blue eyes brighter than the summer sky.

When I reach for her this time, she doesn't pull away.

*

❀❀❀❀❀❀❀❀❀❀❀❀❀❀❀❀❀❀❀❀❀

The train swoops onward through the night, swift, silent. Have we crossed the border into France yet? I can't tell. I have been on too many trains, crossed too many borders this year. Maybe the thrill of it all is finally wearing thin.

Tanglewood seems like a dream, a place I imagined or conjured up from nowhere. It's only six weeks since I packed up my rucksack and moved on, but it feels like forever.

I think I left something behind me there, something important, essential. My heart, my soul, my sense of adventure . . . Let's just say those things have been missing in action ever since the day I said goodbye to Honey Tanberry.

I didn't want to leave. I have six months of travel left to me before I am due back home in Sydney; I have a university place waiting for me there, to study philosophy and politics, starting in February. The idea of that used to excite me a whole lot more than it does these days.

I'd spent three blissful weeks at Tanglewood, but suddenly I wanted more. It's that kind of place . . . a place that feels like home, even to a teenage Aussie kid with Sri Lankan heritage whose closest family are half a world away.

I was young and in love and I didn't want to walk away from all that. Who would?

❀❀❀❀❀❀❀❀❀❀❀❀❀❀❀❀❀❀❀❀❀❀❀

'Come with me,' I said to Honey. 'We can travel around Europe together, see Paris and Berlin and Madrid . . . go wherever we want to. We can eat ice cream and hire a scooter in Rome, throw coins into the Trevi Fountain and make a wish . . .'

I knew what I would wish for, even then.

'Shall we?' I asked again, although I knew what the answer would be. I watched Honey's blue eyes darken like a stormy sky.

'I have school,' she said sadly. 'It's my A-level year. I can't just take time out, even though you know I'd love to . . .'

I blinked. When I first met Honey, eighteen months ago in Sydney, she was allergic to the very mention of the word 'school'. It was enough to bring her out in a rash, wipe the dazzling smile from her face. Now, school was the thing that threatened to keep us apart.

'Take a year out,' I suggested. 'Like me!'

She shook her head. 'Ash,' she said. 'It has taken me almost seventeen years to see the point of school. Now I have – now I'm actually working – I'm not going to mess it up. Don't ask me to do that!'

Hope fizzled in seconds. It hadn't been a serious suggestion,

344

not really – I knew the practicalities. I knew it wasn't possible. I just couldn't help giving it a try.

'It's OK,' I said, backtracking. 'I wouldn't ask you that, of course I wouldn't. It's just that I'm going to miss you so much . . .'

'I'll miss you too,' she said.

'What if I just stay a while longer? Hang out here for a month or two, get a part-time job?'

She smiled. 'And miss your chance to see Europe? How long have you been planning this trip? You have to see it through. Go, Ash. Have adventures . . . but email me, tell me all about it. It'll be almost as good as being with you.'

I doubted that very much.

'I wish I could go, Ash,' she repeated. 'Or that you could stay . . . I'd keep you here if I thought I could, but you'd soon feel restless, start to resent me. I'm not going to be the one who keeps you from your dream, OK? This last month together has been amazing, but we can't get sidetracked. Don't throw away the adventure.'

I would have thrown everything away for Honey, but I stayed silent.

'I want you to do the right thing, that's all,' she said.

The trouble was I didn't know any more what the right thing was, and I still don't. The fun seeped out of the plans I'd made; seeing Europe had lost its appeal without Honey by my side.

She came with me as far as the railway station in Exeter to wave goodbye.

'Remind me why I'm going?' I asked, as we waited for the train.

'Because it's been your dream for as long as you can remember,' she told me, laughing. 'And because you only have six months before your uni course begins. Don't waste it.'

'Yeah. About that uni place . . .'

Honey put a finger to my lips.

'Don't say it,' she told me. 'No cold feet, OK? You have a place at university for the course you wanted most in the world. I know you might be having second thoughts right now, but that's exactly why you need to stick to the plan and finish your gap year. Go see Europe. Have some adventures, see some sights . . . If you miss this chance, you'll regret it, I know.'

'But . . . I'm not sure philosophy and politics are what

346

I want to study any more,' I admit. 'Maybe I should be studying English? Or journalism? Or maybe I should just get a job in a coffee shop until I've worked out what I should be doing?'

'Go and explore,' Honey said. 'Have fun, see Europe, soak it all up. And do some thinking, Ash, about what you want from life. That's what a gap year is all about.'

The train came in and I hugged her tight, and then I was on the train and waving as it drew out of the station, and I didn't need a gap year to know I was leaving behind everything that mattered to me.

2

I try to sleep, using my backpack as a pillow, but it's not comfortable and after a while I give up and sit up again, my cheek pressed against the cool glass of the train window. I watch an unknown city slip by, a blur of white lights in the darkness.

I don't know where I am any more. I'm not sure I even care.

I have ticked a few boxes on my travel itinerary these last few weeks, seen a few sights. I took a ferry and a train to Amsterdam and cycled around the city on a hired bike and stayed with Daan and Cas and Mika, three philosophy students who were living on a barge. We'd met at the backpackers' hostel where Daan worked and bonded over philosophy. They had a spare bed for the week, so I moved in and paid a few euros less than I would have at the hostel. It was a win-win situation. Daan and his mates had three late-night parties in less than a week, wild nights where the barge filled up with an unlikely mix of hipster students and mad musicians. I blogged about the chaos and emailed Honey to tell her about the parties; I knew she'd have loved them.

On the last night, a bunch of crazy art students turned up and started painting the inside of the barge with red and gold paint while one of the musicians, a girl called Astrid, played live saxophone over the sound of vintage punk rock on the sound system. There was no way I was going to sleep with all that going on, so I sat up on deck in the moonlight and got chatting to a German student called Ernst who was driving back to Berlin the next day.

That's how I came to take a detour, because a free lift across Europe and a free place to stay while I was there was not something to turn down. While I was in Berlin I bought a coffee from a little internet cafe and ended up with a job for a week, covering for some guy who was down with the flu. My German is very patchy, but three years of making lattes and flat whites and Americanos at the cafe

✿✿✿✿✿✿✿✿✿✿✿✿✿✿✿✿✿✿✿✿✿✿✿✿✿

on Sunset Beach in Sydney meant I could handle their very bad-tempered coffee machine when nobody else could.

I made some money and a few new friends, and I stayed with Ernst who turned out to be the perfect tour guide. I saw what was left of the Berlin Wall and looked at some art and went to some gigs and sat in the parks beneath the September sun. I visited the museums and took lots of pictures and wrote a few blog posts about the city and a whole bunch of emails to Honey. Those emails were upbeat and chatty and packed with the kind of quirky detail I knew would make her smile. I wanted her to see the city as vividly as I did, but the irony of it all was that Berlin only really came alive for me when I wrote about it for Honey.

I didn't want her to pick up on how much I was missing her, but I was. I missed her like mad, wished that she was with me. It was like an ache inside me, all of the time.

After Berlin, I went to Vienna; then Zurich, Milan, Nice, Marseille, Barcelona and Madrid. I tried to enjoy the adventure, the gap-year odyssey I had been planning since forever, but somehow my travel blog and the emails to Honey became the bit that mattered most. It was all about

✿✿✿✿✿✿✿✿✿✿✿✿✿✿✿✿✿✿✿✿✿✿✿✿✿✿

taking the right photo, finding the right words. I wanted to make it real, make her see what I was seeing, feel what I was feeling. I was bringing each new place to life so Honey could share it with me.

Somewhere in the back of my mind, the idea began to unfold that maybe writing – journalism – was something I could do. If I decide not to go ahead with the philosophy and politics course, I will look into journalism degrees. Maybe in Sydney . . . or maybe not.

Anyhow, right now I am on the night train to Paris, wondering how I can capture the magic of the city I wanted us to explore together in just a few words and pictures.

I reach into the inside pocket of my rucksack and bring out a crumpled letter. It's from Honey, posted once she knew I was going to be staying at the internet cafe in Berlin for more than a week. It arrived on the last day I was there, and I've read and re-read it every day since.

I open out the letter, smooth the page flat. Honey's letters are small works of art – the page is inscribed with her vivid slanting handwriting and perfect line drawings of the happenings at Tanglewood. There's a jokey sketch of Coco playing violin on horseback and the sisters running for cover with hands over their ears; a sketch of Summer and Skye sharing the hammock and being fanned by Cherry holding a big palm leaf; a sketch of Fred the dog and Humbug the sheep in Paddy's chocolate workshop snaffling all the truffles. There's even a picture of me in shorts and sunhat, rucksack on my back, striding across a map of Europe, ticking off city names on a list and leaving a trail of postcards behind me.

Those pictures make me smile.

On the last page there's a sketch of Honey sitting on the windowsill in her turret room at Tanglewood, a tear rolling down her cheek and so many tissues at her feet it looks like she's sitting in a snowdrift.

'I miss you,' Honey has written.

That one doesn't make me smile. If we miss each other this much already, how will it feel when I'm back in Australia at uni?

Long-distance relationships are hard work. We've managed to keep things going for eighteen months so far, but I am not sure that being parted for another three years would be a good plan. I take out my mobile and google university courses in Exeter, the nearest big town to

Tanglewood, but the Wi-Fi signal on the train is hopeless and I abandon the search.

It's no good anyway, I know.

I am way too late to apply for courses in the UK . . . The uni term there starts in just a couple of weeks' time, so there's no way I'd be able to get a place. Not for another year, at any rate.

I push the thought out of my mind and fold up the letter again. It's getting very worn round the edges, so I am extra careful as I slide it back into the rucksack pocket. I stifle a yawn and check my watch. It's past two in the morning.

This gap year was all about finding myself, but lately it seems to have had the opposite effect. I am lost, adrift, hurtling through the darkness far from everyone I love.

I lean back in my seat and close my eyes, and this time I sleep.

3

The train arrives at Gare Austerlitz just after nine, and I step out into a bright Paris morning, my Rough Guide handbook in my hand. I've already emailed ahead to book a place at a backpackers' hostel in Montparnasse, so I make my way there. As I walk, I breathe in the aroma of freshly baked bread from the *boulangeries* and the rich dark coffee aroma drifting out from the cafes. I grin at the sight of the shuttered windows and wrought-iron balconies and the sound of French being spoken around me. How long will it take me to tune in to the city, to get the hang of it? For now, Paris is pure thrills. I check my map, turn into a side street and arrive at the hostel.

The receptionist is a pretty tawny-haired girl called Teresita, an Italian student on a gap year just like me. Her smile is big and welcoming, and I grin back, the buzz of this new city starting to build.

'You will like it here,' she tells me. 'Good hostel, very clean, very friendly, and the breakfast is good. It's just four people per room, so you won't be swamped, and we've got a night warden so it's pretty quiet and orderly. You cannot check in until four, but I can put your rucksack in our safe room if you want to head off and explore?'

'Thanks, that'd be great,' I say. I hand it over and head back out into the streets of Paris, free to roam.

I eat my breakfast in the Jardin du Luxembourg, a huge park with a fancy palace plonked in the middle of it. I walk past kids launching model sailing boats on a huge octagonal pond, and as I come out of the park cafe with warm chocolate croissants and a paper cup of chilled orange pressé a line of stocky ponies with small children on their backs passes by.

I find a patch of grass and sit down to eat in the sunshine, close to the old-fashioned carousel. Last night's doubts and worries have melted away to nothing, chased into the shadows by the buzz of a new city. Suddenly I can't wait to start getting to know this place.

❀❀❀❀❀❀❀❀❀❀❀❀❀❀❀❀❀❀❀❀❀❀❀

Paris – it's like a surprise birthday present waiting to be unwrapped. Although I've read more about it than almost any other place on my itinerary, the city itself is still a mystery that only I can solve. I leaf through my Rough Guide, studying street maps and places I want to see, then close it abruptly and push it into a jacket pocket. Sometimes, I want to forget about plans and itineraries and how many cool sights and museums I can tick off in a few days. Today, I just want to wander.

I drink the last of the orange pressé, brush the sweet pastry flakes from my fingers and jump up from the grass.

Away in the distance to my left I can see the Eiffel Tower reaching up into the hazy blue sky, and I know the River Seine is somewhere ahead, so I head out of the Jardin du Luxembourg and let chance take me along the little streets. I am near the Sorbonne University, so there are lots of young people around . . . It's a studenty area. There are students talking in excitable French as they stroll along the roads, students clutching books and hurrying to lectures, students sitting at pavement cafes reading, writing, sipping espressos. The term must have just started, and a bit of me wishes I was a part of it, one of the students making their

✿✿✿✿✿✿✿✿✿✿✿✿✿✿✿✿✿✿✿✿✿✿✿

way through the narrow streets of Paris to class. It's a pity my French isn't up to scratch.

Could being a student back home in Sydney be as cool?

My heart sinks, and I push the thought away.

After a while I find myself down by the river, a broad sweep of blue flanked by little stalls selling prints and pamphlets and souvenirs. Across the water, on the Île de la Cité, stands the cathedral of Notre Dame with its Gothic towers and willowy spire and circular stained-glass window.

I'm smiling again now, eyes wide at the beauty of it all, savouring the aroma of falafel and chilli and grilled halloumi cheese from one of the riverside stalls. There's a shop called Shakespeare and Co., which sells books, books that spill out on to the pavement on tables and shelves. It looks like an Aladdin's cave, and I step inside, browsing among the shelves. The books are all in English, and I pick up an ancient copy of F. Scott Fitzgerald's book *The Great Gatsby* because it's one of Honey's favourites and a book she's studying for A level. She told me that Fitzgerald and his wife Zelda lived in Paris for a while back in the 1920s. 'Just imagine,' Honey had said. 'How romantic? We'll do that, one day. You can write and I'll paint.'

❀❀❀❀❀❀❀❀❀❀❀❀❀❀❀❀❀❀❀❀❀❀❀❀❀

I don't know if that will ever happen, but I will wrap the book and post it off to Honey, a small souvenir of Paris.

I pick out a postcard too, to send to my sister Tilani and her family back home in Sydney. The kids are collecting them, charting my travels on a big map pinned up on the living-room wall. I haven't seen them since I set off in January . . . That feels like a long time ago now.

Since then I've been to India, Sri Lanka, Turkey, Greece, France, Germany, the Netherlands and a few places in between. I've loved them all, but the three weeks I spent in Somerset with Honey was the best of the lot. Whatever happens in the future, whatever I decide to do about my uni place and however things work out with Honey . . . well, I know I won't regret this year of travels and adventure.

The lilting sound of a flute cuts through my daydreams, and I glance up sharply, turning my head towards the sound.

A small child in a raggedy sundress the colour of emeralds runs past me, laughing, and vanishes down a narrow side street away from the hustle and bustle of the busy Paris waterfront. As I watch, I see her running across a cobbled

❀❀❀❀❀❀❀❀❀❀❀❀❀❀❀❀❀❀❀❀❀❀❀❀❀

alley, dark hair thrown back, looking up towards a shuttered window. Is that where the music is coming from?

I step into the side street, into the alleyway, into another world.

4

Silhouetted in an upstairs window bordered with shutters, a young woman is playing a silver flute. Her hair, long corkscrew curls of blue-black, catch on a sudden breeze and flutter out against the white-painted shutter. The same breeze takes her haunting music and lifts it into the air so that it slides across the city's rooftops.

It sounds like magic.

The little girl in the green sundress is dancing now, whirling around on the cobblestones.

Abruptly, a wrinkled, claw-like hand closes over my elbow. '*Puis-je vous dire la bonne aventure, monsieur?*' a crackly voice enquires.

'Sorry?' I blurt. 'I don't speak French. *Je ne comprends pas!*'

A wizened old woman is at my side, her face tanned and

360

leathery, dark eyes glinting. 'Engleesh?' she asks. 'Engleesh boy?'

'Australian,' I say.

'Ah, of course. Your fortune? You wish to know your fortune? I can see, I can tell. I have the sight.'

I take in the woman's crimson dress, her black fringed shawl embroidered with roses. Her greying hair is scraped up into a makeshift bun and her ears are studded with gold. She looks like a caricature of an old-time fortune teller.

'No, I'm good, thanks,' I say, but she isn't listening. Her hand grips my elbow harder, trying to steer me across the cobblestones.

'You have many questions, no?' she persists. 'About the future? I see this in your eyes, Australian boy. I can help!'

She lets go of my elbow, dark eyes challenging me.

Behind her I see a doorway with a curtain draped across it, a painted sign advertising fortune telling propped against the step. I have many questions about the future – it is true. The flute music wraps itself round me like a spell, and the little girl in the green dress dances over and leans against the old woman, wide eyed. They're waiting to see if I want my fortune told. Do I?

361

❀❀❀❀❀❀❀❀❀❀❀❀❀❀❀❀❀❀❀❀❀❀❀

One thing my gap-year travels have taught me is that when adventure appears right in front of you, you'd be crazy not to go with it.

'I don't have much money,' I say, a last half-hearted protest as I fish a five-euro note out of my pocket. 'Is this enough?'

'*Mais oui!* Of course!'

I follow the old woman and the child to the curtained doorway, stepping into a dark room smelling of incense and furniture polish. On every surface shadowy statues from several different religions huddle together with ornate candlesticks and crystal balls, beaten-brass singing bowls and bundles of dried herbs. The old woman indicates a couple of wooden chairs pooled in sunlight from the doorway, and I sit down.

The eerie flute music drifts in through the open door as the old woman perches beside me, her face serious now. She looks at my palm, frowns at my face and then sits back, nodding.

'I can sense many questions, many dilemmas, Australian boy,' she says. 'Fate has brought you here today.'

'Yes?' I prompt.

❀❀❀❀❀❀❀❀❀❀❀❀❀❀❀❀❀❀❀❀❀❀❀❀

'You are at a crossroads. Lost. Wandering.'

I bite my lip. 'That's right,' I agree. 'Lost. Wandering.'

She looks at my palm again, her fingertip tracing the lines etched there like a claw. A shiver slides down my spine and my heart begins to thump.

'I can see what you must do,' the elderly woman declares. 'You must walk a different path now. The route you have planned out will not take you to your destination . . .'

I swallow, leaning forward, almost afraid now of what I might hear.

A silence falls between us, invisible but heavy enough to touch. I know instinctively that what the old woman says could change my life forever.

'So?' I prompt again.

The old woman sighs.

'You must expect the unexpected,' she says, eyes narrowed wisely. 'Something is coming to an end, but something new will take its place. Your next big challenge is just around the corner.'

I blink.

Whatever I expected, it wasn't this. A handful of clichés and platitudes? My shoulders slump.

'This makes sense to you?' the old woman checks.

'Um . . . yes . . . no . . . maybe?' I falter. 'Is there any more?'

She stands up, shrugs. 'No more,' she says. 'This is what I see. I hope it answers your questions, Australian boy.'

She is ushering me back towards the door again, as keen to be rid of me now as she was to lure me in a few moments ago.

'I'm not sure it's totally clear . . .' I say.

'The meaning lies within yourself,' she replies briskly. 'I can see the truth, but it is for you to work out what that truth means. You have the answers already. You will see.'

I find myself outside again in the cobbled alleyway. 'But . . . hang on . . . I have lots of questions, like you said before. Can I . . .?'

'If you have the questions, you have the answers,' the old woman replies. 'If you want to talk about your future, look for the girl with stars in her hair. She can help you to decide it all.'

The curtain drops abruptly and I am left alone, feeling more confused than ever.

The sky has clouded over and the alleyway is no longer

bathed in golden light, like something from another time, another place. It's just a dirty Parisian side street with sweet packets littering the pavements and a couple of skinny cats slinking around in the shadows.

All the mystery has seeped away.

The child in the green dress is sitting on the doorstep of the fortune teller's house, drinking Coke from a can and playing on some kind of smartphone. The flute music has stopped; the only sound now is the distant hum of traffic, and when I look up to the shuttered window there is no sign that anyone was ever there at all.

5

It doesn't matter how streetwise I think I am, how much of a seasoned traveller . . . I have clearly just fallen for the biggest scam in the book. I must be seriously gullible to have spent five euros on such a rubbishy prediction . . . at least I didn't part with more.

Expect the unexpected? Something is coming to an end but something new will take its place? The next big challenge is just around the corner? The predictions couldn't be more cheesy. They probably fit half the population of the western hemisphere, and of course the only thing around the corner from the cobbled alleyway is the busy riverside street.

What an idiot I am.

I start walking again, heading across the Pont Saint-

Michel to the Île de la Cité , and as I cross the river the feelings of embarrassment drop away and I'm laughing, shrugging off my own stupidity.

Already I am planning the jokey email I will write to Honey, describing my disastrous visit to the fortune teller, turning it into a story, an adventure. I've catalogued everything about the last few weeks in emails to Honey, everything except the loneliness anyway.

I went off radar for a fortnight earlier this summer, when I was on my way to Tanglewood. There was some mad TV crew filming a reality TV series about Honey's family, and they paid for my train fares across Europe and an overnight stay in a posh hotel in Exeter just so I could turn up at the Chocolate Festival the Tanberry-Costellos were holding and feature in some big reunion. The boy from Australia finally reunited with his British girlfriend after eighteen months apart . . . It was TV gold.

It meant I got to save money and see Honey a few weeks earlier than planned, so I didn't complain, but the catch was that the TV company wanted me to stop emailing and texting so I didn't accidentally give the game away. It all worked out really well, except that Honey will never let me

❀❀❀❀❀❀❀❀❀❀❀❀❀❀❀❀❀❀❀❀❀❀

forget that I went all silent on her. I've made up for it since with a whole slew of texts and emails of course.

I lean on the parapet of the bridge and flick through my texts. There were loads from yesterday, a whole text conversation while I was waiting at Madrid station, letting Honey know I was on my way to Paris at last. I told her the hostel I'd chosen, my plans for the first few days, my ideas of heading off to Denmark, Norway, Sweden and Finland next before flying back to Tanglewood to spend Christmas with her.

Her mum and stepdad made it clear I'd be very welcome, but still . . . It's months until Christmas. I'm not sure I can stick it out till then.

Off to take some pictures beside Notre Dame, thinking of you, I text to Honey now. *What are you up to?*

There's no reply. She will still be in school, painting self-portraits or taking a drama class or studying American literature for A-level English. I head off to capture the best and coolest images of Notre Dame, to lose myself and shake free of the uncomfortable fortune-telling experience.

Later, I find an internet cafe back on the Left Bank and order coffee and a baguette while I upload my photos and write a new blog post about the magic of Paris. I check my

❀❀❀❀❀❀❀❀❀❀❀❀❀❀❀❀❀❀❀❀❀❀❀❀❀

emails, but there's nothing new from Honey. Maybe she's busy with homework or is doing something with her sisters.

We Skype when we can, maybe once a week or so, depending on where I am and whether I can get access to an internet cafe at the right time of day. We plan the Skype talks and set a time by text. Suddenly, even though nothing has been arranged, I want to talk to Honey, hear her voice, see her face. I want to tell her properly about my strange encounter earlier.

I click open the Skype icon and enter my details, then ring through to the Tanglewood computer; the whole family use the same Skype log-in. After a couple of rings, the call is answered and a couple of faces appear on screen – Skye and Coco.

'Hey!' Coco greets me. 'How's it going, Ash? Where are you now? Spain, was it? Or France?'

'Paris,' I say.

'Cool,' Skye says. 'Honey's out, I'm afraid. She won't be back till late. I think it was some kind of . . .'

'Study group,' Coco chips in.

'School trip,' Skye blurts at the same time. 'To see a play. Shakespeare or something.'

'That's what I meant.' Coco nods. 'A sort of study-group school trip. Right?'

'Right,' Skye agrees.

I frown. The sisters are looking a little uncomfortable, a little awkward . . . I get the feeling they are not telling the whole truth.

'OK,' I say, brushing the thought aside. 'Well, no worries. Just tell her I called . . .'

'We will!' Coco says. 'As soon as she gets home. Definitely! Not a problem! Summer's not here either . . . She's started at Rochelle Academy, and she's loving it. It's very weird without her. Would you like to say hello to Humbug?'

There's chaos while Coco attempts the task of lifting her pet sheep up towards the screen. Fred the dog gets involved and then Charlotte leans in, waving and wishing me luck, and Paddy appears in the background telling me about a new truffle flavour he has created that seems to involve baked apples, blackberries and cream.

It's probably my imagination, but something about the whole thing feels a little off, a little forced. The general mayhem is typical Tanglewood stuff, but today I get the feeling that everyone is just too bright, too chatty, trying too hard.

I'm about to say goodbye and hang up the call when Cherry sits down next to the computer, grinning and asking if Paris is as cool as everyone says.

'Cooler,' I promise. 'Weirder too. But cool, definitely.'

'I can imagine!' she sighs. 'Honey will be so hacked off to have missed you. I'll tell her you called!'

I bite my lip.

'Where did you say she was again?' I ask.

'Um . . . it was an art trip, I think,' Cherry says. 'Some exhibition in London. She'll be back tomorrow, apparently . . .'

'Sure,' I say. 'Well, I'd better go now. Nice to talk to you . . . Tell Honey I'll call again soon . . .'

'Of course,' Cherry says. 'Bye, Ash! Have a brilliant time!'

I cut the call, shut down the computer and walk out of the internet cafe with a sick, twisted feeling inside, wondering why Honey's family have suddenly started lying to me.

CARTE·POSTALE

Turn
Around
x

6

When the crazy old woman from earlier told me to expect the unexpected, and that something was coming to an end, did she mean my relationship with Honey?

I am not stupid. I know all too well that long-distance relationships suck, and that a fiery, impulsive girl like Honey must find them especially hard. What if she has had enough, got tired of a boyfriend who is never around? There must be loads of boys at her sixth form who would love to take my place.

Honey has told me herself that she doesn't have a good track record when it comes to picking boys. She went through a very rough patch after her dad left and her mum married again; she rebelled every which way she could. What if her old hell-raising ways aren't over after all? If she's out with some boy-band-lookalike bloke with a six-pack and a motorbike? If she's forgotten about me?

It would explain why her family were so jumpy, so over keen with the bright chat just now. It would explain why she wouldn't even consider coming travelling with me. It would explain a lot.

Can a leopard ever change its spots?

I fell in love with a rebel and a troublemaker and tried to tame her . . . What if she didn't want to be tamed? Honey has turned her whole life round since the months she spent in Australia . . . Just when it seemed like her life had spun so far off course it couldn't be hauled back again she decided to take control. She enrolled in sixth form (at a different school from the one that had expelled her) and started studying for A levels, and her grades so far have been amazing. I can't take credit for any of that . . . Honey is a strong and determined character. She's changed things all by herself.

But maybe I'm just not a part of the future she has planned out.

Dusk is falling and the streets are bright with fairy lights and street lamps. There's a warm yellow glow inside the cafes I pass as people gather to talk, eat, fall in love. Paris is the prettiest city in the world after dark, the loneliest when you are on your own.

I catch sight of my reflection in a cafe window, a small slightly built Asian boy with a taste for travel and a way with words. Back home in Sydney, there were a few girls who thought I was good-looking, but I wasn't interested in any of them. I just wanted Honey.

Now I can't help wondering why a girl like that – a girl who could have anyone she wanted – would bother with a boy like me.

I thought we had bonded so tight that nothing could come between us, two kids whose dads had both left them, two kids looking for something to believe in, something to trust, and finding only each other. Maybe I was wrong.

I turn the corner and walk into the hostel courtyard.

I need a hot shower and a good night's sleep, and a new plan for tomorrow. A new plan for everything, perhaps.

It's the same receptionist on duty from this morning – Teresita, the Italian student with the tawny hair and the big smile. Right now, I can't find one to match it. I hand in my bag-check ticket and she takes it and goes to the office

✿✿✿✿✿✿✿✿✿✿✿✿✿✿✿✿✿✿✿✿✿✿

to find my rucksack, sliding it across the counter to me along with a room key card.

'Oh . . . and I have this for you as well,' she says, handing me a postcard of a Parisian starry night.

'Huh? I don't see how . . .'

I turn the postcard over. Just two words are written on the back, in the lively, sloping handwriting I know so well.

Turn around . . .

I look at Teresita and she looks back at me, grinning. 'Go on, then!' she prompts.

So I turn round. Standing just behind me is a girl with tousled blonde hair, a huge rucksack and a beautiful face that shines with glee.

'Honey!'

She drops her rucksack and I drop mine, and the two of us hurl our arms round each other, hugging and laughing and hugging again as if we will never let go.

7

In the end I check my rucksack in again and Honey ditches hers too, and we head out into the Paris night together.

'I can't believe you're here!' I say. 'I tried to Skype you earlier, and everyone was acting really weird. I can see why now. They were covering for you!'

'I wanted to surprise you,' she says simply. 'I wanted us to see Paris together, like you said!'

We walk along the riverside beneath the twinkling fairy lights, hand in hand. I point out the quirky English book-shop I discovered earlier and hand over the novel I bought for her, then tell her about the cobbled alleyway I found that felt like stepping back in time.

'It was somewhere near here,' I explain. 'The kind of place you might never find even if you knew exactly where to look . . . It was like a piece of magic, Honey, honestly! Flute music and a little girl in a green dress swirling around on the cobbles, and a crazy old lady who reckoned she could tell fortunes . . .'

Honey laughs. 'Trust you, Ash!' she says. 'You find adventure and magic everywhere you go! I've missed you so, so much. I absolutely love your emails – they make every place you visit come alive!'

'I sent you an email about the alleyway,' I tell her. 'I'm guessing you haven't read it yet?'

'I left my phone on the kitchen table at Tanglewood,' Honey confesses. 'Typical, huh? Did anything else happen?'

'Never mind,' I say with a grin. 'You can read the whole story when you get back. The email tells it better than I could!'

She shrugs. 'You're good, Ash – too good. Those emails showed me just how much I was missing out on!'

'I think it's what I want to do,' I say. It's the first time I've ever said this out loud, but the minute it's out there I know it's true. 'I think I've picked the wrong uni course. I don't want to be an academic, poring over thick books and writing scholarly essays on obscure philosophical questions. I

❀❀❀❀❀❀❀❀❀❀❀❀❀❀❀❀❀❀❀❀❀❀❀

want to be a journalist, travelling the world as a reporter, making the world come to life.'

'Journalism?' Honey questions. 'Really?'

'Yeah . . . I think so. I've loved the thrill of moving from place to place, but not just for the sake of exploring – part of the thrill has been taking photos and making it all come to life on my blog and in my emails. Does that make sense? I've loved it!'

'It makes perfect sense,' Honey says. 'And I'm glad about that, because I have something to tell you. It's a bit major, Ash. You'd better sit down . . .'

The smile freezes on my face, and anxiety seeps in again. Expect the unexpected?

We sit side by side on a bench looking out across the river, and Honey starts to talk. She tells me that she missed me like crazy, hated the thought that I would go back home to Sydney to study on the other side of the world. She hated the thought so much that she filled in an application form on my behalf for the London School of Journalism, attaching a folder of email and blog print-outs as evidence of my writing.

'I know I shouldn't have,' she is saying. 'I know it wasn't my business, that I should have asked, but it was only an idea to start with . . . I knew it was too late for this year, but I thought that maybe if they offered you a place for next October you'd at least have a choice between that and Sydney. I just thought –'

Hope and fear pulse through my veins.

'Did they?' I interrupt. 'Did they offer me a place for next year?'

Honey looks up at me, her face stricken in the soft glow of the fairy lights above.

'No, Ash,' she says, and my heart plummets.

'They're not offering you a place for next year,' she continues. 'They're offering you a place for THIS year. Like . . . next month. If you want it, that is!'

'W-what?' I stammer. 'How come? Are you sure? I mean . . . SERIOUSLY?'

'Seriously. They loved your writing, really loved it. Apparently someone deferred at the last minute, and they've given the place to you . . . along with a scholarship. So yell at me if you like. I know I shouldn't have done it, but . . . well, I did!'

Expect the unexpected . . . something ends and something fresh begins . . . a new challenge is just round the corner . . .

✿✿✿✿✿✿✿✿✿✿✿✿✿✿✿✿✿✿✿✿✿✿

'You did it for me?' I whisper, pulling her close. 'I can't believe that. You're awesome, Honey Tanberry!'

I am laughing so much that Honey's anxious face relaxes at last and she joins in, and I pull her to her feet and we run down to the water's edge. We stand for a moment looking out across the river, and when she turns her head away I notice that Honey's hair is tied back into a fishtail plait woven with silver stars that glimmer in the moonlight.

Look for the girl with stars in her hair. She can help you to decide your future . . .

I take Honey's hand, still laughing, and whirl her round and round on the pavement in time to the echo of what sounds like distant flute music . . . although I may just be imagining that bit.

ASH KHATRI · LSJ STUDENT CARD

8

In the end, my year of travelling comes to a halt a few months early, but not before I got to spend a wonderful, magical weekend in Paris with the girl I love.

We went up the Eiffel Tower, had dinner in a cafe where F. Scott Fitzgerald and Hemingway used to drink, saw the Moulin Rouge, went window-shopping along the Champs-Élysées, wandered around the cathedral of Sacré-Cœur and walked beside the river in the moonlight.

We packed a lot in, and it's just as well because it took me all weekend to actually believe what Honey has told me. I have a place at a prestigious university to study something I know I will love, and none of this will bankrupt my family because I have savings and I have a scholarship, and the minute I find digs in London I will get a part-time job

❀❀❀❀❀❀❀❀❀❀❀❀❀❀❀❀❀❀❀❀❀❀

in a cafe. My skills at taming the most unruly coffee machines are second to none, plus I can fix a mean fruit smoothie.

Could it be any better?

OK, London isn't especially close to Tanglewood, but it's a whole lot closer than Sydney would have been – I can head down to Tanglewood for holidays and Honey can come up to London for wild weekends and sightseeing and general craziness.

Telling my sister and her family was tough, but Tilani was happy for me. She has been the best sister ever, looking out for me since I was tiny, after our dad walked out, babysitting when Mum was working. Later, when Mum died, Tilani took me in, even though she'd just married Sam. The two of them never once made me feel like I was a problem, a burden . . . We were family, pure and simple.

'You're amazing, Ash, always remember that,' Tilani said when I called to tell her about the change of plan. 'The best little brother in the world. I'm going to miss you like mad, but I'm so, so pleased for you . . . What an amazing opportunity! I know there's a whole big wide world out there for you . . . Go and explore it, little brother. Have fun, have adventures . . . live your life! I'm so proud of you, Ash, d'you know that?'

I guess I know it now.

I grew up thinking I had a broken family, but it turns out that wasn't true. I have my sister, my brother-in-law, my nephew and nieces . . . plus Honey and all of the lovely Tanberry-Costellos – even the friends I've met on my travels, especially Daan and Ernst. Family is more than just blood ties, after all . . . it's the people who are there for you, the people who care.

Anyway, my nomad days are over – for a while at least.

I now have a bedsit flat (the size of a large postage stamp) in a student house in Kilburn, a job in a little Italian cafe just round the corner and a bike borrowed from Paddy, who says he never used it anyway, to get around London on. All this in a couple of weeks. My life has turned upside down, but in a good way.

And now I am standing on the steps of the university, the borrowed bike shackled firmly to the railings behind me, clutching a rucksack full of books and a new laptop, about to start my very first day. I've been so busy there's been no time for second thoughts. Every day I've felt more

❀❀❀❀❀❀❀❀❀❀❀❀❀❀❀❀❀❀❀❀❀❀❀❀❀

thrilled by the idea, excited to be living in London, studying something I know I will love . . . but I'm not kidding myself it'll be easy.

I remember watching the French students in the streets around the Sorbonne in Paris; I remember the old fortune teller, with her cheesy lines that all came true. Well, here's the big challenge that's just round the corner . . . It's a good job I like challenges.

A few students file past me as I stand on the threshold, all of them looking older, cooler, more sure of themselves than I am. Just for a moment I feel out of my depth, scared that there's been some mistake. I falter, wondering suddenly if I can do this, and then my phone buzzes in my pocket and I take it out and check the message. It's from Honey.

Hey . . . thinking of you, Ash. Good luck! xxx

The nerves recede like shadows in the sun, and I grin and walk up the steps and into my new life, my future.

Are you a  **Cathy Cassidy** superfan?

Can't wait to discover all the news about Cathy and her amazing books?

Then the brand new

is for you!

Tune in and you can:

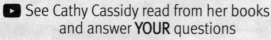 Watch video blogs from *CHERRY*, *SKYE*, *SUMMER*, *COCO*, *HONEY* and *SHAY*

See a **NEW** video every time you visit

Enter fun surveys to win **FAB** prizes

See Cathy Cassidy read from her books and answer **YOUR** questions

Watch book trailers, music videos and much, much more!

Visit **www.youtube.com/CathyCassidyTV** today!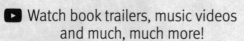

Welcome inside the world of

the chocolate box girls

*A **delicious** scrapbook of f[...] creative ideas from **Cherry**, **Summer**, **Skye**, **Coco** and **Hon**[...]*

♥ ***Host*** a chocolate[...] themed sleepove[...]

♥ ***Design*** a flower headband

♥ ***Create*** a cupcak[...] sensation

And many more ideas for every seaso[...]

A whole year of **Chocolate-Box-inspired ide**[...]
– which one will you make first?

CHERRY CHOCOLATE FRIDGE CAKE

Cherry says... ♥

We can't all be good at everything. We have our own skills, and mine seem to be daydreaming and writing stories, which is fine with me. It's not easy for me to be part of a big, blended family where everyone else is great at baking, though, because, trust me, I'm not! I am way too easily distracted and more than once I have walked away from the kitchen only to cremate a tray of cupcakes or burn my chocolate brownies to a frazzle. Ouch.

This recipe is my trademark sweet treat; it's a no-bake cake, so even I can't go wrong! Luckily, it's also wickedly chocolatey and everyone loves it. Charlotte showed me how to make it when I first moved to Tanglewood, but the idea of adding cherries was all mine!

YOU WILL NEED:

- 225g digestive biscuits
- a strong plastic food bag
- a rolling pin
- 100g butter
- 200g milk chocolate
- 3 tablespoons golden syrup
- a large heatproof bowl
- a saucepan
- a wooden spoon
- 225g tinned, stoned cherries, drained and chopped
- a baking tray
- baking parchment

METHOD:

1. First put the digestive biscuits in the bag and smash them to small crumbs, using a rolling pin (great way to get over temper tantrums).

2. Place the butter, chocolate and syrup in a large heatproof bowl over a pan of simmering water. Stir with a wooden spoon until just melted.

3. Quickly add the crushed biscuits and the cherries and mix well.

4. Line the baking tray. Pour the mixture into the tray with baking parchment. Put it in the fridge until set (overnight is ideal, but it should be ready in a few hours if you are really desperate!)

5. Cut into squares and serve; it tastes far too good to be this easy.

Instead of cherries, use chopped fresh strawberries or raspberries or add mini marshmallows, dried fruit and nuts or Maltesers. Instead of milk chocolate, try dark or white.

Look out for another special treat from Cathy . . .

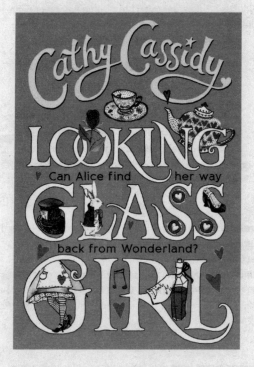

Alice nearly didn't to go the sleepover. Why would Savvy, queen of the school, invite someone like *her*?

Now Alice is lying unconcious in a hospital bed.

Lost in a world of dreams and half-formed memories, she is surrounded by voices – the doctor, her worried friends and Luke, whose kisses the night of the fall took her by surprise . . .

When the accident happened, her world vanished – can Alice ever find her way back from wonderland?

l started with a Scarecrow

Puffin is over seventy years old.
Sounds ancient, doesn't it? But Puffin has never been
so lively. We're always on the lookout for the next big
idea, which is how it began all those years ago.

Penguin Books was a big idea from the mind of
a man called Allen Lane, who in 1935 invented
the quality paperback and changed the world.
**And from great Penguins, great Puffins grew,
changing the face of children's books forever.**

The first four Puffin Picture Books were hatched in 1940 and the
first Puffin story book featured a man with broomstick arms called
Worzel Gummidge. In 1967 Kaye Webb, Puffin Editor, started the
Puffin Club, promising to **'make children into readers'**.
She kept that promise and over 200,000 children became devoted
Puffineers through their quarterly instalments of *Puffin Post*.

Many years from now, we hope you'll look back and
remember Puffin with a smile. **No matter what your age
or what you're into, there's a Puffin for everyone.**
The possibilities are endless, but one thing is for sure:
whether it's a picture book or a paperback, a sticker book
or a hardback, **if it's got that little Puffin
on it – it's bound to be good.**

www.puffinbooks.com